LOOP

A PULSE-POUNDING NOVEL OF SCIENCE-FICTION HORROR

WILLIAM KELY McCLUNG

FALLING UP
PUBLISHING

FALLING UP
PUBLISHING

ISBN 979-8-9851700-0-9 (Trade Cover)
ISBN 979-8-9851700-1-6 (Hard Cover)
ISBN 979-8-9851700-2-3   eBOOK (ePub)

Library of Congress Control Number: 2022900738

Publisher's Cataloging-In-Publication Data

Names: McClung, William Kely, author.
Title: Loop : a pulse-pounding novel of science-fiction horror / William Kely McClung.
Description: First edition. | Midlothian, Virginia : Falling Up Publishing, 2022.
Identifiers: ISBN 9798985170009 (softcover)
Subjects: LCSH: Application software--Social aspects--Fiction. |
Genomes--Social aspects--Fiction. | Journalists--Fiction. |
International Criminal Police Organization--Fiction. | Artificial intelligence--Fiction. |
Deception--Fiction. | LCGFT: Science fiction. | Horror fiction. | Thrillers (Fiction)
Classification: LCC PS3613.C35876 L66 2022 | DDC 813/.6--dc23

"The Man I Love" Lyrics by Ira Gershwin (Public Domain)

"House Of The Rising Sun" Lyrics by Unknown (Public Domain)

Typeset and Cover design by:
John Clayton@ heAring eYe doG CreaTive

For information contact:
kely@williamkelymcclung.com

First Edition: March, 2022

Falling Up Publishing
Midlothian, Virginia, 23112 USA

To a future where we vanquish monsters
faster than we create them

RMY XAI

01101000 01100101 01101100 01101100 01101111

ASH — MORE THAN SMOKE, less than dust. So fine it floated on currents in the air made by their passing. Even behind the cloth he wrapped around his face to keep from breathing it, you could tell it had no odor, and yet his tongue was coated in a thick film that along with the absence of smell, *the nothingness of it*, tasted of death. Little noise, as if sound waves from outside the bubble, a roiling, near primordial stew of flora and fauna little touched by man, knew to stop at the perimeter.

The only sound that registered from within was his heartbeat, and the pattering of small, naked feet from the three children leading him.

They showed no fear, just a knowing beyond their years that he was the one who would relentlessly track and solve the mystery, find answers they could then share with friends and family and their own children in some distant future, and use to make sense of mankind's cruelty to mankind.

The *bubble* — he had no other metaphor for comprehending it as he couldn't shake the idea he was inside a large floating sphere within the high rainforest — was maybe two-thousand meters across. It had no transition. There was life, thick and rich and strident and verdant, with all the sounds and smells and colors of the central African rainforest, and then there was... none.

Perhaps if he had looked closer, a transition line could be found. To the naked eye, at least to eyes overwhelmed with the enormity of the sight, it was as surgically precise as if cut with a laser.

Could a laser have done this? The precision made it seem possible. Was there a laser beam two-thousand meters across that could be aimed at the jungle to vaporize everything down to the soil and loam packed beneath their feet? That seemed... less possible.

As incongruous as if there had been a working Starbucks set in the middle of the clearing, a spot of color called from the otherwise colorless ruins.

Alika, the smallest of the children, sometimes hard to assign an age as nutrition was rarely ideal, but no more than five or six, squatted on her haunches to poke at the doll. A white child's doll, manufactured in China. No nod to where they were, or having plastic with skin tones that might have reflected their surroundings. Instead, blond hair and a bit of colorful cloth. Somehow barely scorched, just the slightest bit of frizzed up fiber that survived what must have been immeasurable heat.

Mbangue pulled her away, looked up to the man to gauge his reaction. Instinctively, with no conscious thought, he knew the man had lived far longer than his own eight years, and so was an invaluable resource for their survival. The man nodded, less with his head and more from a shift of the gray in his eyes to blue, and Mbangue shrugged his permission for the little girl to pick it up.

With the instincts of a veteran cameraman, Ndoka, the eldest at ten, kept the little digital camcorder rolling. He'd clutched the camera and picked his moments ever since the man had first shown the boy how to use it days before in trade for this secret location. It was the boy's sense of mission that had encouraged the man to keep following him on their two-hour trek, filled with doubts, but enchanted by the three children's determination to share their find.

Alika smiled. As bright and cleansing as the sun. Thrilled with her prize. The three children fawned over the doll as happy and excited as if they had discovered an equally sized diamond.

It was Mbangue who looked up long enough to follow the man's eyes back to the dirt. The gleaming bones of a small hand, no bigger than their own, made even smaller without flesh, shone from beneath the dirt and ash.

Mbangue kicked dust and dirt and ash over it, and in doing so, uncovered a fragment of what would later be determined as a ceramic carbon fiber nano-tube composite.

The boy saw the man's eyes. Caught the importance. Pulled the cloth back up over his nose, and knelt to paw the dust as methodically as if he were a seasoned member of an archaeological dig. Careful, the reveal painstakingly slow.

Maybe seven inches by nine, less than a square foot.

Ndoka kept the camera rolling. Sensing the import of the find as the man knelt and reached for it. Stenciled in letters familiar, but in a language the boy couldn't read. Black shapes inked and stenciled against the less-black composite material. Maybe part of the lettering missing. RMY XAI.

The man could guess at least part of it, but would reserve judgment for now. He stood, dropped the fragment in his backpack. He'd seen enough. And like the children, maybe too much. More than most men, first from the inside, and now with over a decade from without.

Two thousand meters. An easy estimate based on experience of how many people and animals — men and women and children, dogs and chickens and goats — vanished in a flash of light.

He knew he'd have to follow the trail. Had some idea where to begin and an early idea of who to call, to at the very least point him further along the path. He felt time slip and shift, as nebulous and tenuous as the dust swirling over his boots.

He tried to absorb the horror of what was left, had the briefest of undefined premonitions of a world on fire, and made the conscious decision to go forward, not backward.

It would be up to others to follow the threads back in time with some obscure, forensic investigation. Congressional hearings and political debates. International hearings and tribunals. Scholarly dissertations on ethics and morality and burgeoning medical advances. A doctoral thesis on the subject in someone's near future.

He had no idea, and couldn't care, they'd discover that the beginning, for at least one telling, and a small but integral part of the puzzle, would be traced to the thirty-eighth episode of season one of Pokémon, *"Dennō Senshi Porygon,"* airing in Japan on the night of December 16th, 1997.

He only knew he had a part to play in a future that rushed at him with the ferocity and power of a charging rhinoceros he'd once faced and barely survived, of trials like those faced in endless wars in which friends and comrades fell, of tasks he'd once executed as orders and walked away from with both public honor and inner shame.

Africa. Thirty-five hundred people. Vanished in a flash. *But why?* He knew it could happen again. Knew this remote blip on a map in the middle of the African jungle wasn't the beginning, but it would be up to others to bring those responsible to account.

His way was forward, and his part of the story started now.

ONE

01001010

PISS-YELLOW STREETLIGHT DRIFTED in from broken windows across the stairs from above. Not enough to see, but enough one could imagine the faces that went with the voices shouting in terror from below.

"Shut the fucking door!" A young woman's voice, or a girl, but too much assurance to be a child.

A man. "I'm trying, I'm trying. Jesus Christ!" Used to giving orders. "Grab that chair and try to brace it!"

Another man's voice. Strident with hysteria. "I've got it. I've got it!"

"Wedge it under the knob — "

"I know how to block a fucking door!"

The girl again. "I'll get it, just don't let them in."

A big echoey boom of something heavy throwing itself against the door from the outside. Multiple somethings.

A scream and shouting and footsteps and their bodies climbing over each other up the stairs. One flight. Two. Stumbling and falling over each other in panic and fear.

Below, a wailful scream and pounding on the door. Underneath it all, a tortured growl that resonated with something primal and elemental. An ear-splitting sound that filled the staircase, maybe half a dozen flights below and another half-dozen above, made all the more terrifying with the undercurrent of something once human vibrating within the awful sound.

The three figures climbed and clamored up the steps, falling over each other and into the murky light.

Clouds of breath condensed in the bitter cold, and for a brief moment, bound them in a common humanity as much as their fear and the struggle to escape whatever attacked from below.

The bigger man was maybe a businessman of some status, or a high-powered attorney. His custom white shirt; sweat-stained in fear and exertion and dirt. One sleeve of his disheveled suit, 1500 dollars of bespoke fabric and tailoring, torn and dangling, but his three-hundred dollar tie snuggly in place.

The smaller man, with the look of a rock climber or a long-distance runner, neither of which he was, struggled to push past the girl and looked as if he was climbing up from the 70s as much as the stairs. Long hair bounced and fell from his head like a bed of angry snakes, almost hiding the scraggly beard that sprung from his chin like weeds in a poorly tended garden. Denim shirt and jeans, high dollar sneakers. Prescription glasses some would have called spectacles, used for effect as much as reading. Near his physical and mental limits. His movements jerked and strobed as if he were lit under a disco ball.

The girl, impossible to tell if she was twelve or twenty, a waif dressed as if she'd grabbed blindly from a basket of toddler's laundry or the Salvation Army's donation bin. An orange bikini top under a green-on-purple zig-zag hoodie, cut-off camo pants and mismatched knee high socks, one with pink stripes and one with neon-green polka-dots. A wild mop of dark curls held in check with a leopard-print scarf on top. Combat boots below. Owning it like a designer's entry onto the Paris runways.

The katana, an oversized samurai sword on the back of her small frame, completed her ensemble.

She slid past the two men with ease and came up short on the next landing as the two men staggered past her.

A door burst open, and three more men stumbled out. The six people crashed into each other with shouts and curses, then disentangled long enough for the fat man — well below six feet and closing in on three hundred pounds — to turn on surprisingly light feet to slam the door shut behind them.

At his side was a badass figure of a man, at least what could be seen of him in the dim light. A western-styled oilskin duster, two bandoliers of large-caliber bullets across his broad chest, a shoulder holster with a 9mm Beretta, and what looked like a flintlock pistol tucked into a wide belt.

The door was being forced open and he threw his weight against it as the others recovered from their shock and surprise.

Muffled and resonate through the steel barrier. "Let us in! Please. For God's sake, let us in."

"No, no, no. Don't let them. They were bit, I can tell." The admonishment came from a young, geeky-looking kid with Gina's Pizza embroidered on his red striped shirt and again across the red ball cap over his greasy blond hair.

The waif looked at the desperate, bloody hand trying to claw its way in from the other side, and threw her own ninety-three pounds into the mix. She hit the door hard, bounced off, and fell to the floor, but the additional force was enough the door slammed shut and locked from the inside.

A howl of pain came from the opposite side, and three fingers, sliced with near surgical precision between the steel frame of the door fell to the landing, and in her mind squirmed like worms in front of her.

The yell of pain from the other side of the door dropped to a low moan that mirrored the sound of icy wind whipping from somewhere above them.

The door shook and rattled from a last effort of desperation that threatened the steel frame.

Then came the screams.

First of terror, and then of pain. The horror resonated in the marrow of the six, quickened the blood that coursed through their veins.

The sounds transmorphed into something beyond pain. And then they stopped.

Light, sudden and intense and orange and red, reached out in forked tongues from the half-inch gap beneath the door, and just as suddenly, was gone. The six fell back to catch their breath and take stock, willed the locked door to stay closed.

Silence of the moment gave way to heaving breath, the gulping of cold air, thundering heartbeats.

"Jesus," Attorney said.

"Who the fuck are you guys?" Hippie pulled away from the others and glared. "You can't just invite yourselves in. This is our spot."

The light in Bad Ass's eyes changed ever so slightly, but enough Hippie stepped back.

"Fuck off. You don't scare me." Hippie tried to inflate his skinny chest.

BAMM!

Something crashed into the door. Snarling, growling, gut-wrenching human screams became something else. The roar and screech of a baboon on full attack folded with the power and piercing squeal of a train car against steel tracks. A sound that became... *other.*

The pounding resumed. Whatever threw itself against the door had to be breaking bone against the steel.

Hippie was one of those who tried to hide his terror with non-stop jabber. "Without those pocket cannons, you ain't so tough."

Bad Ass pulled out the Beretta. A simple but practiced move. Held it out. Long moments...

Hippie reached for it, forcing his fingers to close on the grip, but was shaking so much, Attorney snatched from of his hand.

BHUMP BHUMP BHUMP...

Pounding directly beneath their feet made them scatter and stare at the floor. The outline of an emergency exit, a trap door was set in the cement of the landing.

A woman's voice, muffled from beneath the floor, cried out. "Lass mich hinein!"

BHUMP BHUMP BHUMP...

Hippie pulled back against the wall. "Don't let her in."

Fat Man stepped onto the trap door.

No foreign-ass-muffled-voice woman was getting through there! Looked to Bad Ass.

"Whatcha think?"

Waif took in the strained looks. "We could use some estrogen in here."

The voice beneath them pleaded for help.

They all looked to Bad Ass, promoting him to leader.

"Please?"

Bad Ass nodded, and Fat Man stepped off.

Waif knelt to figure out the clever inset latch, and on her way down saw Bad Ass was missing a leg.

Blood seeped from his knee where the rest of his leg should have been. Instead, a hastily made bandage wet with blood and a ridiculous peg leg made of a rough two by two was strapped to his thigh with tie-down straps.

The trap door sprung open like a jack-in-the-box, and a mostly naked young woman, in cropped t-shirt and blue panties over the lithely corded muscles of a serious athlete — *maybe a dancer* — scrambled up from below.

Wild blond curls bounced back and forth as she absorbed details of the wide-eyed group staring back at her.

A young girl. Dressed as if she was determined to display every available pattern of a discount fabric store. High cheekbones and the hint of Asian blood along with the sword on her back made her look like an anime character. Cute. Competent. Smiling.

A fat man. Struggling for breath, but cherubic blue eyes, *Avatar-blue*, welcoming her to their little band.

A hippie, working to control his panic and failing. Jerky movements, withdrawals or overwhelming fear short-circuiting his coordination. She had the briefest impression he knew her. She frowned. Sure he was guilty of *something*.

Her eyes were drawn to the one-legged man. His energy and confidence were expansive and filled the room. Even with one leg, he moved with the grace and deliberation of a man well aware of his strengths. The blood at his knee told her the event had just happened, a day or two at most, but would not define his abilities. Like the others, she was drawn to and comforted by his presence. She watched as he took her in as well, gazing back without guile or agenda, reshuffling the band's roles to create the strongest team.

Attorney drank in the unforgettable body. Saw one bloody foot wrapped in the bottom part of her torn off t-shirt. He stopped on the eyes — as blue as her panties — glaring back. She looked ready to bolt — *or tear his face off.* He swallowed hard and stepped back.

Her eyes darted to Pizza Boy.

"He's infected." A German accent. Only Bad Ass caught the slight inflection that hinted she might be from somewhere else.

Pizza Boy shrank against the wall.

"No-no-no, I'm not! I'm not bit! It's just the way I look — "

"I didn't say you were bit. I said you are infected. I can smell it."

"Fuck you, bitch."

"We don't know he's infected," Fat Man said.

"He might be!" Hippie looked ready to run. "He has the look."

BOOM! Something slammed against the door. The echoes filled the staircase with the screech of Hell's banshees on the other side. Even with the door between them, it was hard to talk.

More crashes from below as if the attacks were coordinated and timed with those across.

"Up, up, up!" Bad Ass led the way on his unlikely peg leg. Waif seemingly attached to his hip, reached out to take Dancer's hand, making sure the girls stuck together. Fat Man in the way of everyone else. Hippie, Attorney, and Pizza Boy brought up the rear and tried to squeeze past his bulk.

They all came up short as Bad Ass and Waif stopped to look out an open window.

The alley four floors below them. Their perceptions had been distorted — not as high as they'd thought.

The only light came from a couple of emergency lamps mounted outside on the building they stood in. Old school. Pre-halogen. Sulfurous yellow. Shadows rendered in muddy blacks beneath the weak bulbs reflected off ice and drifts of snow along the oily street.

Their view from the rectangle of the window made them feel they were watching from the safety of a movie theater. The roars and screeches and pounding below bounced off the walls where they stood and resolved in marrow-shaking surround sound.

Movement drew their eyes. Even if you knew what you were looking for, it made little sense. A jerking, snapping, careening motion that seemed to propel the… *what?* They were new enough to the ecosystem they couldn't possibly have a formal name yet.

"Jesus. Loopers," Waif whispered.

Okay. *Loopers.* Good enough. The two girls crowded on either side of Bad Ass to watch as the Loopers skittered and clawed their way into the wide alley. Two arms, two legs. Human at one time. Twisted as if they'd been torn off and stuck on backward or inside out. The joints — elbows and knees — seemed to work in both directions and not quite under control as if they were still learning how to walk. And run. And climb up the dark alley walls.

A scream drew their eyes to the opposite end where a young couple, maybe in their early thirties, careened from around the corner and ran onto the dark street.

Waif pushed forward, ready to shout a warning, but before she could get a sound out, three more of the infected — *Loopers* — come from behind, chasing them. Or maybe, *herding* them.

The man fell, and the woman helped him up before tripping over discarded trash and falling hard.

The woman hit the icy pavement; layers of skin torn from her hands, and twisting her knee. She'd been a runner in college and knew this pain. Forced to withdraw from the Olympic trials she'd trained her entire early life for. She knew her leg wouldn't carry her weight no matter how terrified she was.

Her husband tried to lift her and saw they were trapped. Desperate for a weapon. Garbage cans, broken bottles, stacks of plastic pallets. He spun one way and then the other, screaming and cursing at God for deserting them to these unholy creatures.

A pipe against the wall. He pulled and kicked and twisted until it came free in his hands.

He spun to defend his wife just as the first Looper attacked. It seemed to come from one direction, jerked to the side and then backward before snapping left and diving for the man. He caught it full against its head. It staggered but rolled and spun in place, then launched itself eight feet into the air to come down with a frenzied attack.

He did his best to keep it at bay, landed a few superhuman blows delivered from his last reserves of adrenalin. Overmatched and ill-equipped. After all, he was still human.

The creature ripped the pipe from his hands, slashed at his throat, and as he fell toward his wife, another launched itself off the wall from high above and slammed him to the street.

The woman sat in the center of the alley. Praying quietly to the God they'd just cursed for abandoning them. Seemed to fold into herself as blood, warm and wet, landed across the back of her neck. She barely flinched when her husband's arm landed beside her.

Closed her eyes as the sounds of skittering movements gathered around her — the feet and arms and hands of the Loopers on the icy pavement sounded like the scurrying of insects against a cardboard box.

Dancer pulled Waif away, the screams mercifully cut short after a wet, broken frenzy of tearing flesh and cracking bones.

Bad Ass forced himself to watch. He'd seen horrors before and their aftermath, but this was like seeing an explosion rip bodies apart in slow motion. Gut wrenching, but still he watched.

If there was a lesson to be learned, a weakness to be found in witnessing the couple torn apart in the savage attack, a way to defend or kill or destroy these abominations, he wanted to know it.

Bad Ass saw the terror in Waif's eyes beside him and turned back to the group as they leaped away from Pizza Boy.

"Damn," the boy said in surprise, staring at his hands.

As the other five watched, Pizza Boy lit up with an internal glow. For an instant, they could see his skull and bones outlined beneath his skin. The flesh blistered and bubbled; spontaneous eruptions burst open from the heat as his arms twisted in their sockets.

WHOOSH! His body ignited like a match hitting coals doused in lighter fluid. Just as quickly, the flame was gone, and they watched in shared agony as his joints coiled and bones cracked.

The torment was too great to scream, but as he continued to be ravaged and wracked with unspeakable pain, a soft, terrifying keening from inside him grew in intensity until it threatened to shatter their eardrums.

Waif struggled to pull the sword off her back. Dancer backed away from the threat and heat as Attorney pulled uselessly on the Beretta's trigger, the mag already empty. Hippie and Fat Man pressed back against the walls.

Bad Ass snatched the Beretta from Attorney's hands. Shoved it back into his shoulder holster. Handed the flintlock to Waif. Pulled the sword from the scabbard tied to her back.

In a motion almost too fast to see, the katana whispered around his body and sliced across and down, cleaving the tortured boy nearly in half.

The split body hovered on the landing, smoldered and smoked. The halves slid apart and they had the briefest glimpse of the fire still burning inside.

The others stood in shock — *the transformation of boy to monster happened faster than they could process* — as Dancer side-kicked both halves down the stairs.

They watched what was left of Pizza Boy tumble and fall until a renewed frenzy against the doors below woke them from their stupor.

"To the roof," Fat Man shouted.

They scrambled up the final flight, piling up behind Fat Man and Bad Ass hobbling on his wooden leg.

The air outside hit them with the force of a train. The bitter wind cut deep. Bad Ass pulled off the duster, and with a flourish, spun and wrapped it around Dancer's naked shoulders.

A quick search of the rooftop, air conditioners and ventilation systems, yielded some pipes and a few loose boards the six-man band gathered to brace the door behind them.

Bad Ass and the two girls made their way to the edge of the rooftop and looked down on the alley as a dozen Loopers began heading toward the building on which they stood. Five floors down. No way off from here unless they grew wings.

Hippie had the same idea and result, and turned away from the far rooftop edge overlooking the street.

Attorney and Fat Man were on their way to the third side of the rooftop when a wall of dust and gravel and snow was driven into their faces.

THWOU THWOU THWOU... A black Huey, impossibly huge and dragon-like in the night, rose from below the roofline to drive the two men back.

Halogen spotlights danced over the group as bullets stitched a line across the rooftop in front of Fat Man. Gravel and shrapnel spit across his face, and he put his hands up in defense and surrender.

The chopper's HUD revealed the motley crew of misfits below them. Three with their hands in the air moving toward the middle of the roof. The fat man, a 70s hippie reject, and a big man in a torn suit.

In defiance at the edge of the rooftop, a young girl in a hoodie and combat boots with an antique pistol clutched in both hands stood between a barefoot woman wrapped in a western duster, and a one-legged man with bandoliers of bullets across his chest and a Japanese sword in his hand.

The HUD switched from infrared to thermal as the pilot scanned the six, then returned to normal view with isolated facial and body tracking.

"DROP YOUR WEAPONS AND MOVE TO THE CENTER OF THE ROOF." On loudspeaker. "DO IT NOW."

The gunner knew the power of overwhelming force and intimidation, and stitched another line of 20mm rounds from the Gatling gun across the rooftop. The deafening noise echoed off the buildings in cascading waves beneath the whine and thwump of the rotors.

"DROP YOUR WEAPONS OR YOU WILL BE SHOT."

The three ran toward the west side of the rooftop with the illusion that the next building was close enough to jump. Waif grasped Dancer's hand as they all pulled up short. Not likely.

The gap would be a challenge on the best of days, and impossible for a one-legged bad-ass with a Samurai sword. *Still ...*

Knuckles white, Waif gripped Dancer's hand harder and looked to Bad Ass.

Bad Ass looked from the military chopper overhead to the far rooftops and buildings twenty feet away.

Gradually backing away from the edge before he looked back to the girls and smiled.

"Ja?" She'd only been around him ten minutes and his response, proving he was insane, made her like him even more.

"Yeah."

Waif shook her head and grinned. "Okaayyy then..."

"MOVE AWAY NOW."

Bad Ass looked to Fat Man who could only shrug. Hippie and Attorney stood together, covering their eyes from the rotor-wash and blinding searchlight.

"WE WILL FIRE."

Bad Ass looked around. The darkened town dotted in fires... sloppy wet snow falling through the searchlights... the chopper hovering above them representing everything that had gone wrong but that he was determined to fight against.

More bullets ripped up the rooftop in front of them. All three felt bits of tar and asphalt pepper their legs. Well, *leg* for Bad Ass. They shared a look, psyching themselves up.

Do or die!

Waif grinned, lifted the flintlock. Not hard to aim, the flying machine above them was massive. She pulled the trigger.

Click. *Fizzzzz*. BOOM. *Score!*

The recoil lifted Waif off her feet, and Bad Ass snagged her by her hoodie as she flew by.

Sparks flew off the steel above. No damage, but enough to make it veer away for a moment. *But just a moment!*

The chopper flit out two-hundred meters, banked hard, made a wide circle, and headed back. Fast.

Dancer and Waif sprinted toward the edge. Picking up speed. Bad Ass on his one real leg doing a great job of keeping up. *Kind of.*

They jumped.

TWO

01100001

THE SPACE WAS NOT designed for quiet. Taken as a whole, even in a snapshot of time, one would have said the rich symphony of sound that filled the expanse was young, vibrant, and filled with promise.

A winter-white sun shone down from the domed glass ceiling on the Nerds, Geeks, Greeks, Hot Chicks, Janes, Targets, Standers, Bees, Hiltons, Slackers, Stoners, Jocks, and Jockettes. Eating, talking, flirting, hiding, cramming, sweating, and fronting. Nearly everybody on their phones. Texting. Candy Crush. TikTok. Snapchat and Fortnite.

Sprawled in a padded armchair, staring at the screen of his phone, a good looking Afro Nerd bolted upright. "Whoa, whoa, whoa... check this shit out."

Hot Chick crowded in, set herself over the arm of the chair. "Let me see." Slid down to his lap. She squirmed against him until she was happy with the result.

Afro Nerd, Dockers shirt buttoned to the top and a plastic pocket protector, glanced up from behind his Clark Kent glasses and did his best to pretend she wasn't affecting him.

"Pretty cool," Jock Strap said from a chair nearby, distracted and looking down at his own phone. He made a swap and watched as dozens of friend's headshots and selfie snaps morphed into one.

Held up his phone to show off the result. The photo smiling on screen, a good looking nineteen-year-old, *mostly* looked like him, but more handsome than ever.

Hot Chick and Double D winked at each other as Double D set herself on his lap.

"Do me."

"Been trying to all year."

"Hey!" Hot Chick pretending to be mad.

Double D shimmied and squirmed, making sure he had a view of her ample breasts. "Well, the year's not over yet. You still might get your chance." She looked at his phone. Some kind of app that allowed him to move pics in and out. Looked like a game. "How's it work?"

Afro Nerd spoke up for both girl's benefit. "He puts you in his family tree." Grabbed a quick snap of Hot Chick, and moments later, slid it into place. "Like, maybe he makes you his great-grandmother."

Jock Strap did the same with Double D.

Looked kind of boring. "Weird." Though the app worked under the hood, the fun was in watching it happen. Jock Strap's face broke apart, reassembled, morphed again, and updated as she watched. He angled the screen, anticipating her reaction. "Whoa... pretty cool. I want to try."

He handed her his phone, and she moved herself down a level to "grandmother." On one side of the app, her face was broken apart into a thousand facets and analyzed; on the other, the percentages of his genetic makeup updated across his picture.

The result this time was more dramatic; his face only changed slightly, but his hairline shifted, and his chin looked like it belonged under a superhero mask.

"Sweet. If you *did* look like this, I'd have done you already."

Hot Chick handed her phone across to Afro Nerd. "Download this to my phone."

"Give me a sec."

"Me too." Double D used her thumbprint to log onto her phone. "What's it called?"

"Loop."

In the hall, heading to class, the four kids with their heads buried in their phones like everyone around them.

"I can't find it," Double D pouted.

Afro Nerd took her phone. "That's because it's not out everywhere. Some kind of targeted rollout."

An Eavesdropper, "They tried in Europe somewhere. Germany I think. People were fighting over it so much they pulled it."

Another hall surfer. "Africa too."

Another voice. "What's to fight about?"

Someone nearby, "Purity of the races and shit."

"Fucking Germans."

Afro Nerd ignored them, thumbed in an address, held the phone up to do a biometric scan of his real face as they walked, and logged onto an obscure site. "Another sec." A moment later, he handed her phone back.

Double D scrolled through her apps, launched it.

"Why *Loop*?"

"Run it and see."

They entered the class. Large theater seating. The cliques taking their places. The slap of books on desks, and the rustle of coats, backpacks, pads, and papers.

"Okay. It's up." Hot Chick said. "Now what?"

"Check the menu. Scan for your best pic and run genetic markers and diagnostics."

"This shit can't be accurate," Bigger Jock said as he took off his coat.

Sweet Cheeks looked up from her phone. Same thought she always had — *Wow, Bigger Jock was big!*

"My mom did one of those DNA test things, and this is pretty close."

Hot Chick sat down beside her. "You already did it?"

"Last night. Took some time." Sweet Cheeks brought up the app and held up her phone. "Ta-da!" Her new profile pic. It looked nothing like her.

Hot Chick scrunched up her face. Tilted her head. "I guess it looks like you."

"The *perfect* me."

Bigger Jock looked disgusted. "My friend's mom did that ancestry DNA shit, and found they were 3% Jewish and 5% African."

"Baby got back," Double D said, confirming her tits and ass were still there before she pushed her way past them. "Shit had to come from somewhere."

Four Eyes, a row away, watched on his phone as it took away his glasses and straightened his nose. "Nice. How's it doing it?"

"AI." Afro Nerd set out a tablet, lined up pens and paper to take notes for class. "Government databases and 20 billion pics and videos to draw from. Breaks apart your facial structure and calculates your genetics."

Eavesdropper chimed in. "That's the shit from China. I wouldn't trust them for a second."

Another voice, "You know they gather all that shit for a reason, right?"

A girl dressed in a basket of toddler's laundry and combat boots entered the lecture hall. A colorful scarf held back a wild mop of luscious curls that almost reached her butt, her backpack nearly as big as she was. The guys did a terrible job of hiding that they were checking her out while she found her place a couple of rows back.

Small enough to curl up in her seat, she pulled an old school Game Boy from her backpack.

A smoking hot Asian Chick rolled her eyes, and Hot Chick turned back to see her boyfriend's goof grin.

"Seriously?"

Jock Strap shrugged. "She's kind of hot."

Double D punched his shoulder. "Yeah. In a *'I'll help her clip your nuts kind of way'* if you don't wipe that shitty grin off your face."

"Yes, Granny."

Down in front, the professor walked in. Jeans. Denim shirt. High dollar sneaks. Moved like he was lit with a strobe light. Started setting up his lecture while his TA began setting up his media presentation.

Hot Chick peered over her boyfriend's shoulder, still fucking with his phone.

"So put me in," she said. "I can be on the other side of your family."

"Gonna mess up my genome."

He slid her picture over, and his profile shuffled and morphed again. Held up his phone to show the results.

"Okay. You are now my other grandmother."

"You're banging your grandmother?" Asian Chick.

Jock Strap beamed with pride. Put his arms around Hot Chick and Double D. "My two GILFS."

Double D's face with a WTF look.

Some Random Guy chimed in. "A granny I'd like to — "

"Gross." Hot Chick elbowed her boyfriend.

"Just *one* of the things you like about me," Jock Strap said.

"Whoa. Check this shit out." Loud, from the back of the hall as Nerd Bros shared something on their phones. Porn no doubt.

"I could go for bigger tits," Asian Chick said. "And maybe a tan."

"Ain't getting mine," Double D pushed her chest out. Batted her eyes. "Unless you ask real nice."

Sweet Cheeks nodded at Afro Nerd. "Maybe he can be like your great-great-great-grandfather."

"How many people can you put in?"

Nerdy Guy a row up, "Six generations but you can't change your parents."

"Figures."

"So six generations is like, what? Forty? Forty people minus your parents is thirty-eight," Hot Chick said.

Jock Strap shook his head. "Six generations is forty? Is that right?"

"No. Sixty-two." Afro Nerd corrected. "Without your parents. Sixty ancestors."

Asian Chick held up her phone to show her progress. "So you guys are now all in my family."

"I think it's better to be mixed," Hot Chick said. "It's where we're all heading anyway."

Double D looked to Jock Strap. "So we can mix up the races?"

"My family is pure for like, at least five hundred years," Bigger Jock said. "I do wish I was bigger though."

Sweet Cheeks and Asian Chick on the same page. "Add Daryll."

"I don't mean like that!"

Afro Nerd looked up and grinned.

"Shit's too complicated," Hot Chick said.

Daryll, Afro Nerd, shook his head. "Not really. AI and machine learning do all the heavy lifting. Just move Keven out and slide Mark in."

"Ha!" Double D said. "She already did that shit!"

Hot Chick glared. "Slut."

"Skank."

Both girls stuck their tongues out at each other. Giggled.

Hot Chick concentrated on her phone. Rearranged pictures again. Determined. And then beamed. "And now... *I... am... perfect!*"

She held up the result of her work. The picture on screen *was perfect!* And still looked *exactly* like her.

Group in the back was getting loud. It looked like a Battle Bot team was gathering around the Nerd Bros. Checking out a phone. Talking over each other.

"Yeah. You do it too much and you go up in smoke." Big Nerd Bro made sure he had everyone's attention, playing it up. "And then it gets *really* bad. Cirque du Soleil - *zombie edition.*"

"People get addicted and forget to eat and shit. Start attacking everybody."

"Bullshit."

"Ewww." Little Nerd Bro swooned and covered his eyes.

"Don't look at your screen or you die."

"Fucking *Ring* crap."

Hot Chick's phone dinged. A text link. Opened it and started watching. Her face went white before Afro Nerd saw her and leaned over.

Her posse concerned and crowded in to see. She dragged her thumb and started the video over.

Waif pretended not to be taking in everything around her. Kept her head down to her Game Boy.

"Bullshit," Sweet Cheeks said.

Asian Chick turned away. "Looks pretty real to me."

Jock Strap rolled his eyes. "Yeah. So was Spiderman."

The professor was writing on the huge chalkboard —

THE ROLE OF MACHINE LEARNING TO INFLUENCE
POLITICAL CAMPAIGNS ON SOCIAL MEDIA

— while his TA finished setting up the projector.

"Okay, settle down. Today, we're going to start exploring — "

"Professor Hall?" Some random guy shouted. "Have you seen this?"

His TA was glued to her own phone as a ripple went through the crowd.

Another guy yelled out. "Put it up on the screen."

"Yeah. Put it up!"

Professor Hall nodded and his TA pushed the video onto the screen as it lowered into place.

No sound yet, but lights dimmed as the helpless man on video was going up in flames. People on the video screen scattered but were pulling out phones and turning back to record and take photos. An instant later, the man's arms and legs began twisting and contorting in their sockets.

Waif stared like everyone else across the lecture hall, transfixed by the silent horror.

Not a sound or whisper from the class other than a few sharp intakes of breath. A few spontaneous sobs, from young men as well as young women, as the camera pushed in to capture the gory details. Skin blackened and bubbled, smoke and steam burst from the rising lesions. An arm snapped, and jagged white bone jutted from the burnt flesh as blood spilled from the rupture.

The sound kicked in mid-screams and crackled through the lecture hall speakers with raw intensity. The yelling and shouting of the panicked crowd on video soon echoed through the lecture hall but was quickly overtaken by screams of agony from the man twisting and smoldering on the ground.

The camera jerked, and was jostled and hit as it pushed in to catch another glimpse, until the man on the ground sprung up and grabbed at the closest people. The view spun in a blur to join the running crowd, the little microphone quickly overwhelmed with the cries and shouts of terror.

THREE

01100010

FOURTEEN STORIES UP MADE it the highest floor of the highest building in the city. The office took up the entire top floor other than a thousand square feet subleased to a document translation service specializing in large corporate contracts with the Chinese.

A symbiotic relationship. They were sometimes able to send each other work, but just as often had to maintain professional and confidential separation.

At fourteen floors, six stories higher than the next tallest building, most people would have called Mazeville a town, not a city. And they'd mostly be right. It had only been a couple of decades ago when the main drag, Grant Street, got its second traffic light.

The second renaissance of growth hadn't really started until a massive endowment was given to the local university ten years before. At just under four-thousand students, the liberal arts college had some renown for shaping the views of three graduates that had gone on to win congressional seats, two federal judges, and one sitting Senator.

Not long after the Senator had been sworn in, the school's reclusive benefactor built his home and a small, private research lab on the hills defining the northern perimeter of the town.

Secrecy and security were paramount, but it was rumored to be one of the more advanced computer labs and artificial intelligence research centers of the world. Considering the owner, it made sense. Most assumed it was in service to the military. Others imagined it more like Frankenstein's laboratory.

No one in the town or the local college, and certainly not in this office, cared what they did as long as the money continued to flow.

The name on the door and the nameplate in the lobby said *Lance and Sons & Associates.*

Two Suits, one Dark and one Light, and a good looking Skirt, were scattered around a polished conference table that could easily seat twenty, and sometimes did. But it was getting near the end of the year, and besides those on vacation or teleconferencing from home, the office had been quiet since the CDC's guidance and the Governor's efforts in taming the recent global pandemic.

Success generated from their global clients, these three made up significantly less than half of the firm's attorneys. The clerks, legal secretaries, and aides required to meet in the office would be kept to a minimum until life around the world returned to normal.

They waited for the boss, the only one of the *Lance and Sons* too young to retire. He still had dreams of saving the world; besides, he had a daughter who had decided to follow his footsteps and get her education at Stanford instead of staying close to home.

The Skirt poured herself more coffee. The good stuff she imported and brought from home in a polished stainless steel thermos. Though she was always willing to share, the Suits knew better than to expect her to pour any for them. Theirs came in paper cups with plastic lids from the bakery where they had grabbed the donuts. Good by college-town standards but a distant second to what she brewed at home.

Another suit entered, a big man in fifteen hundred dollars of luxurious cloth and bespoke tailoring, a custom shirt, and wearing a three-hundred dollar tie. The back half of his name on the door, *the son that still worked for the firm.*

Privileged and used to the good stuff, he went straight for her thermos.

"Morning, Lance."

"Jackie," naming the Skirt for us. "Who's the ADA on this?"

"Neils."

"She's tough, but fair. Take Rob with you. I think they have a history."

She glared at Dark Suit. He shrugged an apology. Obvious to everyone they shared more than a professional relationship.

Jackie was a gem, and Lance had broken off their own brief, ill-conceived affair long ago.

Rob had been with them just over a year, and only *separated* from his wife, not *divorced*, so Lance enjoyed watching him squirm. The extra tension he was orchestrating for the court room might work out in their favor. Or not.

"Maybe we get lucky and it rattles her cage a bit."

Light Suit spoke up. "There's more coming out on that video. CNM is reporting that it's not an isolated event."

It was the second time in two days he'd brought it up. They were used to his flirting with the conspiracy theory du jour.

"Won't go anywhere," Rob said.

Jackie's phone vibrated, and spun on the table.

"Once these things go viral," Rob continued, "no way to track them down,"

Jackie checked the text, and reached for the TV remote. The big 4K screen at the end of the room came on to cell phone capture of a man lying on the street still smoldering. CNM chyron showed LISBON, PORTUGAL.

The solemn reporter was inset to the side and speaking. " – be disturbing to watch. The authenticity of this video has not been confirmed by CNM, but this marks the fourth known recorded incident. Further reports are coming from across the globe, but we have no new information to share at this time."

The charred figure on screen bent backward and was nearly folded in half as he writhed on the street. Arms twisted and bent, from the heat or some other force, seemingly ripped from their sockets to turn on themselves.

The screams of agony from the man, made even more disturbing with the low fidelity of the mobile phone recording, and the increasing panic and shouting of the crowd, made it seriously hard to watch.

The crowd was half-committed to turning and fleeing, but like a car wreck on the side of the road, couldn't tear themselves completely away. Many with obvious cell phones and cameras recording the event. One man, a passing first-responder, or maybe even a doctor, stepped forward to help the young man.

As he knelt over the wretched figure, the body launched from the ground. The moment of terror and frenzy was only in half-frame and nearly obscured by the fleeing crowd as the good Samaritan was literally torn apart with the superhuman strength and fury of his attacker.

Mostly a blur of images, but the compressed sound remained relatively clear. Screams and yells — the chaos of absolute terror.

"Jesus," Rob said. He glanced around the room to make sure he wasn't the only one unnerved.

The broadcast cut to the perfectly composed face of the news anchor. "Let's listen in."

The White House Press Secretary stood behind the official lectern in front of both federal and district flags. A woman off to the side repeated each word in sign language for the hearing impaired.

" — intelligence sources are telling us early indications are that this is nothing more than a tasteless if convincing publicly stunt for the release of the newest Jackson Micheals' film due later this summer."

Jackie hit the mute button. You didn't have to sign to know what was being said.

"Like anyone is ever going to trust the media again," Light Suit said.

Rob leaned back in his chair. "Looked pretty fake, right?"

"Looked pretty real to me," Light Suit said.

Rob hid behind his coffee. "I mean that kind of shit can't be real." He looked to the others. "Right?"

"Wrong," Jackie said. "First they're going to find out it's real, and then they're going to find out the government is behind it."

Light Suit took the last chocolate donut. "And that's only after thousands of deaths and years of denial." He looked to the boss. "Whatcha think? Worth looking into?"

Lance frowned. "Let's make sure we have everything we need for the discovery." Turned to Jackie. "When's the grand jury?"

"Should hear today," she said.

Lance looked at Light Suit and gestured at the replay of the chaos on the TV. "Let's not spend a lot of time on this. But take a fast look and give me your first take on it all."

The door opened, and an older woman peeked her head in.

"Tim?" Only the secretary got to call him by his first name; she'd been there years before he'd even finished law school.

"You have a Colonel Bradley on the phone." She looked at the donuts and smiled. "Save one for me."

"All yours," Jackie smiled back.

Everyone pushed back from the table. Jackie handed the box to the woman, who smiled and closed the door behind her.

"Get the number from Maureen for General Connelly out of State," Lance said.

Light Suit was excited. "For?"

"See if he'll meet us for a drink. If this goes anywhere beyond a hoax, we might want some leverage to see what we can pry out of the situation."

"Anything else from me?" Rob asked.

Lance sat down, reached for the remote.

"No. Just stay available for Jackie if she needs you on this."

"You got it, boss."

The energy in the room was up, you could feel it.

He changed the channel, and the screen cut into the same video playing on another network. Turned the sound back up and watched the people run.

FOUR

01100010

A SOLID WALL OF MONITORS. In a snapshot, it might have been a high-end showroom with an unimaginative display, stacked five high and four across all selling the same model. A real-world examination would reveal they were next-gen, at least five years ahead of the market. 12K, 16bit, but it was the integration with the computer brain that fed them that made them cutting-edge tools.

Scattered throughout the rest of the room were dozens of computers, spectrum analyzers, AI frame reconstruction, facial recognition and bio-metric data matching, a huge high-def map updating in real-time with a variety of transmission and packet data, and of course, the Lab Coats that manned them all.

Music played from invisible speakers in the ceiling. As high-end and technically perfect as the video monitors. *"The Man I Love."* A sweet voice on a sweet song recorded in a bygone era.

"Someday he'll come along..."

Manning the computer that controlled the video on the main screens, sat a woman in a lab coat with a glorious mane of auburn hair piled high on her head. She made adjustments to the video and isolated a three-second loop.

More screams and yells filled the room.

Stopped in mid-scream.

"And he'll be big and strong..."

Scream. Scrub backward.

"The man I love..."

Yells, screams, terror.

She rewound the scene further. We've seen this video before, playing forward with the chyron below it saying Lisbon, Portugal.

The good Samaritan torn apart on the leaked viral video became whole, walked backward to rejoin the shocked crowd. The attacker jumped up from the ground, his arms twisted and bent backward, twisting in their sockets. They soon popped back into place, and burnt flesh absorbed the flames and smoke, and moments, later he looked like any normal young man sitting on his scooter across the street from an outdoor market.

Cars and pedestrians moved backward in time as the man ignored them and focused on his phone, maybe waiting for someone. He looked up as a young woman walked away backward from the market crowds then kissed him before rejoining him on the scooter. It backed out of frame until the Lab Coat began running it forward again.

"... I'm sure to meet him one day..."

The tape stopped after the woman kissed her man goodbye and glided across the street toward the market. The video again inched forward, frame by frame until the man pulled out his phone.

"... Maybe Tuesday will be my good news da ..."

Two shoes, wide and worn with seams ready to burst, but spit-shined and polished, danced to the music. The man inside of them thought of himself as stocky. As a boy, his mother convinced him he was *hefty,* and once he squeaked through basic training, the Army mostly let him make up for it with intellect. The dancing, Thursdays twice a month at the nearby Mazeville community center, his only exercise these days.

Well under six feet, his lab coat looked like a small tent. Those who worked for him respected him too much to call him *fat,* but at nearly three-hundred pounds, it was the simplest description.

Surprisingly light on his feet, and made even more buoyant with charm. His blue eyes danced across the lab as lightly as his steps.

"How ya holding up, Mads?"

The auburn beauty froze the video. Glanced at her friend and commanding officer, long enough for him to see her tears before she turned away.

"... of the man I love..."

He gently squeezed her shoulder, trying to comfort her, the video taking its toll.

"How far are you on the new one?"

Mads turned back to the computers, put up a new video that looked like it had been taken in Africa. A small town. A market. Then a hospital, or more accurately, a makeshift clinic. What passed for government buildings. A police station. The mayor's office. The streets in front of it.

A wider view showed the traffic. A dilapidated car held together with prayers, duct tape, and baling wire, chugging down the broken street and belching black smoke. The others it passed were little better except a comparatively new Mercedes sedan parked in front of what passed as city hall.

The door on the lab opened and five men came in. Two in everyday battle dress with sidearms and automatic weapons cleared the way for a Colonel, a General, and a man in a suit tailored to fit his impressive physique.

The lab coats, a mixture of enlisted and civilians, mostly ignored protocols of salutes, but visibly straightened as they continued their tasks. An older scientist came to attention, and pointed across the room.

The two armed men stayed by the door, as if someone might escape, while the other three made their way past the work stations, lab tables and desks, then turned the corner to approach Mads and the fat man.

The video screens in front of them showed a dozen other shots of the African town.

Men and women with baskets balanced on their heads or strapped to their backs, and sometimes both. Others pulling wheelbarrows as big as cars while still others filled and replenished the carts and tables of colorful goods and produce for a thriving market. Foot traffic dodged cars and trucks while small children added to the chaos by playing tag or soccer in whatever space was left.

Establishing shots. Maybe somebody had been preparing a documentary. Or a news story.

"Whatcha got for us, Carm?"

The fat man turned and was half-way through a salute before the General waved him off.

"Colonel Mike Bradley, this is Major Carmine Marelli. Carm's been our lead on this from the beginning, and his number two, Captain Madison Lewis."

"Major."

"Colonel."

"Captain."

"Colonel."

Madison, *Mads,* reached out her hand to shake the Colonel's and saluted the General.

"General."

"Captain."

The Suit rolled his eyes. "So what you can you tell us?"

The Suit - no introduction — name, rank, or position — but the General nodded his permission for Mads to speak freely.

"The video has been stepped on a dozen times and lost too many data packets during the generations of transmission to be sure it's genuine."

"I thought digital meant perfect copies."

"Not *perfect*. Close enough if done in a laboratory setting, but not in the real world with conversion, compression, and the variety of distribution channels it went through to make it here."

"So it could have been faked?" Colonel Bradley asked. "No way to prove it's real?"

She thought there was a tinge of disappointment in his voice and wondered what that was all about.

Looked away and back to the screens. "The video is degraded, and with little reference for verifiable reconstruction. The events are outside of any known documented parameters."

Carmine and the General trade looks.

Mads continued. "But we've isolated the audio, and by first reconstructing the original background noise with advanced machine learning and virtual warehouses of sound recordings, we've been able to further reconstruct the sound and use that for verification." She shrugged. "Of course it would best if we had the original video."

"Can you bring up the spectral view for me?" Carmine asked.

The video replayed on all screens but two. One filled with the waveform of the sound, and the other, with billions of dots representing the sound frequencies the two military scientists read like a newspaper.

The outside video switched to black and white security footage. From high on a wall, inside the city hall. Unremarkable. A secretary behind a desk. On her mobile phone. She reluctantly set it aside long enough to pick up the receiver of a multi-line desk phone. Transferred the call. Low rez, the sound captured by the security camera compressed to almost intelligible white noise.

Back to her phone. A couple of people entered, signed in, and a couple of others passed through frame to leave. Back on her phone — like half the people around the world these days, addicted.

Nothing happened for maybe thirty seconds. Then...

The secretary cried out as if shot, arched her back and rocked across her desk. Papers and phones went flying. She snapped back, in the grasp of an invisible hand, her neck and head twisting as if possessed. She screamed in pain, held her hands out in front of her as they suddenly began to smolder and smoke. And an instant later, a whoosh of flames, rendered white-hot in the poor resolution of the black and white video.

As the video played, Mads made adjustments, and the sound became more and more clear. Soon, the crackling of flames and the splitting of flesh along with an inhuman moan of pain filled the speakers as if they stood in the room with her. Impossible, but they could almost smell the burnt flesh and taste the smoke in their mouths.

The flames went out on their own, and they watched and heard her arms twist beyond their limits and break in their sockets.

People streamed from the offices, hugged the walls and ran for the exits. The secretary fell and writhed on the floor, then seemed to bounce into the air, clawing at people as they fought to get past. One woman was jerked completely off her feet and slammed against the wall with brutal, superhuman strength.

A man, who they would later learn had been the Mayor, was the next victim. The secretary grabbed at him. Ripping and tearing, grabbing, biting, and twisting in a frenzy the video couldn't keep up with.

Armed guards – soldiers – ran in and unloaded automatic weapons, and the secretary and Mayor were ripped apart in a spray of blood, mist, and bullets.

"Where is this?" The Suit asked. Dispassionate. "Besides Africa?"

The General looked to Carm who looked to Mads.

"That hasn't been verified. We're doing our best to track it down."

"How does this compare to the original event?"

Carm took over. Half the screens went to Lisbon, the other half to Africa. He punched in timecode and both videos jumped to frames just before the infected person spasmed and began going up in flames.

Frame by frame. Young man on a scooter. Secretary sitting at a desk. The timing was too close to be coincidence. At ninety frames, *three seconds,* the first sign of flames. The immolation lasted just under seven seconds before the flames were out and blackened arms and limbs began twisting in their sockets. At fifteen seconds the person was incapacitated by unbearable pain and writhing on the ground. Ten seconds later they attacked whoever was closest in a frenzy of near superhuman effort to devastating effect.

The General looked like he was going to be sick. "What's your opinion, Carm?

"They're both real."

"Fuck."

"Yeah. Fuck."

The Suit stood at another workstation behind two technicians wearing oversized goggles.

Hundreds of faces went by. Facial mapping, deconstruction, recognition and reassembly. The screens populated with digital readouts of AI estimates for genes and non-coding DNA. Another screen showing the 3D representations for newly constructed mitochondrial and chloroplast DNA strands into new facially matched genomes.

The lab techs sensed the Suit behind them and froze the screens.

"You're better off if you don't watch too closely," Carmine offered.

Colonel Bradley and the General joined them.

"So this is the app the kids are using?"

"We're diving a bit deeper, but, yeah."

The military men traded looks.

The Suit caught it, and Mads and Carm noted that he did. "And have we determined where the app came from?"

"Not yet," Carm said. "We're concentrating on the underlying technology that enables it."

"We know where it came from," the General said. "The damn Chinese stole the technology from us."

Uncomfortable fidgeting from the science side.

Mads spoke up. "Ummm, yeah. But we stole it from them first."

Carm stepped in before the General exploded. "All due respects, Sir. Once it exists, once it's out there in the ether, it's out there."

"Existential bullshit," Colonel Bradley said. "New-age justification for leaks of top-secret material."

Mads defended her boss. "Yeah, maybe. But it's still true."

The Suit looked at them in disbelief, as if he was just figuring it out. Made a show of it. "Jeeesuuuus Christ! Heads are going to roll, gentlemen. You guys invent this shit and never consider the ramifications of your technologies. Well, not this time. Mark my words, heads will roll."

The General ignored him. "The only question is, how do we put it back in the bottle?"

"No," Colonel Bradley said. "I think the real question is, how did it end up on Play Tunes or whatever the fuck it is? I want to know who created this... *Loop?* And how we shut it down?"

Mads shook her head. "It's out there, Sir. And spreading. Think of this as any other virus. A cold or the flu. Or last year's pandemic."

Carmine took over. "Except we think this one has two possible points of transmission." He looked around to make sure they were paying attention. "*And both appear to be lethal — *"

"Nine billion social media accounts." Mads pointed to the wall of screens. Twelve different video captures we hadn't yet seen of events from around the world, videos of people going up in flames, doing that Cirque du Soleil zombie thing, and attacking everyone.

" *— and people eating each other,*" Carmine said.

FIVE

01100101

SHE KNEW PEOPLE THOUGHT she was hot. People had been telling her she was cute since the day she was born, long before she understood the word but could respond to the positive feedback loop of their wide smiles and the flood of warmth in their eyes. By the time she was twelve, she was still cute, but starting to pick up on a variety of meanings and nuance, and soon, well before she entered college, she was just hot.

But at twenty-one, she still had her doubts. Not that she ever shared them or would admit them out loud. But like anyone anywhere with connections to the Internet, she had access to a million other hot chicks to compare her every body part with and to discover her *flaws*.

Any failings or gifts weren't her choice. She hadn't picked her hair or eye color. Genetics. Hadn't chosen how tall she would be, or the potential of her intellect. Natural selection. That she had what most people would have thought of as perfectly shaped and balanced C-cup breasts instead of gravity-defying D-cup tits. *Or was it the other way around?* Her family tree was lush and beautiful and strong.

She'd been a senior in high school before she found out her mother had posed for some scandalous paintings in New York, and that her grandmother had been Miss August on a pin-up calendar during the war.

Long legs, a perfectly rounded ass, and great tits. She knew she was lucky to have them. So did every boy in every class, and every girl she went to school with. She was the one they compared themselves with. A superhero without the uniform. Didn't try to deny it, not even to herself. Still, she was not... *perfect*.

Right now she was concentrating on her mouth. Could be just a fraction wider. And of course, her lower lip could stand to be the tiniest bit fuller. The same lip that right now she was chewing on with her perfectly straight, white teeth. Something she was not born with, but could be happy her parents had recognized the need for braces when it looked like her bottom teeth might not be coming in toothpaste-commercial perfect. Her mother understood the need for perfection in this imperfect world.

Wearing a pink, silk-blend spaghetti strap camisole beneath the luxurious down comforter she'd pulled up to her chin. She was propped against thick, soft pillows against the padded headboard. One hand on the phone, the other beneath the comforter. She was finding it hard to concentrate, rolled and pinched her nipples for the pleasure and pain, distracted but determined. Had been at it for a while.

"Oh, yeah. Just... like... that."

Moved one of her friends in as her great-grandmother and watched her face deconstruct then reassemble and morph with the subtle new changes.

"Soooo... fucking... close."

Switched out another pic. Opened another app. Scrolled for just the right face to add.

Back to Loop.

"Right... there. Ahhh... that's good. Yeah... just like that."

Her genome updates and her eyes changed ever so slightly.

Scrolled through her pics again. Added Asian Chick. *Now that girl was hot!* Watched her cheekbones rise and her hair darken. Still blond, but richer, deep honey instead of the golden butterscotch she'd been blessed with. The arch of her eyebrows shifted, her lashes thickened, and her eyes opened even more over perfectly sculpted cheekbones.

The changes were slight, anyone else would have had trouble finding them, but she was in love with her new face!

She locked it in, hit the update, and *Save New Profile* button. One hand maneuvered the icons on the phone, one hand drifted lower.

The face on the phone deconstructed — *it was all for show as it happened 'under the hood' with trillions of calculations per second* — while her real body writhed in pleasure as the computer that was her brain fired millions of its own signals.

She gave in… her foot shot out from under the covers, toes curling, foot arching, lifting off the bed.

"So… fucking… good…"

Eyes rolling back into her head, biting her lip, head twisting and rolling to the side as she gasped for air.

Waves of pleasure continued to build, each one rolling into the next until she could no longer keep them separate.

Hand dropped the phone, fingers clawing the air. The other, clenching tight as she brought it to her mouth and bit the back of her hand. Back arched. Anyone watching would have thought she'd break in half.

She screamed. Fell back to the bed. Ripped the cover from her legs.

Jock Strap! Big, goofy grin as he looked up from between her legs.

He loved seeing her mouth open, eyes clenched, arms and legs straining against themselves. Damn, she was hot!

She grabbed at his thick curls, pushed him back down, and ground against his face.

Found just the right fit, and held him to her as the warmth and waves of pleasure continued to roll up from the deepest part of her.

He still hadn't learned to read when she'd had enough or needed more. *What the fuck?* She didn't always know either. But he was a talented and enthusiastic student. Had an amazing young hard body she could work with, and at nineteen, was ready anytime she was. She held him close, thighs clenched tightly around his head, waited until he was struggling for air, and dragged him up by his hair to pant in her ears and grind against her.

"You are getting so good at that."

"Yeah?" Eager to please. Though she knew his efforts were still all about him and he had so much to learn, she understood the need to stroke the fragile ego of the male animal. *And why not?* It was so easy to do..

"Soooo good."

"Cool."

 He tried to kiss her, but she pulled away. Not that she disliked the taste on his tongue. She just couldn't give in to *everything* he wanted. He settled for a kiss on her cheek and propped himself up beside her.

"My turn."

SIX

01110010

SHE TOOK IN THE spacious room, not *intimidated* by it as it had been designed, but still impressed. That she had been told to wait here was as transparent and deliberate as if she been hit in the head with a hammer, and after the whirlwind series of events and flights to get here, she felt like maybe she had.

She spent the time searching for any clues that might give her an edge.

Dark woods and fine furniture, high ceilings with ornate, hand-carved crown moldings, and walls with matching panels of exotic woods and wainscoting.

The chair behind the desk could double as a throne, while the massive desk itself was polished enough she could see her reflection in the wood. Blue eyes and a wild mop of blond curls gazed back — tools to be used like any other.

Three high walls of floor-to-ceiling library shelves, and a fourth with framed, Magnum-quality photos — she recognized that many were. Brokering peace deals and cease-fires with Heads of State. Bringing medical supplies to doctors in the rainforests of Central Africa. Arranging heavy equipment and wielding a shovel in efforts to speed recovery crews in flood-ravaged coasts of South East Asia. Trekking with new vaccines up the Amazon. No one could deny the billions in philanthropy and the strides he'd made in helping the disadvantaged around the world. Framed covers from Time, Forbes, and Fortune. Wire and Rolling Stone.

Find a butler in a 1940's black and white film and you had his clone in the long-tailed morning coat, charcoal trousers, starched white shirt, near-black maroon vest, and matching tie of the man who carried in the fine silver tray, delicate bone china cups, and tea service.

"Frau Becker? X wird bald bei dir sein."

"Danke."

Addressing her in German was a nice touch as was the antique Meissen china. She wondered what would have happened if she'd been Icelandic or Hungarian? Probably switch out the help and the dishes just for effect.

Not that she could see the cameras, but she knew she was being watched. "Tell X we can speak English if he prefers."

The butler smiled and poured her tea before backing away and leaving her to peruse the titles of leather-bound books.

She sipped at the steaming tea. Delicious. No doubt engineered like everything else the man was known for.

The reflections in the wall of monitors closely matched the framed covers on the walls downstairs. The posture and the slight trembling of the hands lacked the vibrancy of the man who had conquered the world, but his eyes still gleamed with the intelligence that made him a force to be reckoned with across the globe. Hell, maybe the *universe*.

He watched the woman. Beautiful, and though he was now beyond such concerns, he understood the potential such perceived perfection engendered. There would be plenty of others to make up for any brawn and muscle she might lack, while her intellect and determination composed her primary threat.

He watched her pull down a volume from the shelves. The historian Howard Zinn's opus, *"A People's History of the United States."* One of his modern favorites. There was definitely more to her than a casual glance would have told.

He moved closer to the huge fireplace, large enough he could have stood inside, and let the warmth seep into his bones. Things were moving in patterns he'd long planned but at a faster pace than he'd anticipated. There was much to be done and little time for distraction or censure.

SEVEN

01110111

FIVE MINUTES AND HE was ready to explode. She could feel it in the muscles of his thighs and his increasingly erratic breathing. She did her best to back off. Unlike some of her friends, she loved doing it. Every part of it. He was young and smooth and hard and thick and every part of his body jerked and jumped and reacted to her slightest touch. It was like playing a living instrument, and a lot more fun and responsive than the piano she'd spent ten years trying to learn.

He was so close. Trying to hold back. He was younger than her by over a year, but was a good student, and she gave him plenty of practice. If he could breathe normally, let the tension out slowly, he might be able to hold off. She was the hottest chick he'd ever met, and she loved him in her mouth as much as he did. Well, okay, *maybe not that much*, but fuck... they'd dated for a year, and it was still getting better and better. She was getting more and more creative and lately had been digging for his fantasies. He couldn't imagine there was anything better than this. He wasn't ready to get married or anything, but couldn't imagine ever being apart.

Breathe. In and out. In and out... *shut the fuck up!* Don't think about *in and out!* Maybe football. How many times he'd scored last year. Damn it... not *score*. Maybe getting hit and tackled. Even with the pads, that shit hurt. Imagined himself hitting the ground hard. Dirt in his face and the smell of sweat and the grunts and groans of the linemen as they charged. Oh, fuck! Those were *her* fantasies, not his!

What the fuck were you supposed to think about to take your mind off what was happening? *Maybe stop signs.* No, everybody knew stop signs were erotic. *Red lights.* But weren't those supposed to represent hookers? *Green lights.* Green for go... *wrong thing.* The problem was, when you were nineteen, blessed to be a healthy, seriously good looking athlete, and had the hottest chick in the school working her magic, *everything* was a turn-on.

He saw her phone. Picked it up. Saw her perfect face. *God damn, she was sexy!*

He looked at who she'd moved into her new family tree. Some he knew, some not. Double D, Hot Asian Chick. Frowned. Hey, where was his face? Like he wasn't good enough? Come on... they were going to be joined together *forever*.

Found his pic, moved it back in, settled on grandfather. *Jesus.* That was *too* kinky. Waited until it updated, then tried great-great-grandfather. Watched again how her face broke apart and then began reconstructing. This shit was so cool!

Thousands of images flew by — *how could he know it was actually billions and billions.* Eyes and ears and noses and mouths. Watched the three-dimensional representation of her DNA twist and coil and deconstruct. Saw her face reassemble. Maybe her chin was a bit square, but now he was a part of her forever.

Starting at his toes, clenched hard enough you'd think they'd break, she felt the ripple across his legs, heat rising fast in the thighs she lay between. She let her hands move up, roam over his hard, rippled abs. Circled behind him, then grabbed hard and pulled him in. She swallowed and felt him enter her throat. She could only hold him a couple of seconds but was getting better. Like her parents taught her, if you were going to do something, you might as well do it right. There really was so much still to learn.

She gasped. *Too... fucking... hot.* She tore the covers away, and gulped for air.

Hard to see in the dim light, but she could swear steam rose from his body.

He arched against the bed, clenched the blanket in his fists, and writhed and pressed into the mattress.

Double D had told her they went crazy for the throat thing, but *wow!* She pushed herself away to watch. She knew she was good, *I mean come on...* but not this fucking good! Had to jerk her hands away. He was hot. Like a flame from somewhere deep inside, she watched his body glow just for an instant as if a ship of light rose from the depths below.

His skin cracked and blistered. An instant later, his entire body went up in flames. She gasped and threw herself back, falling and rolling off the bed, cracking her head while scrambling away.

He screamed out. Fought against an invisible force that seemed to twist and shake him in its grasp.

The flames across his body went out but the covers caught fire. Hot Chick screamed and crab-scuttled backward to the walls as Jock Strap's arms began twisting in their sockets.

The arms continued to turn outward. The pressure too great, the radius shattered and ripped through his skin, and still, his arms twisted.

Flames danced and frolicked against the antique wallpaper, then raced up the walls, gathering at the corners of the ceiling as if deciding their next moves. They went for it, and long tongues of flame roiled across the ceiling. Plaster blistered and fell, and Hot Chick staggered to her feet.

Impossible to get to the door. She turned from the inferno toward the window. Pried and clawed at the wooden frame, her nails breaking against the latches, painted and frozen shut from fifty years of new students each semester.

Jock Strap, now in full conflagration, thrashed and screamed out on the bed behind her. The superheated air pulled the oxygen from her lungs, and her once lush, butterscotch tresses crinkled and fizzed. She grabbed for a chair, slammed it with all her might against the window. Glass broke, and the air from outside rushed in to feed the fire.

Four floors, but she would have jumped without thought or hesitation. In front of her, the decorative iron bars, added fifteen years ago when a student had tried to commit suicide, kept her locked in her fiery prison. She pulled and pushed and kicked at the iron with no effect.

Outside, people poured from nearby buildings, stood in the deep snow in coats and slippers, screamed and yelled their encouragement, stared in horror at the shrieking naked girl fighting against the window as the flames embraced her.

Later, when questioned by dubious police and the arson investigators and the ravenous news reporters, eye-witness accounts and mobile phone captures would show the helpless girl grabbed by a twisted, distorted demon and torn in half just before fire engulfed the room and flames exploded from the windows.

EIGHT

01101111

A SHADOW AGAINST THE light, the man walked through clouds of decontaminant. Without the tailored suit jacket to hide the display of weapons, the silhouette of his physique in shirt and tie made him look even more imposing than when he'd been in the DARPA military lab.

Though he carried two illegal Glock-18's, fully automatic 9mm's in symmetrical shoulder holsters, the only real threat he posed to the man watching on, would have been the introduction of outside contagions.

Chemicals were sprayed from micro-jets in the walls every six feet, each formula designed to destroy different pathogens. The subdued lighting was augmented with narrow-spectrum ultraviolet and violet-blue light shown at the precise intensities to kill a broad spectrum of prokaryotic and eukaryotic microbial species and fungal spores. He'd made the journey down the long hall of floor-to-ceiling curved walls so many times over the past five years, he barely noticed any of it.

He stepped toward the wall. There was no need to announce his presence — he knew sensors in the floor, as well as the near invisible cameras in the ceiling and walls — had alerted X long before.

"On. Move to center four."

Inside the room, an image resolved over a quad of monitors in the center of the wall.

Outside, a large, hidden screen in the wall came on. The man waited patiently, outside the steel doors that might have let him in. There was no reason for such interaction, and X was content to speak from inside his chambers.

"Good evening, Gunns."

"Good evening, Sir. It went as you expected."

"How long?"

"I'd give it forty-eight hours to sink in, another twenty-four before they accept the inevitable. A day to act. Call it four days."

X sat propped against the headboard of his massive bed, looking like a small child on the vast expanse of mattress. The bed in turn looked small within the expansive room. The wall of monitors took up one side of the room, with Gunns on the central screens, and various angles of the woman displayed on the others. The massive fireplace burned opposite, while a Cube — every edge precisely sixty-one centimeters, the strange material lit by the glow of the screens and embers of the fire — sat on a simple wooden stand in the middle of the room. Made with a nearly indestructible alloy and woven carbon nanotubes, so black and matte it absorbed the light of the room, and yet, the air around it pulsed and shimmered in time to his heartbeat.

Gunns saw none of that. Nor did he see the man as he was now, sitting on the bed. He saw no trace of decline from the disease that ravaged the body, nor the trembling of the voice.

What Gunns saw and heard on the screen in front of him was much the same man the woman three floors below saw immortalized in photos on the walls. The image, like the speech, manipulated and enhanced by artificial intelligence, tailored for maximum effect based on a determination of the preferences and inherent biases of the individual viewer.

"Let's call it three days, seventy-two hours starting now. Shut it down."

Outside the room, Gunns nodded, and made the long trip back down the hall. No clouds of chemicals or light beams to rid him of whatever pathogens he once carried. Sanitized. Healthiest killer alive.

"Do you think they will forgive us?"

"I do."

They watched the woman downstairs fall. The irreplaceable china cup shattered as she bounced off the desk and crumpled on the floor.

"I'm not so sure."

The butler got up from where he sat beside X watching from the bed.

He turned to fluff up the pillows behind his friend.

"Great achievements take great sacrifice. They'll forgive you. Shall I tend the fire?"

The butler moved across the great room to stir and rearrange the embers. Sparks leaped and danced, climbing over each other to escape up the chimney. Here and gone, their lifespans cut short. He couldn't let that happen to him.

He turned to see two white-suited attendants rolling a padded gurney into the office below.

"Don't stay up too late. We have some trying days ahead."

Ula Becker lay on the floor, her focus narrowing like the shadow of a sunset inching across the floor. From the feet walking toward her from behind stainless-steel wheels and their little rubber tires, to the shattered porcelain vessel of her demise, and finally, to the individual threads of the hand-knotted carpet. Persian, not Turkish.

She'd once studied such things, fascinated by the workmanship as much as the representation of the Divine; the mathematics and multiplicity of the patterns serving as artists' representations of God, the unity of all existence.

She felt four hands lift her. She wanted to tell them to just give her the moment. She'd remember the name of the pattern soon.

From there she'd be able to tell them where the rug had been woven, maybe even the exact village. She'd be fine.

She couldn't concentrate long enough to let them know. Or that she'd been poisoned.

In her mind, she was shouting, "Check the tea!"

In reality, she mumbled and drooled.

"Screens off."

Lying on his side with the warmth from the fire on his back, the reflection of the embers multiplied across the screens lit the room with a soft, warm glow.

He rolled over to where the pulsing energy of the Cube could comfort him, lull him to sleep. Not long, he thought. He'd made so many mistakes. Soon he'd have all the time in the world to make up for them.

NINE

01100011

MOUNTAINS WERE A LONG way off, hiding in the formless distance, but snow reflected back on itself to hint at rolling foothills. Clumps of clouds thickened above and threatened to bring heavier snow over the next few days.

For now, headlights off the hard falling flakes looked like distant stars in the night. With no light other than the pin-prick of a distant farm, and the soft, nearly invisible glow that promised a town somewhere beyond the horizon, he floated in the big sedan as if flying across the sky. He felt, not for the first time driving through night snows, as if he were piloting an X-wing across the galaxy.

If only he could have flown here as fast or direct. Jeep to puddle jumper to a regional airport. From there to a real airport and a real plane. Then another. Across the oceans. Back to a smaller plane. Another regional airport. Then a rent-a-car across the hundred miles he was now driving.

Forty miles of land so flat it was as if purposely leveled. In fact, it had been, so that when rains fell the infrequent times they did, they'd soaked straight into the earth, keeping the farms and ranches from fighting over sparse water rights and the run-off. It wasn't nearly enough. Instead of oil like the lands both north and south of them, pipelines ran the precious water they relied on for irrigation and livestock.

Then thirty miles of gently sloping foothills, the edges and features softened under the heavy blanket of fresh snow.

He drove down, then into and across the basin, where the horizon sat above him with no defined separation of land and sky.

He searched for a radio station. Not easy in the middle of nowhere. Switched to AM and found the end of an oldie. *"House Of The Rising Sun"*. The early Clarence Ashley and Gwen Foster version from 1933.

"...they call the Rising Sun, where many poor boys to destruction have gone..."

Light appeared off the far sloping wall in front of him. Headlights. The first he'd seen in over an hour. Seemed higher than the hills, and a wave of vertigo threatened to take him off the road. He soon righted, and drove on as it approached with impossible speed. Maybe it was flying — a genuine UFO. Maybe he was in a Star Fighter after all.

It took a few more moments for his mind to resolve the image. A helicopter. Coming fast. Soon, he thought he could make out the running lights, which told him the make and model. On a direct intercept course with his own path.

A powerful searchlight blasted on, cut through the night and sliced across the hills as the chopper sped above the vast fields. He strained to look up past the car's roofline until the blinding light caused him to swerve.

The afterimage of the Huey, a huge, flying demon, danced behind his eyelids. Stealth black, no markings, all of which screamed military.

It roared past, the rotor-wash kicking up snow that refracted off the searchlights and scorched his retinas.

His phone rang, causing him to snap his head instinctively toward where it called for attention on the seat beside him, but he only saw the colored lights dancing across his brain.

The chopper dropped and skimmed the snow laden earth, the searchlight blasting into his windshield. He snapped his head away and tried to stay on the road, but powerful beams of light shot on from the side, and his world exploded in pain and confusion.

He had an instant to think he'd crossed a train track and had been smashed full-on as something huge slammed into the driver's side, lifted his car off the road, and crushed his door. Glass shattered and swept across his face in front of the bitter rush of wind and ice that took his breath away as much as the impact.

His wheels came down with an electric jolt to his spine, and he fought to stay on the road. Felt himself slide sideways as rooster tails of snow and ice and sparks arced fifty feet behind him.

The car slowly spun as he hydroplaned across the icy road, and he found himself staring at a huge black truck while it found its footing and began barreling back down on him.

The driver, a silhouette in shadow, waved like an old friend, and then stomped down on the gas.

His sedan suddenly spun completely around, and then again even faster. A 720 spin at sixty miles per hour in the middle of the icy highway. He let it happen, not that he had much choice.

He waited for the slightest bit of resistance of rubber on pavement, then turned hard on the wheel and stomped on the gas. Just enough to find direction as the car fishtailed back and forth down the road.

The chopper overhead turned back, the light fractured and multiplied through his broken windshield. The bitter wind and ice buffeted the side of his face and helped bring him back to his senses. He turned away from the light above in time to catch the beams in the rearview coming on fast.

The truck rammed into him from behind, and he slipped and slid down the road. The violent fishtails snapped his head back and forth, and he felt his spine realign and crack back into place. It was a big sedan, but not much more than half the weight of the huge truck and not meant to be part of a demolition derby.

The truck rode and bucked against the side of his car, and the driver stomped on the gas even more. As if all other sound dropped out, he could hear the individual components of the engine, the combustion of gases exploding in each cylinder, the whine of the belts, and the turning crankshaft as the truck drove him across the highway.

A wheel caught on exposed pavement. It was all the friction needed to redirect the pent-up energy of the moment, and his car leaped sideways off the highway.

Five, ten, fifteen feet into the air. Fifty feet out. It bounced once end-over-end then twisted, spun, and flipped sideways, an Olympic car-crashing performance. Not yet finished, the corner of the front bumper hit the ground before it bounced hard and was launched again. Rolling and tumbling sideways out into the featureless field of snow.

The car fell back to earth and slid another fifty feet on its roof before sliding down a bank into a small river. Sixty feet across, no more than three or four feet deep. Time sat still until it didn't, and so slowly it might have been measured in weeks or months, the lazy current slowly pulled him in.

Pretty sure his spine was intact, but every part of him was overwhelmed with pain. Head still attached, and icy air fought its way back into his lungs as he'd expect. But gravity was fucked, and it took more than a moment to make sense of it.

Upside down. He watched in slow motion. Not a trick of his imagination. The car sat on top of the water and ice, and then very slowly, inch by inch, began to spin and sink until it caught on the rocks jutting up from below.

Great. As a kid, he'd thought to be a magician. Maybe an escape artist. He'd had many days of annoying people until they tied him up just to see if he could get loose. He always did.

Later, by the time he got to handcuffs and chains, he'd discovered girls and football, and lost interest in magic. Probably should have stuck with it. Now, like the great Houdini, he'd die upside down in a water torture chamber.

He was stuck. The agony so strong he couldn't tell which leg it was. Just overwhelming pain that flooded his entire being.

The car continued settling, and the ceiling — *now the floor* — filled with water. His hand hung down into the frigid water.

Intellectually, he knew it was cold, no doubt below freezing, but he couldn't feel it. It was just... there.

Maybe he could sleep for a moment. Let his systems reset. Just one second he thought. Okay, make it two. *No five!* Okay, okay. He'd rest just maybe five, ten seconds...

And then he was out.

The chopper roared overhead, held its position in the air as the truck pulled over to add its lights across the field.

The car had flipped end over end, then bounced and rolled sideways a few times, landed on its roof, cut a fifty-foot long trench through four feet of snow, slid gently to the edge of the stream, and began to sink. The driver watched until steam from the engine stopped. The car spun in the water, achingly slow; half in, half out. It caught on the bottom and stopped. No movement.

The truck driver turned his engine off. Waited until the chopper made a slow pass over the wreck with its powerful light before returning to its place high in the sky, circled once more and took off.

No sound besides the dull FWUPHH FWUPHH FWUPHH of the chopper retreating.

The truck started up and pulled back onto the highway. Searched for a clear radio station. Not easy out here in the middle of nowhere.

TEN

01101011

SHE TRIED TO OPEN her eyes but they felt impossibly heavy. For an instant, the picture of her having to marshal all her efforts just to raise her eyelids seemed ridiculous. And then futile. And then suddenly like a challenge worth taking on. She gave up soon after the first bit of light, magnified and trapped in the prisms of her eyelashes, gave the briefest impression of two aliens working above her.

Great. Abducted by aliens. She'd never live this one down. She wondered if they would dissect her. Maybe grab a steak of the tender parts and cook her up. Any sex stuff was too weird and horrible to think about, though it had been awhile. What the hell did she know? *Brad Pitt.* Surely, he wasn't entirely human. Maybe it wouldn't be so bad. She couldn't open her eyes enough to know if they were tolerable, and gave up.

Sometime later, maybe a year or two, she had the sensation of something moving, and realized it was her fingers. For an instant she thought it was her hand that was moving her. And then had to wonder which hand had moved. Maybe they'd already switched them. Cut her arms off and stuck them on backward just to fuck with her. None of it made any sense. Something to do with computers and tea and zombies and vaccines. She'd rest awhile and try again soon.

Her brain tried to boot back up, and unintelligible noise became alien voices as if they'd been recorded and played back so slowly as to be only sound, not yet words. Not yet processing fast enough to decipher them, but she had the sensation that the two became three. *Jesus, they were multiplying while she lay here.*

Gunns looked at the nearly naked woman strapped to the table. Wasn't sure why they thought they had to strip her just to get a blood sample. Panties and a t-shirt. She had IVs in her arms. Maybe chemicals going in and out. Not his area of expertise. Pads and wires monitoring her heart rate, blood pressure, oxygen levels. The two doctors, if that's what they were, hovered above her.
      "Shut it down."

She could feel her hand. One, but not both. Interesting as she was sure she had two when she came here. *Damn.* When had she come here? And the voices above her. Starting to make sense.

"But there's so much we don't know. So much to learn."
      "You have twenty-four hours. Then it gets shut down. And you with it if you're not out of here."

Her fingers moved. She was sure of it this time. She ran her thumb across her index finger. Left hand. The voices above her were in English. The three above her became two. And the alien shadows resolved into humans. In lab coats and surgical masks.
      Fingers of her right hand moved. She let sensation tingle back into her fingers as consciousness crept into her mind. The Lab Coats were making adjustments to equipment around her when she realized she was strapped to the table she lay on.
      Back online — it all came rushing back to her. The library. The old butler. The tea. She flexed against the restraints. And again.

Was sure she could get her left arm free. And the Lab Coat on her right side was reaching across to make some kind of adjustment. His crotch almost in her hands. If his intent was to get a free hand job, she had a surprise for him.

Okay. *Eins... zwie... drie...*

To the men, it seemed the room exploded. She squeezed with all her might, felt flesh burst and rupture in her hand. At the same time, she pulled her left hand free, jerked the other Lab Coat down, met his face with her elbow driving upward. Her right hand let go, and the unfortunate man dropped unconscious. Not done with the left-side man. She reached across, released the Velcro strap holding her right arm, grabbed the man by his lab jacket, and slammed him into the wall. He bounced off, and as he spun off and fell toward her, she slammed her forearm into his face, breaking his nose and putting him out.

He fell and pulled off a handful of glass vials and bottles with him as he crashed to the floor.

She sat up. Freed her legs. Why the hell was she naked? Well, more or less.

Eased the IVs from her arms. Looked around the small exam room. Grabbed at the charts and reports, the figures and notations swimming in front of her eyes. What the hell had they given her? Strained to make her eyes focus.

Stepped down onto a broken bottle. She cried out and hopped back on the table. *Scheisse!* Her foot opened with a wide gash. *Scheiße!*

She looked around. No clothes. The lab coats too strong to tear. She tore at her t-shirt. Ripped off the bottom half. Wrapped and tied it to her foot.

Vision still swimming, she stared at the floor until she was sure she wasn't stepping on more glass. Eased herself off.

Reached for the door.

It opened before her hand touched the knob. In front, a massive man. Maybe six and a half feet and three-hundred pounds. Muscle piled on top of muscle into a caricature. She fell back, reaching for anything, and her hand closed on a syringe.

She stabbed forward. It wasn't that she moved so fast, the drugs in her system prevented that, it was that he didn't try to block it. The syringe plunged into the thick slab of muscle that covered his chest, but he grabbed her by the hair in one hand, pulled the needle out with the other, and dragged her from the room.

ELEVEN

01111001

DARK AND QUIET MIGHT be creepy for some, lit by the few computers and desk lamps left on, but Mads liked it like this. Empty, with few distractions. The work they did here was sometimes boring, many times tedious — but at others, it challenged and taxed all of their collective brain power.

She wanted to bring her conclusions to Carmine, but not until she had it all in order.

If she was wrong, no foul as long as it stayed between her and the boss. If she was right, she'd need guidance on what to do next. There would be plenty of time for some serious soul-searching; she knew her career in the military would be over. No exaggeration to say her life would change, and hard to imagine for the better. But at least she'd be able to live with herself.

At first, she'd thought the video heavily edited, but after watching a few times, concluded it was mostly edited in-camera, stops, and starts for each angle. Raw, but incredibly skillful and effective, and the subject matter amplified all meaning.

Past a small black girl as her hand reached for a half-buried doll. A young black boy looked up into the camera for encouragement before brushing away dirt to reveal a scrap of metal with partials of all too familiar logos and insignias.

The view stopped. Opened on a new scene, peered through heavy, lush foliage as two jeeps and a 5-ton truck filled with soldiers pulled into the devastated clearing. Heavily armed, ready for war. It made no sense. Who the hell were they going to fight against?

Orders shouted. Mads understood the French, but not the Kikongo creole, as men moved in teams across the barren landscape, randomly shooting at the dirt and ashes.

The camera stopped on a soldier kicking at the dirt. Zoomed in. Revealed a child's arm, partly denuded of flesh, the bone white and garish under the tropical sunlight, no more than five or six, sticking up from the ash. The soldier jumped back just as three of his men unloaded their weapons into the ground.

The camera view jerked to the side and caught a fast glimpse of a hand, a white man's hand, clamped over a small African boy's mouth. Cautioning him for quiet. A fragmented shot on the wide-eyed little girl squatting beside them, doll clutched tightly to her chest, then over their shoulders on soldiers shooting up the dirt.

A helicopter roared overhead. No visible markings. Set down in the middle of a thick cloud of ash and dust. She watched frame by frame as the cloud settled, hoping for any hint of who stepped out, but the little camera veered away.

And then a footrace deeper into the jungle. Flashes of lush rainforest and a narrow path of thick mud.

The camera stopped and the screen went black.

Except for the children and lush landscape, no sign of where the video had been taken. She was waiting to hear from her source. He'd promised more. Much more.

She brought up the Lisbon footage again. One of the early events captured and broadcast through social media across the world. So outlandish and over-the-top, it was easy to explain away. The Reddits and Voats and 4Chans of the world were having a field day. People claiming to have inside scoops, some fantastic homemade fakes, and a couple of elaborate copycats. Even the worst of the productions had followers and picked up millions of views on YouTube. Wild rumors of government disinformation campaigns filled the message boards, while others claimed the answers lie with the expertise of the Russians, the limitless money of the Chinese, the expertise of the Iranians. The tentacles of the Deep State.

Mads was confident it was real, and was now comparing it to footage leaked out of another small town in Africa. Not an isolated event. *An entire outbreak.* Just a matter of time before someone created an aggregate of all the clips, much the way she had, but instead of verification and study, added titles and music and packaged them up as the next indie horror hit.

Another problem was the town didn't exist. At least not anymore.

Her gut told her where this was all going; the voices in her head cautioned her to wait. She had some idea of how she would approach Carm, and if right, some idea how he would react.

He was a genuine good guy, had been her mentor, hell, her *idol* for nearly twenty years. His cherubic disposition belied his razor-sharp mind and relentless quest for knowledge. He must have already suspected.

Her phone vibrated and she snatched it up.

"Jack?" Shit. "Oh, okay."

She hit a switch and the monitors went dark. She went to another workstation. Made some quick adjustments. Hit a series of switches and went to unlock the lab door. Looked up at the big clock over the doors. It always made her smile; one of the most advanced labs in the world, and they used the same giant analog clock that lorded over every classroom in every school she'd ever been in. 10:40 p.m.

Hit the switch that unlocked the outside doors, waited until she could see him outside the lab. Unlocked the door, and greeted him with a kiss.

"Who's Jack?"

"What?" Locked the steel doors behind them. "Oh, just a colleague. Give me just a minute," lifting her phone as explanation, "and then we can get out of here."

Why wasn't he picking up? It wasn't like him. Hell, he was the one who'd started this, the one that reached out to *her*.

She pushed Professor Hall toward her desk, stepped back into the hallway, and tried to call again.

TWELVE

01110011

OTHER THAN A FEW flickering bulbs, the long hallway was empty. It was enough light to show the filthy floor and rock-hewn walls. As much a tunnel as a hall.

Echoes of a one-sided struggle could be heard and soon rounded the corner, where Beast dragged Ula by her hair across the decades of detritus and litter. She fought and yelled and scratched, but still he came.

An instant later, they were joined by another man. Skinny, amped on something besides the moment, fighting to get ahead, then behind, jumping and skipping. He nearly tripped on his own feet and stepped on the woman as he pushed a small video camera into her face.

Beast shoved him out of the way and kept coming, but Skinny was determined to capture every moment. Gleeful and giggling with the challenge.

Close on the pain in her face, closer on the terror in her eyes. A shot of her foot bleeding through the makeshift bandage, the blood of the floor lost in the dust and debris. A great shot of her breasts as her chest heaved from the exertion. A close-up on Beast as he lifted her with one hand by her hair over the broken floor.

The frenzied trio entered a large chamber. A higher ceiling, stone and brick, and past three new computers, monitors, routers, and modems, strung together on a makeshift table. Three chairs behind them.

The woman had no chance to see the set up, or the two young men manning their stations.

Beast dragged her toward a huge door, thick with rust on the iron strapping that held it together. With one hand, he pulled the mighty door open, and with the other, tossed the woman in.

She tumbled across the smaller chamber, crashing into the far wall. Enough it knocked her senseless, but just for a moment.

Her hand grabbed at the debris-strewn floor. A piece of brick. She spun and threw it with all her might. Beast jerked Skinny out of the way — the brick grazed his head and exploded against the wall.

Dazed, but jacked with adrenaline, she reached for more, charged across the floor like a crazed banshee as Beast grabbed Skinny by his scrawny neck and threw him from the room. He stepped out, and slammed the door shut behind him.

Ula crashed into it. She might as well have run into the stone wall. Hanging onto the rusted iron bars across the small window, she pulled and kicked at it.

"Lasst mich raus! Bitte lassen Sie mich raus! Ihr Wichser!"

Giving in to the panic that threatened to overwhelm her, she attacked the door with all her fury. Threw her shoulders against it. Kicked and pounded until it opened the gash on her foot further. Screamed and yelled, but it took just moments to realize she was trapped, the echoes of her shouts and curses her only companions.

THIRTEEN

01000001

MADS WAS WORRIED. She'd been calling and calling. He'd reached out to her for confirmation, and now that she had it, or at least thought she did, he disappears? Maybe he'd changed his mind, though that would be a first. Hadn't happened once in the year they dated. Not once in the years she'd known him since. Not when he was a badass commander in special forces. Not as the — whatever the hell it was he did now. He was *relentless*.

No. Something was wrong, and she was right to be worried. This was bigger than all of them and spiraling out of control.

Phone at her ear, she entered the lab and froze. A thousand thoughts ran through her mind. None of them good.

Hall was at her computer. The wall of video screens was up. The Lisbon footage leaked on the news everyone had watched. The Chinese event that no one outside this lab had seen. Classified footage from India. The African footage.

Four events being analyzed in minute detail.

And what no one had seen, besides her and Carmine, data recorded of each person's activity from just before each event triggered by the Loop app. Theoretical genome and DNA manipulation. Matching images from the application taken at approximately the same time interval before each event. Estimates of brain activity based on machine learning algorithms she herself had written and programmed. No way to know conclusively, but enough she'd convinced Carmine to let her run with it.

It might be as close to a smoking gun as they were going to get.

Stunned, not able to think, she dropped the ringing phone in her lab coat.

"What the fuck are you doing?"

He ignored her. Never a good thing to do with a woman.

Hall advanced the images, just the way she had minutes before he came, just to the point of the bodies contorting and beginning to smolder from inside.

"I said, what the hell do you think you're doing?"

He typed in a command. Every screen began erasing itself. A graphic representation on the monitors of hard drives deleting every frame of her work. Each matched genome. All the synchronized activity.

It was all safely stored in the servers... but then he started typing in new commands.

"Get the fuck out!" She turned and pointed to the door. "NOW!"

He slammed her in the head with a keyboard. He used both hands, and considerable effort, the hard edge smashed just below her skull, catching the back of her neck.

The impact, directly between the atlas and axis vertebrae, rocked her head to the side and she fell like a rock. The side of her skull bounced off the steel cabinet with a sickening crunch of bone and the ringing of steel, and she crashed to the floor.

Professor Hall watched the blood flow from the gash in her head. A twitch of her fingers but nothing else moved. He leaned forward to look down at the crimson liquid slowly spreading toward his feet. Tilted his head. He could almost see his reflection.

Turned back. Typed in more instructions. A rack of servers was blinking, and he made an educated guess. Removed the relevant hard drive, and watched her computer screens flash multiple error messages. Wiped down the keyboard.

He didn't worry about her being found. She was working late and had slipped, or the janitor attacked her, or a hundred other plausible scenarios. The high-end security systems she'd disabled to allow their tryst, meant he was never here.

Besides, it wasn't as if the town didn't have other things to worry about right now.

She couldn't move. Couldn't see or hear. Couldn't feel. Her ability to interface with the physical world was no longer a part of her reality. Just before the final ionic transmissions across the synaptic receptors buried deep in her cerebral cortex failed and dimmed, the connections flashed to a single image of a man, and then formed a single word. *Relentless.*

Chemicals and electricity, there was nothing spiritual about it. She was here. And then she was gone.

FOURTEEN

01101110

THE LARGE CHAMBER WAS nearly as dark as the hallways and tunnels. The only additional light came from the computer monitors, lighting the two boys manning them.

Both early twenties. A Teen Idol nerd and his friend, tall and thin and just as good looking, little more than a Clothes Hanger.

Teen Idol made an adjustment and an instant later, his monitor lit up with a high overhead shot of the woman in her little prison. The Clothes Hanger turned away and adjusted a variety of controls. A third and fourth monitor fired up showing multiple views from inside the room, four in all.

"What the fuck was that about?"

"Fuck off."

Beast and Skinny arguing as they came to join the boys.

"You didn't have to drag her. You about tore her fucking hair out. What the fuck is wrong with you? She's at least as human as you are."

"A fucking stripper? Who gives a shit? You knew what we were doing—"

"The fuck I did."

Skinny pulled the SD card from his mini-cam and slapped it on the worktable beside Teen Idol. A good chance they could edit it in, turn this into a real production.

Beast grabbed him with one huge hand, but Skinny darted forward and slammed his fist into the big man's face.

Beast partially blocked it, and the fist thunked off his thick skull. Beast tossed him across the room where the smaller man bounced off the wall and wobbled to his feet.

"Hey, guys!" Clothes Hanger was on his feet and stepping between them. "Fucking cool it!"

He turned to Skinny. "The girl's fine. You know the Professor said we'd have better luck if we can heighten her emotions. So unless you thought she was going to fall in love with you by the time we got her here, fear is the best way to go."

"We already agreed on all that shit," Beast reminded them.

"Yeah. Scare her. Not torture her."

Beast pushed forward again, but the good looking nerd held his ground between them.

"Come on guys, you want to get paid?" Clothes Hanger turned to Skinny. "And don't try to pretend you didn't know what you signed up for."

He sat back down, turned to Teen Idol who shrugged and shook his head, and turned back to his task.

Skinny and Beast, ready to go at it again, moved behind the boys and watched as they worked.

They watched as the woman surveyed the room. She walked the perimeter, banging on the walls, feeling the brick as if it might open up for her.

She looked directly up into the camera, then turned to scope out the other three. All four set high into the ceiling. The angles made her appear small and helpless.

Settling against a rough wall, she let her back scoot down it until she sat on the filthy floor, hugging her knees.

Clothes Hanger worked some controls, and the camera zoomed in to a wide-eyed close-up as she stared back at it.

Practiced fingers danced over the keyboard and an instant later, a large clock popped up on the screen. 24:00:00. Counting down. 23:59:59... 23:59:58... 23:59:57...

New commands were typed in, and a simple log-in counter appeared. The cursor blinked_ blinked_ blinked_

And the number 1 popped on.

"Yes!"

Almost before the word was out of his out mouth. The number changed. They watched as it rapidly increased to twenty-five, then it suddenly shot up into the seventies. The four looked at each other, held their breath. Wishes granted, the counter jumped into the hundreds.

More adjustments were made, and a request for donations appeared. Bitcoin or Ethereum preferred.

Skinny glanced at Beast. He was still pissed, but this is what he'd come for.

Someone, somewhere, made the first transfer, and the dollar amount came on screen.

Beast grinned and turned back. Like kids in a candy store, the excitement couldn't be contained. High fives all around.

"Okay," Teen Idol said. "Time to raise the stakes." He brought up more computer controls and a moment later, their view of the room was bathed in light.

Ula sat against the wall. Her head a long way from cleared; whatever poison was in her system was still there. Waves of nausea washed over her, and she fought down the urge to throw up even though she knew it would probably do her good.

Rage that had kept her warm was quickly fading into fear and bone-racking cold. She hugged her knees, hanging on to whatever warmth her body produced, and fought to reign in the despair.

Who the fuck were these people? She needed to quiet her thoughts to make sense of it.

She'd come to confront him. X. A visionary. The Messiah. The Antichrist. A hundred people would give a hundred different answers and perhaps they were all right. *But stupid?* Stupid enough to drug and drag her here?

She knew too much about him to imagine it. Retraced her steps in her mind. They all led back to the library. Waiting to meet the man himself — she had questions that perhaps only he could answer. Looking at photos on the wall. Drinking her tea. Something gnawed at her, fought its way through the chatter. The tea. The antique Meissen china. A butler who spoke perfect Germa —

— she was blinded by light.

"Go for it," Teen Idol said.

Clothes Hanger hit the switch and three more projectors came on. One for each wall. UDH, 5000 lumens each. The walls prepped in silver paint to give them maximum reflection and brightness.

A new window appeared on the monitors. The Loop app. The girl's face front and center. Moments later, the AI's first mapping of her DNA based on her facial structure appeared.

Complex machine learning would constantly update and refine the estimate as it worked to increase the accuracy. They had a database of tens of thousands of relevant images they could feed it. The boys had worked hard to create an app that would automatically try different combinations.

The counter continued. 23:51:42... 23:51:41... 23:51:40.

Logins were low six figures, and donations, disappointing, but crossing their first one hundred. *They had plenty of time.*

FIFTEEN

01100100

His head throbbed in time to the pumping of his heart, admittedly slow, but strong enough to wake him. Black became gray became less gray. Then everything in shades of white.

The car rested on its top, and the ceiling had filled with water, edges crusting with ice as water flowed from front to back. The windshield, what was left of it, was thick with ice, huge starbursts and crystal configurations that would have delighted any child. He began to sense a world of color within the patterns as increasing daylight refracted off prisms of ice.

The car had flipped and bounced across the field, each impact finding some new corner to crumple. *Random physics in random motion created random outcomes.* He'd read that somewhere, and it made sense now. The windshield he was looking through was reduced to a triangle of fractured light about a foot by a foot and a half.

Driver's door buckled inward, the passenger door intact. The passenger airbag had deployed, no sign of the one that had been designed to protect him. What had been a spacious interior was reduced to a small, misshapen box. *A pretty shitty coffin if he didn't get out soon.*

He rolled his head in circles, his neck still worked. He twisted to see what held him up.

His right leg. He'd been slammed back and forth by the impacts, nothing broken, but the sedan bounced and folded and twisted. Only half his leg was visible. He turned and pulled himself toward the tiny triangular porthole of light until he saw a foot sticking up in the air outside. Snow piled up six inches on the upturned boot.

Inside, the metal of the car came to a sharp crease where the windshield had been, and his leg, from the knee down, was presumably trapped on the other side of it.

No visible blood. It didn't seem possible not to be severed. No pain. And that worried him. He tried to think what his options might be. They rolled over him in slow motion like the fog of his breath.

He could hang here until someone found him. Another couple of months of snow and cold to go. If someone stumbled on him before spring, they'd find him neatly frozen upside down. It wouldn't take long to discover who he was, and they could say, *"here was the fool who thought he could save the world."*

Maybe wolves would come by and gnaw his leg off from the outside, then he could hop his way to town. Just thirty or forty miles. Did wolves live around here? He'd heard they were making a comeback. Maybe a fox. Beavers in the river. Wasn't sure if they were above making a meal of a human leg. Might have thought it was just another frozen log and used it to build their dam, but probably smart enough to be hibernating. *Rabbits.* Rabbits *liked* snow.

He remembered watching the rabbits hop through snow as a kid, and tracking them just to see where they lived. And to prove to himself he could do it.

In summers, he would creep close, sometimes taking a whole morning. At twenty feet, he'd spring up and chase them across the fields. He was fast. *World fast.* Zig zagging and turning with every direction change.

It didn't happen often but once in awhile, he'd manage to actually scoop up one of the furry creatures, but then let go even faster as it kicked and fought in his hands. Maybe they were dangerous, he had no idea at ten. In all his years, he'd never met anyone who chased and caught rabbits by hand who lived to tell about it.

Yeah, once upon a time. He had the feeling that his running days might be over.

Now, he just needed a fluffle of rabid, carnivorous bunnies to come by and free him.

If no one found him until the thaw, any flesh left would be rotted and putrid. Might take a few extra days to figure out who he was after the vultures and crows picked his bones clean. Dental records and DNA were on file; they'd get there.

More light as the world turned. He thought he could see his phone. Lying under six inches of freezing water in what had been the roof over the back of the car. Teasing him. Not a chance in hell he could reach it. Miles and miles beyond his grasp.

His head throbbed. As much from the poor selection of options as the pressure of blood that would surely cause him to stroke out if he didn't freeze solid first.

Too much to think about. He let himself drift —

Flying across the endless galaxy. Master of his destiny. Then the alien UFO. Then rammed by the massive attack ship of the Empire.

Needed his lightsaber. He'd make quick work of the leg. Get back to base and let them attach a new one, like Luke's, better than the one he had. *Easy-peasy.*

Dreams became thoughts became plans became decisions. Instead of waiting for wolves to gnaw his leg off from the outside, he could try to cut it off from the inside. *Hey, it's just a leg.* He had lots of buddies who had lost more. A few where a leg had been the only thing left. And others where…

Bullshit! He was fucking strong, damn it! He put his good leg against the crumpled steel. Twisted to get his shoulders braced against the top. Just fucking lift the goddamned car off his leg and slide it out.

Icy water sloshed against his neck and into his ears. The cold helped him focus. One, two, three, GO! He gave it everything he had. Felt his spine compress, bones popping against each other and crushing the discs that separated them, his good knee grinding as muscles in his thigh and hip gave direction to everything he had left. His heart pumped and he thought his head might explode, but he grunted and roared and dug deep and found even more.

Nothing. Not a fraction of an inch. He collapsed. Let the chill of the water bring him back to his senses.

Okay. Fuck it. It had been a good leg. Served him well. A bit beat up and scarred like the rest of him, but now it was him or his leg.

He'd have to cut it off while he still had the strength to do it. *If* he had the strength. *And with what?*

He was trapped inside a box of metal and glass. Had to be something. Safety glass didn't give him anything. And the dash was mostly plastic to begin with. Designed not to have anything sharp. The thin chromed molding around the windshield was metal. Bent and twisted away from the broken glass, the shiny metal called to him.

He reached for it. Pulled at it. Bent it against itself. It seemed to take all his remaining strength to bend it back. Another reserve he discovered to crease it. Worried it back and forth until the stress began separating metal and it suddenly broke off into his hand.

He ran his thumb across the back. Hands numb. Couldn't feel a thing. But it looked like an edge.

Okay. No lightsaber in sight. He'd have to make do with the world's dullest knife.

The light dimmed and he knew he was running out of time. How long had he been here? He felt his beard. Had been more or less clean-shaven when he arrived. Did increased blood supply make whiskers grow faster? He couldn't feel anything in his frozen hands but it sounded as though no more than a day's growth as his rough palms crossed his chin. Fifty grit sandpaper at most.

He needed a tourniquet. His other foot hanging almost down in his face. Shoelace might work. His frozen fingers pulled at it. Double tied. A minute. Five. No way could he make his hands work enough to untie it.

His belt. A buckle wasn't nearly so complicated a piece of machinery as a tied, frozen shoelace.

Even that took more effort than he would have imagined, but it was soon wrapped tight around his lower thigh. The thigh he hung upside down below.

It took a dozen drags of his make-shift butter knife to get through his jeans. Peeled away the fabric. Started in on the flesh.

He knew it was a one-shot deal. Once he started, there could be no stopping. He cut as hard as he could and watched the flesh part. Blood seeped in to fill the wound, and dripped down into his eyes. He didn't really need to watch anyway. Afternoon light fading, his eyes literally only saw red. The blood splashed onto his face, hot against his skin, into his mouth and up his nose, threatening to drown him in blood. Mind drifting but hands kept sawing.

It was black outside when he dropped into the water. The splash seemed to wake him as if he'd been sleeping for hours. Part of him remembered sawing at his leg, the parting of flesh. First skin, then layers of fat and muscle — not much around his knee — and finally chopping and sawing at tendon and ligament.

He heard himself scream in frustration and anguish, railing against the flesh that held him in place, filled with hatred for his weakness and the limb that threatened his life. He'd made his peace in losing it before he started, yet it refused to release him. Then he couldn't wait to be rid of the cursed thing.

Sometime in the night, he won the battle, his fear of weakness the only thing that kept him alive. He twisted in his miniature coffin. He unlocked, then kicked at the mangled passenger door. Again. It opened enough he knew he could slide past it. He remembered he had a coat somewhere.

Took a minute, but he found the coat. A giant frozen sponge. Doubled back for the phone. Another ordeal to reach it. If it still worked somehow — was waterproof as advertised — maybe they'd want him for testimonials. If not, he was definitely calling customer service and getting his money back.

He crawled up the bank. The snow and ice a protective layer between him and the razor-like bramble beneath it.

He sat up. The sight of his two legs sticking out was something he'd seen every day of his forty-three years. Having the view changed, no lower leg, no foot below it, no matching boot, caused a wave of vertigo to wash over him.

His head cleared. Too cold to feel pain. Still, things had to be done and done now. He tightened the belt around his leg. Afraid to loosen it. What if all the blood just drained out of him right here in the snowy field? He should have been dead. Not the first time they'd tried...

He had his thick coat. Waterlogged and frozen stiff. He did his best to wring it out. Still waterlogged and frozen stiff, but it was all he had.

No moon. No light. The clouds and mists of snow enveloped him in formless gray. He knew the ground was below him. And the sky above. The world hadn't changed.

He needed rest, warmth, care, and food.

Reached into his coat pocket. *Ha!* A protein bar! He tore at the wrapper with frozen hands, his thick fingers not working. He chewed on the end until the paper tore and he tasted the artificial *everything* on his tongue. Chewed the wax paper up with it. How could it hurt?

It took time to make his jaw work enough to grind the frozen paste, but the sweetness on his tongue let him know he was alive. At least for now. The bastards hadn't killed him, hadn't stopped him.

Trying to balance in the deep snow on one leg was maybe easier than without the snow, but it still took forever to get to his foot.

Endless fields of gray going white as day tussled with the night to give form to the landscape. Like a blank piece of white paper in front of his eyes.

The highway should be close. He could crawl to it, flag down the first vehicle that came by... get to a hospital. He concentrated. No sound other than his labored breathing. No landmarks other than the wide stream that held his car. No idea if it ran east or west, north or south.

He stood on his one leg long enough the sky slowly brightened. From dim to less dim. Still no clue.

Frozen with indecision. Frozen in the cold wind and snow. Just... fucking... frozen. *Jesus, already.* Make a fucking decision.

He fell to his stomach and began crawling.

Time to save the world.

SIXTEEN

01000010

IT WAS ONE OF those days when the sun took the day off. Clumps of snowflakes, like little pre-made snowballs, plopped onto sidewalks made crunchy with refrozen snow.

She unlocked the padlock on the outer security gate door. Fought against the ice and snow to fold it open. An accordion of frozen steel. Opened the front door and quickly locked it behind her.

Stamped her combat boots free of ice, and caught a glimpse of herself in an oversized, gilt-framed mirror. Looked a bit like the world's most colorful snow ninja until she began unwrapping the layers.

She dropped the backpack. Then the hat, cap, and face wrap. Scarves, outer jackets, and mittens. That left her with fingerless gloves, an oversized hoodie, and a bright orange tie-dyed sari wrapped over her powder-blue-camo combat fatigues. At least one of every possible clashing color and pattern known to man was visible.

Flipped a light on over the cash register where the owner's handwritten instructions for the day waited for her.

Jessie, if there's too much snow,
you two lock up early and go home. Your call.
Have a great weekend — Sid

Jessie went straight for the coffee pot. Locally roasted and ground, but the pot she brewed was triple strength, and would be poured over an almost equal amount of sugar.

As the heady aroma filled the shop, she turned all the TVs on. Morning news, Saturday cartoons, local programming.

She let the caffeine and sugar speed through her veins and warm her bones.

Clocks on the wall and those lined up on the simple wooden shelves all came close to showing the same time, while a paper calendar on the wall by the cash register noted it was monthly inventory day. Shelves of computers and tools, worn books, VHS tapes and scuffed DVDs, cameras, and second-rate jewelry. Kitchen appliances, vintage mixers and toasters, silver and silver plate, and mostly full sets of wedding china.

It could all wait. She had almost two hours before she had to open up.

In the back, half a dozen vintage arcade games. Pac-Man, Space Invaders, Asteroids. Black Knight and Eight Ball deluxe, two of the greatest silver ball monuments ever made. Near mint condition.

Beside them, the third coup of Sid's pinball acquisitions — a modded out but otherwise museum-quality edifice, calling her name to *"the dimension of imagination,"* a mainstay of top-ten lists of all-time wide-body flipper boxes everywhere, Midway's Twilight Zone.

SEVENTEEN

01100001

A HIT SINCE ITS debut on April 1 of the same year, "Dennō Senshi Porygon," *Computer Warrior Porygon*, the 38th episode of Poketto Monsutā, or *Pokémon,* as the rest of the world would come to know it, was broadcast on December 16, 1997, at 6:30 p.m. across thirty-seven stations in Japan and was seen by over four and a half-million households.

By 7 p.m., the calls to hospitals were already starting to build, and before that Tuesday night was over, Japan's newspapers and news stations would report nearly 700 young viewers were transported by ambulance for nausea, headaches, shortness of breath, and a wide range of myoclonic seizures, to local hospitals and clinics.

Though most recovered on the ride in, some 150 children would be admitted to hospitals for further observation, while two spent weeks under medical care before returning home.

All in all, and with what was later to be determined as a mass hysteria event built up from news media and schoolyard word of mouth, some 12,000 young people across Japan complained of a variety of symptoms.

The incident — its aftermath, the legend, misinformation, subsequent legal action, and changes made to world-wide broadcasts, media and video games creation — would take nearly two years before being brought to the attention of then Lieutenant Carmine Marelli by one of his colleagues, Second Lieutenant Madison Clark, a junior officer and the aunt to two young boys whose mother was concerned about this new Japanese programming that was sweeping the nation.

It struck a chord, and the beginning of an idea began to form. Already documented with anecdotal evidence and hard research begun in the 30s, the idea that outside stimulus could trigger electrical and chemical reactions within the body in the form of photosensitive epileptic episodes was well documented.

As the ability to map the functions of the brain increased, so did the understanding of the role of photic stimuli and manipulation — duration,   color,   and   frequency — and   the mapping of specific responses to specific regions of the brain.

The abstract that Lieutenant Carmine Marelli wrote as his doctoral thesis on vaccine delivery, the idea of using sight and sound to coax the body into producing a wide range of targeted responses in both electrical and chemical reactions — insulin, or white blood cells, or the increased production of adaptive immune responses to target viruses and even cancerous cells — to in effect, create its own individualized vaccines and medicines, came to the attention of the military, and the visionary artificial-intelligence pioneer, Alliard X.

Both reached out. Though X had the advantage of seemingly endless resources, the military already had hooks into him. Soon, as Captain, and then as Major, Carmine found his work perverted from saving the world into finding military applications and weaponization.

Exponential advances in both machine learning and artificial intelligence were now making his original concept a very real possibility. Facial recognition technologies became familial and genetic bio-mapping, while targeted vaccine delivery became targeted bioweapons systems.

Somewhere along the way, a part of the technology, with no thought or understanding of the danger, maybe developed independently and in parallel, found its way into a social media app. Of course it was addictive; from the graphics to the sound, it was designed to be. And now, good or bad — *fuck it,* it was all bad — it was out there.

Numb, Carmine sat on a high lab chair. He watched the Assistant MEs roll Mad's body out of the room on a steel gurney. Cold and antiseptic, exactly why he wanted to do research instead of practice medicine. He wasn't made for so much death.

The lab was a joint project of both the government and private sector with congressional civilian oversight. Uniformed Military Police stood at ready, looking over the lab, but let the civilian cops do their jobs.

The crime scene techs and forensics, suited up like they were in a space movie, had been there most of the night and morning. Considering what was going on in the world, not the kind of place that could afford to lose a day, but seemingly every surface was covered with fingerprint dust and blocked with crime scene tape.

They finished their final photos. The clicks and flashes reminding Carmine of the strange world that had brought them to this point.

"What can you tell me about what she was working on?"

The detective looked around the high-tech lab. Pretty sure he wouldn't understand it anyway, but he needed to ask. And again, since the big guy didn't seem to hear him the first time.

"Major Marelli. I know you're upset. Can you tell me anything about what the Captain was working on?"

Carmine looked at him. It took him some moments to realize sound was coming out of the man's mouth. Maybe asking him a question.

"Everything we do here is classified."

The detective had been warned. He knew the drill. His presence there was a matter of form. He'd only be in trouble if he actually found something, and then it would have to be turned over, and any memory of it sworn to secrecy under threat of early retirement or worse. Any real investigation would only begin, if at all, after he left and signed off.

Logs and check-ins showed the woman liked to work by herself. But somewhere in the night, the ME's first impression said before midnight, she'd let someone in. No other way to make it into the lab. Maybe a friend or a lover, someone she felt she had to keep secret. Or maybe she was being blackmailed or selling classified technology.

He'd already watched the last night's security footage. Nothing from the outside; most of the cameras trained inside the lab had been turned off, and still others, erased. A hard drive missing.

Someone had hit her. Hard enough she'd fallen and maybe hit her head again on the way down. Hair and trace tissue evidence left their imprints. The autopsy would show more about the order of what happened, but on its own, had little chance of revealing the who.

"Okay. You decide you have anything to say, give me a call."

He handed over a business card. "Number's on there," he said, mostly to fill up the time. One more chance to gauge the man's reactions. He felt bad. The Major genuinely looked devastated, and as fat as he was, totally deflated.

Looked one more time at the blood on the floor. Hoped the big guy would call a bio-hazard clean-up crew, and not take it on himself. Some stains lasted more than a lifetime, no matter how hard you scrubbed.

He walked out with the rest of the civilians.

The two MPs stood their ground on either side of the door.

Carmine made sure they saw him toss the Detective's card in the trash can. It missed and fluttered to the floor.

He slid off the stool, struggled to bend over and pick it up... and saw the phone. Mad's phone. The one with the silly stickers on it, on the floor under the lab table.

He knew his bulk blocked any view the MPs had. Got on hands and knees, dodged the puddle of blood and reached for it. He dragged it closer with one finger until he could grab it, all while making a show of dropping the card in the trash.

Got his feet under him, and used the stool as a crutch to help him stand. *Now what?*

It made sense to turn the phone over to the detective. Who knew how they'd missed it, but they might find out who she'd seen last. Maybe even find the killer. But first, he wanted the chance to talk to whoever had been feeding her information. Then had to hope they weren't the same person.

He needed to get out of here. Go home. Make some dinner. Make a fucking plan. Was reaching in his desk drawer when he felt the presence behind him. Left the phone inside and traded it for his keys.

Turned around to face Colonel Bradley.

EIGHTEEN

01101110

THE VIEW FROM THE ground made the barn look huge. It was the first thing he'd seen in hours that wasn't white.

He lay in an acute slice of mid-morning light that stretched from the open door across the cold wooden floor. Cold, but not as cold as the seemingly endless fields of snow. The murky grays and browns of the barn welcome after the hours of reflected light.

He could hear, but not see pigeons above him fluttering in the rafters, cooing their concerns about the frozen apparition that had invaded their home.

The sharp smell of livestock burned the inside of his nose and filled his mouth with the taste of leather. He was thankful for it, and the warmth rising from below.

So... his eyes and nose and ears worked. He was alive. His eyes soon adjusted enough he could see into the shadows. Workbenches, a wheelbarrow, and a stack of buckets. Saw a long wooden table. He crawled to it, pulled himself up.

He struggled to get the coat off. Nearly frozen to him. Saw some dry coveralls hanging on a peg, not his size and not a chance he could have pulled himself into them anyway. Not until his hands and legs thawed. He hopped to the wall, pulled them off and wrapped them like a shawl around his shoulders. Fell back to the table, and took stock of his surroundings.

The barn was big, not huge, and well made. Massive, hand-hewn timbers showed it had been here a long time. Bales of hay. He was tempted to crawl deep into the straw and sleep. But if there was a barn, with animals snorting and oinking and mooing and clucking below, then surely there was a house nearby.

An ancient tractor, a newer one beside it. Tools on the wall. Hammers, saws, and an axe. Hoes, and a pitchfork.

He looked at his leg. His jeans and boot caked in melting snow and ice. Then at the half leg. Took him some time to get his fingers working but he loosened the leather belt. A raw, ugly wound at the end of a thigh that was now rapidly swelling. Blood dripped from the ragged flesh as it began to thaw, and he reluctantly tightened it back up. The throbbing and pain hitting hard, reminding him that he needed real heat and real care.

Hopped to the wall and grabbed the hoe for a crutch. Awkward, but he was new at this. Hobbled to the big double barn doors. A clever pulley system that made it easy to open.

The doors parted on well engineered tracks. Fifty feet in front of him was a two-story farmhouse. Like him, it had seen better days, but right now the blue smoke drifting from the chimney promised everything he needed inside.

He reached for the axe. You never knew. Lifted it off the wall and turned back.

He stumbled and hopped, his instincts sending him reeling backward even before his mind caught up to the little red-haired girl standing in front of the barn doors.

Almost fell, steadied himself with the hoe long enough to laugh at his reaction. She was cute. No fear, just a child's wonder and curiosity.

He had a moment to question if she was anything more than a trauma-induced hallucination, but thought he should probably say hello anyway.

A shadow swept up from behind him just before he was slammed over the head, and it all went dark.

NINETEEN

01100100

No high score today, an obvious sign the universe was out of whack.

She'd started with an easy stretch on Asteroids, warmed up on Space Invaders, and put in a serious workout on Twilight Zone. Tougher than it looked.

Twelve minutes and counting. The right flipper slapped the steel ball high. It spun through the mid-lanes and racked up double bonus points, ricocheted and bounced, and dropped onto the baby flipper where she tossed it back into the Power Field. It rang and clanged and dinged, caught on and bounced around the magnets, went crazy on the knocker until it kicked out and fell straight to where she caught it on her left flipper.

She had one last door to nail, but instead threw it to the Gumball. Two balls sat waiting in the Lock, and she needed one more, or even just a good shot up the left ramp in time to trigger another round of multi-ball play.

Biffed with the left. Missed high and dropped back through the right lanes. An easy catch, and she completely blanked. Drained it. Dead center. Opportunity missed.

Only four-hundred million, two-hundred thirty-five thousand, seven-hundred thirty-five. A long way from Roy Wills' masterful billion-point score.

You would have thought she was in training for some secret back-alley underground pinball battle or even a shot at the IFPA's World Pinball Championship, but nope. She preferred to keep her skills to herself.

Some people might call her a retro gaming nerd. A pinhead or a plungeroo. Or a Pac-Man addict.

She was none of these things. *Or maybe all of them and more.*

She'd first approached the games as a representation of a simpler time, stirring memories of when her dad used to take her to the bowling alley arcades on a Saturday morning. She'd have a pink or purple mini-camo cargo pocket full of quarters to occupy her time while catching glimpses of her dad playing in the leagues.

Only later did she realize why her mother always had to pick her up on Saturday afternoons, and why she'd wake up Sunday mornings to see her dad passed out on the couch. Or in his car. Or lying in the yard. Turned out he was a loving father, a half-ass bowler, and a first-class drunk.

People liked her, gravitated toward her, but she couldn't bring herself to play the step-and-fetch-and-press social games that would have ingratiated her with them.

First, was the fact she looked younger but was older than most of the other students. Second, she had an insatiable thirst to understand people. No one in particular, at least not yet, just humankind as a whole. And third, according to a Gypsy fortune-teller she'd met at fourteen, she had an older soul. Not like, *Egyptian mummy old,* just fifty years or so...

The retro games and analog culture were part of her doctoral thesis and studies, as was the monitoring of the AI class, that she hoped to someday use as a way to codify the social norms and interactions that were reshaping society at exponentially alarming rates.

Well documented that the last twenty years had produced a population addicted to online activities, willing to trade privacy and personal freedoms for the illusion of joining a global collective even while privately retreating into the comfort of perceived tribalism.

The recent worldwide pandemic had exacerbated those elements of society, adding to the near-cult-status of figures that were increasingly determining policy across the globe for real-world problems in everything from the response and threat of the current and future pandemics, to climate change, social equality and equitable justice, and our reluctance for meaningful response.

Her studies specifically examined the addiction loop of near-instantaneous feedback and validation, *yes, Twitter, yes, Facebook,* through computational complexity theory. Decision problems reduced to a yes or no, a 1 or a 0, a positive or negative response, to a given input stream of otherwise meaningless and irrelevant data.

The rebellion against societal progress, the deepening of political chasms and social rifts were accelerating, becoming more and more sharply divided and potentially violent.

She wasn't feeling it today. She'd pushed herself this far, but it was time to call it quits. She bumped the machine with her hip harder than the tilt settings allowed, and the steel ball fell like a rock between the flippers.

She'd cool down on Pac-Man, and think about her upcoming day.

Sid said it was her call on getting out early. Not much to get out to.

Though she wasn't consciously listening to the cartoons, restored black and white movies, or the national and local news playing up front, the constant rehashing of the fire and death of two fellow students was bringing her down. They weren't close friends, but still... she felt bad. She'd had zero desire to be a part of their little gang, but they'd been fun to watch, and in their own clueless way, innocent.

Now, besides the newest WHO projections of pandemic deaths and variants and the ongoing issues with the vaccines, you could add in rumors of a mystery virus that turned people into homicidal zombified pyromaniacs — and that was *before* they started chewing on you and tearing you limb from limb.

She knew not to believe any of it at face value. She laughed at herself — LOOP — face value — but it all sounded too fantastical. The viral videos were such low quality, and she had a good idea at how far the technology of deep fakes and VFX could be pushed. Creepy as fuck for sure, but come on, a smartphone app?

But she also knew there was precedence, Pokémon came to mind, and that nagged at her big time. She glanced at the clocks. Still had fifteen minutes.

Didn't see the shadow racing by outside the door as she took a sip of cold coffee and fired up the game.

Wacka... Wacka... Wacka... less about the overt metaphor of Pac-Man's consumerism and endless hunger than a seemingly simple mathematical puzzle. Like everything else she looked at, it became a mandala, hinting at patterns within the larger universe.

She paused, backed up, gobbled up some cookies, trapped and pounced on poor Clyde.

Wacka... Wacka... Wacka... besides, it was fun.

...

Banging on the outside gates brought her back to reality. The clocks more or less said a quarter after eleven. Jeez! A full hour past time to open up.

She stopped by the cash register, grabbed the keys from the drawer, and unlocked the door.

"Thought you were coming early today so we could get started."

"Sorry," and in case she was *'snow-blind'* and somehow missed it, "snow."

Numbnuts held up the bag. A peace offering. The world's best donuts. As famous for the fact that they hadn't closed a day in twenty years, even on Christmas, as for the made-to-order-donuts with dozens of homemade topping options. Caramel and Granny Smith apple for her. He knew better than to show up late without a bribe if he wanted to keep his job.

She switched on the rest of the overhead lights and turned on the OPEN sign in the window. Looked through the neon PAWN SHOP at the still gray day, the wet snow falling harder. Flipped the OPEN CLOSED sign around on the door.

They'd either be dead because of the snow, or busy because of the holidays.

"Think we can get out early today?"

She turned, ready to ream him out. He was already plopped on a stool, staring at his phone, drinking a Mountain Dew, and eating his donut. Poster Boy for slackers everywhere.

Didn't have the strength for it today, she let her breath out slowly. "Let's see what happens."

"Okay. Cool!"

TWENTY

01100101

HIS EYES OPENED TO the hallucination again. It sat staring at him in the form of a little girl. Six he guessed, though he didn't have the experience to really know. What the hell? It was *his* hallucination — *she was six*. Messy red curls pulled back with a green ribbon. Cute as all little girls were. Preternaturally bright blue eyes. Perched on a little yellow chair. Eating a biscuit dripping with melting butter and honey. Crumbs stuck to her little pink lips.

She seemed real enough, but he closed his eyes and willed her away. He'd open them again in some hotel, maybe along a Mediterranean beach — that's where he'd been heading the last time things made sense — a beautiful woman sleeping beside him, curtains blowing in the warm ocean breeze, and with two good legs.

Smells of bacon were strong, as was coffee, and baking biscuits. The smell of burning firewood, dried pine and oak, and maybe a hint of soap. His hallucinations were detailed, he'd give them that.

He could hear movement. Couldn't determine what it was. Not ocean waves. Not the breathing of a lover curled up beside him.

He opened one eye. Was just as cute in half-vision. A dusting of freckles on her nose. Impossibly long eyelashes. *Fuck it.* Opened the other.

Behind the girl was a woman at a fireplace. Back toward him, a wild mass of red curls swimming around her head, she hummed to herself while concentrating on a large iron skillet and stirring up the wood in the fireplace. Beside her on a small table was a plate of biscuits. They looked like blue-ribbon winners at any county fair, stacked three high, beside a bowl with butter and a Mason jar of honey, and a plate of crisp bacon.

The movement of his eyelids wore him out. He felt incredibly heavy, weighed down, even the lifting of his chest to breathe felt labored. He let his eyes close. Tried to shut out the sounds that he had now assigned meaning. His imagination was out of control. He needed to go back to sleep, reset, and try again. *The woman in the Mediterranean hotel seemed like the way to go.*

The woman turned to her daughter. Less than arm's distance away from the stranger, but she wasn't worried. He looked like he was still asleep, or more accurately, unconscious.

"Do you want another one, honey?"

The girl nodded. Her mother buttered up another one of the blue-ribbon biscuits, drizzled it with golden honey gathered from their own beehives, and traded her daughter's empty saucer for a new one.

Instincts, the lizard part of his brain, gradually lifted him from the dark depths of his unconsciousness, and into the light of reality. Fighting to breathe, his tongue thick and choking off air. He gasped for oxygen, found none, and forced himself to breathe slow and steady through his nose.

The little girl was still there. Still staring at him as if he was a puzzle to be solved. *Good luck with that.* Well-meaning amateurs and professionals alike had tried and failed.

The woman was occupied at the fireplace, her back toward him. Singing softly. He couldn't catch the words but it sounded like a hymn. The flames danced in front of her and distorted her silhouette while making the mop of red hair glow and writhe with a life of its own.

His eyes went to a crucifix, big for a house, perched high on the wall above the fire. Christ nailed to the cross, twisting in the shadows and embracing the ecstasy and pain of sacrifice.

He tried to turn. Couldn't move, still heavy with abject fatigue and exhaustion. Twisted his head and saw more crosses and crucifixes on the walls, dancing in fire and candlelight. Some, incredibly detailed and lifelike, some, little more than sticks and twigs tied together with string and wire.

He was covered in thick blankets, heavy but not possibly enough to be weighing him down. His arms felt pinned to his sides and he realized he was naked beneath the blankets.

Tilted his head until he could see he was wrapped and bound to a sofa with heavy chains. The links an inch thick, they would have held an elephant and were wrapped around and around, holding him in place and squeezing the air from his lungs. He tried to yell out, and only then realized a thick strip of cloth gagged him.

The little girl kept at her biscuit. The mother, the red hair said she *had* to be, turned and smiled, then returned to her task.

She put the heavy iron skillet deeper into the fire. Added more wood. It was starting to glow but she wanted to be sure.

The woman stood above him. Pulled the blanket from his legs. He could only imagine the raw ugly wound that met her. He hadn't felt this helpless trapped in the car. He tried to shout, tell her this wasn't the way.

He watched through unbidden tears as she calmly put on some huge mittens. Like what men wore working in steel foundries. Turned back to the fire and lifted the white-hot skillet.

As if from the outside, he watched himself thrash and scream and fight. In truth, he could barely breathe much less move as she brought the iron skillet closer.

"Close your eyes, honey."

He locked eyes with the girl as she smiled and nibbled her biscuit.

The woman held the iron to the raw flesh. It sizzled against the skillet. Burned and smoked. The man, despite the bonds, seemed to levitate from the big sofa. He twisted inside the chains, screamed out against the gag, and passed out.

She circled and rolled the pan, making sure to seal and burn the ragged edges. Pleased to discover the smell of his burning flesh wasn't that much different than the bacon.

It was nice to have a man in the house again. Sure, he only had one leg. Well, really, one and a half. But he was a *man*.

She'd cracked him over the head in the barn; first thought to leave him there or maybe feed him to the pigs. She'd picked up the axe with every intention of using it but her daughter shook her head no, so they'd dragged him through the snow into the house.

Covered in blood up to his neck. She'd stripped and cleaned him, pleased to find everything else was intact. Slabs of muscle across his chest, cords of muscles for arms. How long had it been since she'd touched any part of a man?

Fought against the impure thoughts, thankful her daughter couldn't read her mind. Though sometimes…

Still, she was embarrassed. *HE* was always watching. She fell to her knees and begged forgiveness before covering the man with blankets and chaining him to the sofa.

She wondered where he'd come from, what might have happened? And how long she could keep him.

Forced herself to return to the task at hand. Nothing to do but do it. She worked until the job was done.

She untied the gag — good thing she'd tied it on. She would have hated for her daughter to be subjected to what she could only imagine were blasphemous curses and the vilest of language.

Fixed herself a cup of coffee, ate a slice of bacon, slathered butter and honey on a biscuit for herself, and pulled her chair up beside her daughter to watch him sleep.

TWENTY-ONE

01110010

JESSIE MOVED TO THE next set of shelves and continued checking items off her list.

Started with the TVs. Big, small, mostly cheap, but a couple had been expensive in their day. CRT's and early flat screens. Even one 50" 4K.

Still on. Endless channels. Cable service was cheap in Mazeville. The tragic fire again. Lot's of rumors about the cause, all with some obscure connection to a pirated smartphone app.

Conspiracy machines ramping up *bigly*. The usual gamut of theories on Big Brother and Big Tech and Artificial Intelligence taking over the world. The end of days. Terminator machines would be next, currently mapping their human targets with autonomous cars and drones. The app, *this Loop thing*, was nothing more than a software update to the microchips already delivered worldwide inside the Covid vaccines. Triggered by new Chinese satellites secretly launched from somewhere in Africa. Interviews with the organizers of nationwide protests on government overreach and the ever-increasing intrusion into privacy. Blaming the Democrats. Blaming the Republicans.

The CEO of a Wall Street start-up was touting his genuine lab-replicated Neanderthal DNA as the cure for all modern diseases. Somehow not getting it that Neanderthals had the same high mortality rates and shortened lifespans as the rest of early hominoids. And that was *before* they were phased out of the gene pool. *Didn't really seem like the best bet to her.* And last, before she was far enough away to tune it out, a web portal where people could pay to be freeze-dried and shipped to Mars where they'd later be thawed out to colonize the planet.

Numbnuts' eyes left his phone long enough to engage.

"Pretty wild, huh?" Back to his phone.

Jessie moved to the next shelves. Checking the items one by one. Computers, keyboards, gaming consoles, electric guitars, chain saws, leaf blowers, socket sets, screwdrivers, a samurai sword —

"This would probably go faster if you helped."

"I would, man. But you know, I don't want to like, get in your way or something."

She was tempted to throw something at him, plenty to choose from, her hand was moving toward a hammer, but she went back to it.

"Hey, did Sid leave our checks?"

He wouldn't have lasted past lunch if he hadn't been a distant nephew of the owner. When she'd first seen him, back at the end of summer, she'd thought he was kind of sexy in that hopeless slacker way that she was sometimes attracted to.

Tall, thin to just before the point of looking malnourished, shoulder-length blond hair that looked like it belonged on a California surfer dude, and a scraggly little beard that gave him the Shaggy Rogers look.

She liked vegan looking hippies just fine, especially with all that lush hair, but by the time he'd opened his mouth and finished his first sentence, she'd ruled out all possibilities.

One o'clock. Only one person had braved the elements long enough to peek in, asking if they had the newest impossible to get SONY PLAYSTATION. *Ummm…* No.

"Hey, Numbnuts, maybe you could take out the garbage?"

No response.

"After the garbage is out, I'll get your check and you can take off."

"Oh, okay. Cool!"

She signed off on the monthly inventory. Made her notes. Left a reminder to Sid about the stamps.

The Nazi stamp collection they'd taken in a month ago could now probably be sold on eBay or on a dedicated collector's site. Someone would want them, especially the mint pane of 1941 Hitler-Mussolini stamps.

What Sid pointed out to her when she'd shown him, and what the woman who'd brought them in missed, was the true value of the 1923 Weimar Republic overprints. Originally 200 marks, covering the cost of foreign and domestic letters under 20 grams, the printing of new stamps at the time was out of the question. Cheaper to print on top of the old ones. Sky-rocketing inflation and wildly fluctuating values saw the stamp officially "overprinted" and re-issued at 2,000,000 marks.

She couldn't fathom the numbers, and even less when Sid recounted his grandmother's stories of billion-dollar Mark notes and half-trillion Mark loaves of bread.

He told her the pair of unused, mint quality stamps might fetch as much as three or four thousand dollars. Maybe more.

Jessie needed coffee. Maybe she'd spend the afternoon reading.

They had a small selection of well-worn books no one besides her had cracked in thirty years. Stevenson and Verne, Grimm Brothers and Lewis Carroll. A nearly complete set of Dr. Suess for good measure.

Got water for the coffee. She wasn't a coffee snob — well, okay, *maybe she was* — but one of the easiest to solve and most overlooked requirements of a good brew was the water. Not the chemically laced and mineral enhanced liquid that came out of the faucets.

She carried the pot to the five-gallon glass dispenser of distilled, ozone polished, 11% hydrogen, 89% oxygen combination everyone else called water. Nothing more. Nothing less. She knew those percentages were off a few hundredths, but fuck it, close enough.

Went to dump the old coffee filter. *Damn it, Numbnuts!*

She pulled out the plastic garbage bag, not even half-filled, but *"take out the garbage,"* meant to take out *all* the garbage.

Hurried to the back door.

The blast of arctic air almost took her off her feet. Ice and snow whipped across her face and drove her back. She had to shout twice to get his attention.

"Hey, Numbnuts!

She watched him use all his strength to crack the snow-topped lid high enough he could push the half bag he carried into the green enameled dumpster. He turned toward her. Snow was really coming down and drifting against the alley walls. The idiot without even a coat — she might have missed him behind the curtain of winter if she hadn't known he was there.

She raised the bag in her hand. Ventured half a dozen steps and tossed it as far as she could.

The bag landed with a dull plop between them.

Numbnuts smiled and waved, shrugged, then slipped, slid, and staggered his way to it.

And screamed.

He fell to his knees. Close enough she could see his hands blistering and turning black. An instant later, flames raced up his skinny arms and his entire body burst into flames.

A blood-curdling scream of pain and terror, and as she watched, his clothes either went up in ashes or melted on his body, leaving him naked and burnt. As the flames went out, his arms twisted in their sockets, elbows bent backward until she could hear bones cracking and flesh splitting. His back folded and snapped him to one side, and then back again.

He fell on his back onto the snow where he writhed in agony and the ice melted around him.

Jessie couldn't think. Rewound and ran the day back in an instant. Yep. It was real. She was here. In a snow-filled alley with... *whatever it was.*

She backed up, slipped, and fell hard onto the snow. One moment standing, and in less than the blink of an eye, flat on her back gasping her breath.

She crabbed backward and watched as Numbnuts, now *roasted nuts* for sure, began trying to stand. His arms twisted and circled around him as if they belonged to some other creature, while his legs tried going all directions at once, preventing any forward progress.

Jessie made it to her feet, slipping and sliding in the snow, getting her feet under her and finding her balance, just as Numbnuts mastered his legs.

She jumped for the door, slipped on the tile, was slamming the door when she glimpsed what had been a lethargic numbnut slacker just moments before, launching itself high into the air.

The steel door clanked shut and the locks snicked into place milliseconds before his body slammed into it. The latch held but the impact buckled the door and knocked her off her feet. She hit the back wall, bounced off, and landed on her knees.

She stared at the door as the thing outside smashed into it again and again. The steel door and frame combination, fire-rated for three hours and with a PSF hurricane rating of 65 — *it could withstand winds up to 160 mph* — but BOOM! She watched the 16-gauge steel deform as it was pounded inward.

Just when she thought he might actually break through, he stopped. Silence deafening. The trickle of newscasts and old movies from up front working their way into her consciousness.

Jessie made it to her feet. Stepped as quietly as she could across the wet tile and put her ear against the door.

Nothing.

And then she heard it. A scurrying, clamoring sound against the door, up the wall, and across the roof.

She sprinted toward the front. Slid across the floor to the cash register for the keys. Dropped them. *Jesus!* Coins and pens and receipts going everywhere. She scooped up the keys again, ran for the door.

Could hear Numbnuts above her as she ran. She made it in time to see him, or what was left of him, leap to the ground. His jump took him onto the snowy sidewalk where his momentum slid him far out into the street.

A car, only doing twenty, slammed on its brakes and slid into the strange, burnt, twisted figure scrabbling and sliding in the middle of the street.

Numbnuts was launched into the air but landed mostly on his feet. Twisted and spun like a giant spider, jerking, scurrying, and finding its footing on the frozen roadway.

The woman in the car stared, then remembered to stomp on the gas, but her car spun on the ice.

Jessie put all her effort into getting the door closed. The iron accordion gate was frozen in place. She kicked and pulled and shook it with all her might. Ninety-three pounds fueled by fear. It broke free of its bonds, and she pulled and pushed and slid it shut.

The car's rear end slid into another parked car where the grating of metal on metal screeched like amplified nails on a chalkboard. Numbnuts leaped on the hood of the car, and the woman leaned into her horn. No need, the creature that had once been Numbnuts was focused on the pawnshop.

Jessie fumbled with the keys, tried to get the padlock open. It opened and she shut the shackle back on itself... but missed the hole. Turned the key and opened it again, twisted it back over the hasp, and locked it home just as Numbnuts slammed into the steel grating.

She fell back on her ass and watched in horror as the creature attacked the gate with much of the same desperation she'd used to close it, but with near superhuman strength.

The gate twisted and deformed and bent in his hands, but the steel held. She looked to the iron frame where it was bolted into the brick and mortar. Watched as concrete dust fell and bolts began shaking free.

Back on her feet. She pushed the tempered glass door shut against him, dodging his frenzied grabs and attacks through the bars. No way could she get the glass door closed.

She fell back, out of breath and with tears in her eyes from frustration. Stepped back. Tried to think. The fucking television blared about how it was all a hoax. Fake news. Not to worry. They'd send the military and straighten it all out. The authorities explaining it had all been a big misunderstanding.

The tools. A chainsaw. *How the fuck do you start up a chainsaw without cutting off your own legs anyway?* Leaf blowers, socket sets, screwdrivers, a samurai sword...

The twisted burnt flesh pulled and twisted, and then stretched to grab her as Jessie chopped down with all her strength.

The sword sliced through the arm as if it hadn't been there. It fell and twisted on the ground as the creature screeched out and attacked with an all-out assault of desperation.

Jessie backed up, screamed and ran the sword into the creature's heart.

For an instant, almost face to burnt face, she saw a glimpse of humanity in its eyes before they closed and the abomination fell to the ground.

Jessie pulled the sword out, let it clang to the floor as she renewed her efforts to shut and lock the door.

Not easy as his arm and shoulder — *his attached arm* — was caught in the gate. She tried not to look at his face. The surfer hair had gone up in smoke, and his blackened flesh oozed and cracked as she pushed and shoved until he was pushed further onto the sidewalk, and the door took its place in the jamb.

All she could think of as she turned the key was, *they were real.* Jabberwockys and Bandersnatches and all the fucking Snarks. Boojums for sure.

Maybe she *had* entered the Twilight Zone, but this shit was as real as real gets.

TWENTY-TWO

01110011

WHAT WAS ENVISIONED BY city founders as the most modern of infrastructures in the 1840s, elaborate basements and underground tunnels dug for the transportation of goods and the *"invisible"* support of their supply chains, with a lower layer of catacombs utilized for cold storage in the days before refrigeration, and then lower still, the advanced sewage systems for the burgeoning town of Maizeville, sections of the tunnels, excavated caves and coal mines, were older than the town itself.

Much like the cities of New York, Chicago, and Boston it was modeled after, the underground soon boasted miniature train and cable cars carrying the citizens to elaborate ballrooms and concert halls complete with frescoes and stunning mosaics, chandeliers, and viewing galleries.

The founding of the university in 1910 saw the elaborate brick arch with the university name, and press releases with photos sent to newspapers across the globe, with a misspelling of its name.

Rather than facing up to the embarrassment, the town council quickly decided to embrace the new moniker, and sent out further press releases to the effect it had all been planned in honor of the elaborate hidden infrastructure. Maizeville, named after the distribution of the grain which had put it on the world map, became *Mazeville*.

As pride in the town above grew, the desire to be safely ensconced underground lessened, though it again found use during prohibition by bootleggers and small-town mobsters, and then enjoyed a resurgence of interest during the heightened tensions between Kennedy and Khrushchev.

Like many cities with lesser-known systems like Louisville, Cincinnati, Atlanta, and Seattle, the entrances and tunnels were eventually abandoned. In constant need of repair and a drain on the city coffers, it soon became expedient to seal them up.

Portions of the tunnels under the university had not so secretly been reopened, and rumors of wild fraternity and sorority parties, elaborate hazings, and drunken orgies, became a source of school pride until the murder of a young co-ed found them once again abandoned.

Professor Hall didn't give a shit about any of that. He'd explored enough to discover access to these chambers, and had taken advantage of it.

Having spent long nights and weekends of the past year underground, his movements now reflected the rats that could be found working their way back and forth from the abandoned sewer depths below to the streets above, and he scurried through the halls and tunnels.

He could still get lost. There were miles of constructed hallways and even more of old mining tunnels. He'd started with a basic map. You could get one in the library. But he was in a sub-basement, really the sub of the sub-basements where undocumented halls and tunnels fanned out like spokes from a cavernous chamber.

The intermittent strings of bulbs hanging from rock ceiling tunnels and brick-arched hallways once guided his way, but as he'd explored and strung them further and further, the more confusing it had become. He'd charted halls and tunnels with their access sealed, some completely caved in. It was like being trapped inside a giant Rubik's Cube, and you could now add the failing bulbs.

He thought he heard voices ahead. Or behind. Or maybe they were just running through his head. It could be hard to tell in the catacombs of Mazeville. Stopped to listen. Made his turn and continued.

He'd had reservations in the beginning, but this is where he could work in peace. Like Frankenstein's laboratory, he could conduct experiments without the scrutiny of those who might question his methods. Underground. Halfway to China.

He laughed at the idea. Closer than you might think since they funded much of his work.

TWENTY-THREE

01101110

GENERAL CONNELLY STOOD AT the sink, staring in the mirror. Searching his eyes. What would a computer see? What would it determine as the essence of the man standing here?

He knew his family tree. Could recite the trunk for six generations. Sixty-four names going back to his great-great-great-great grandparents outside of County Cork, Ireland. Making their stand, and the venerable Ó Conghaile name mean something.

Could a computer find the DNA strand that prepared generations of their men and women to serve their countries? Isolate the genetic component of shouldering responsibility to putting men in harm's way across the world?

Or would it go deeper? Discover the doubts and fears coursing through his veins? Hell, you didn't need a computer, they were mapped all over his face for anyone with eyes to see. Was that strand also in his DNA, or was he the anomaly?

It was no wonder kids around the world wanted to change who they were. So did he.

And now, he couldn't stop thinking about how to cover his ass. Seeds planted years ago — the harvest of those decisions made just hours before he arrived. Unraveling faster than his mind could keep up with, and so now it seemed his thoughts had come to a dead-end. Facing a brick wall with a mounted mirror to mock him.

His kids were grown, doing well last time he'd heard. They rarely reached out to him, and him less to them. But they still talked to their mother.

Publicly, his wife adored him. He knew it was all an act. Or maybe only part of it was an act. They were *comfortable* with each other.

She'd had her lovers, seeking comfort those years he was off saving the world. He could hardly begrudge her that, and to her credit, she'd never let herself fall in love with anyone but him.

Her need for security was perhaps why she married him to begin with. The big strong soldier, defender of freedom. If he could protect American interests across the globe, then surely he could protect her at home.

None of it had really worked out that way.

She was dying, and nothing he could do about it. His sacrifices and efforts would not protect her from the disease that was ravaging her nervous system with increasing frequency and severity. Time was short. The promise of medical breakthroughs at the periphery of their research would not come in time to save her.

He dipped his face in the cold running water. At least it was his face. Tired, lined, beat up a bit. *But his.* Goddammit. How the fuck did the technology get out there? And into a game no less? Fuck, not *even* a game. A stupid vanity app. Vanity combined with wish-fulfillment was the key to its rapid, viral-like spread. You didn't have to change human nature, just tap into it.

He came up for air and was startled to see Colonel Bradley in the mirror behind him.

"Hey, Mike." Reached for the paper towels.

"Hey, Bill."

Dried his face. "What are you doing here?"

He sensed the Colonel's hand darting forward. He twisted and caught a glimpse of the needle-like spike before it was rammed into his back.

The General arced backward in shock and pain. He would have fallen if the Colonel hadn't caught him. Didn't have the balance or strength to fight as a syringe was jammed into the side of his neck. Bradley pulled him backward, guiding him to one of the stalls. Sat him on the toilet and watched him die.

Closed the door. Wrapped the syringe in a paper towel, and dropped it in the trash. Washed his hands.

His reflection, strong and confident, smiled back at him.

The General had left him with a mess to clean up, and he was just getting started.

TWENTY-FOUR

01100001

SKINNY TURNED FROM THE iron-barred window of the door to watch the geeksters on their computers. Fingers flew across the keyboards in short, sporadic flourishes.

Teen Idol looked down at his lap and smiled, *a sure sign he was on a mobile device.* The video feed on his screen showed the hot girl in her cell. In panties and a t-shirt. Must have been freezing. But, maybe she was used to it, being half-naked. Running around without her clothes on. *Who was she?* A nobody, a *stripper.* The kind of chick he'd bang every day when they hit the numbers they'd get from their little experiment.

"Jesus. If we can just get her to change on video, we're going to be famous."

His friend looked at him. "Do we even know who she is?"

"Do we really give a shit?"

They both tried to look serious, trying to outdo each other. Burst out laughing.

"Get ready for an explosion of followers. Fame gets you money."

"With enough fame, you don't even need money."

...

Back to the window to watch her. She sat on the filthy floor, her back against the wall, arms wrapped tightly around her knees. He wondered who she was. A drugged-out stripper they'd told him. Drugged when they'd grabbed her for sure.

Inside, the thousands of images fed into the Loop app raced by and were looped over and over, blasting from projectors trained on all four walls. They'd run all night. And still nothing.

Skinny stared at the images. Billions of viable combinations within the parameters of her AI predicted DNA, yet each remained unique to her. Six generations minus her parents. Sixty-two individuals with their own evolving calculations.

The woman looked to be about 110, 115 pounds. Take away the water, and you had maybe 45 pounds left. 45 pounds of what?

At its core, 99% of all the atoms in the body were made up of four elements. Over half the mass was oxygen; a bit over twelve percent was carbon. Of course hydrogen, the most abundant substance in the universe and perhaps 75% of all baryonic mass — *the atoms formed during the Big Bang* — and nitrogen. That left a kilogram of calcium and traces of another dozen elements, micrograms of manganese and molybdenum.

Was that all there was to it? A string of instructions on how to organize the elements and the compounds they formed into the woman that sat in the room? Was that all she was? *All he was?*

"But why doesn't it affect her?" Skinny asked.

"That's what we're trying to find out," Professor Hall said.

Teen Idol scrambled to hide the views counter on his monitor, and Clothes Hanger slid the iPad up under his shirt.

No need. Hall was busy taking off his coat, then dropped a couple of paper bags on the table.

Skinny reached for the bigger of the bags, heavy with four wax-paper wrapped subs. Deep thoughts always made him hungry.

These weren't your typical *"Transparent Turkey"* with lettuce, or *"Hint of Ham"* with their impressively-thin slices of tomatoes cross-bred to last as long as possible with no discernible spoilage or taste.

No, these were sandwiches worthy of the label; certainly more laudable than the degenerate Fourth Earl of Sandwich from which they took their name.

Seriously fresh homemade bread, slabs of meat piled high and heavy, run through the garden with the freshest of blue-ribbon vegetables and tomatoes. Slathered with locally made mayonnaise, and the secret-recipe homemade dressing that made Monico's the envy of college sandwich shops across the country.

The two on their computers bypassed them and went for the Skittles and Red Bull.

"We know the app incorporates advanced machine learning to break down the theoretical DNA strands and resulting genome with a visual stimulus that triggers random neuro-cortical responses, but do you really think there's something more to it?"

"We haven't even proved it's the app that causes the transformation."

"It's the app."

"I still don't buy it."

"What's not to buy?" Teen Idol argued. "But we are missing *something*. A missing element. *A catalyst*. Something that isolates and localizes the response."

"Maybe an additional piece of code targeting the town?"

"Maybe it's triggered by the device's GPS?" Skinny asked between bites.

They looked at him as if he was crazy, or maybe a genius.

Hall watched them debate and argue. He had additional pieces of the puzzle, but wasn't ready to share. He could settle for millions, was spending it in his mind. But, then again... look at Twitter and Facebook. Billions might very well be in reach.

He was still toying with the idea of approaching the pharmaceutical companies; then billions might not be enough. Then the issue would be, how much exposure could he afford?

He hadn't *planned* on killing Mads. It just... *happened.* He had little fear he would be found out. She'd been incredibly thorough, paranoid about security, keeping the two of them a secret, but in the end, she hadn't been able to resist showing off. Enough so, he quickly made the connections between her work and his own studies.

No, the problem was how to document a straight line from his research to logical conclusions that would convince any inquiry that he had somehow leaped ahead of the limitlessly funded think tanks and military research labs around the world completely on his own.

"So maybe some people are immune?"

"If we can prove there's a natural immunity, and we can find a way to induce that, we can find a cure."

"Which opens up new applications — "

" — and means we make history."

The four boys he'd recruited, brilliant students despite their appearance. Luck of the draw. Two winners in the lottery of looks, two losers.

No more one's fault that he looked like a brute than the other who looked like a crack head at the best of times, or the two who looked like models for some exorbitantly expensive perfume. None would be mistaken as geniuses, but they had their moments. What they didn't have, was an idea of his agenda, or the inkling that he'd helped create the app. Wasn't sure how much to trust them. Money, even the *idea* of money, could change people. He needed to tread lightly.

It'd only cost him a few months of dating Mads, pretending he *liked* red hair. Liked the way she smelled. Like the way she tasted.

She hadn't been in love with him, not even infatuated. What she *was in love with*, was the idea of lording her intellect over him. Everything she did was classified, which left her desperate to tell someone her secrets. Indirectly sure, but it hadn't taken long to understand what she was working on. Condescending bitch. Doing her best to help *"her poor little Professor."* Like helping the hungry in third-world countries, or those kids on TV with disabilities. Fuck her. Look at her now.

"How long are we going to give her?" Skinny turned from the door. "It's already been all night. Like eight hours." He wasn't sure of the plan if she turned. Or if she didn't turn. "What do we do with her if she doesn't Loop?"

"Do we even know who she is?"

" — got it!" Beast came from one of the dark hallways. He carried the woman's clothes and was holding up her wallet.

They waited for the rest as he caught his breath. "Interpol." Traded her ID for a sandwich. "Cyber Crimes Division."

"What the hell?" Teen Idol pushed away from his computer, almost dropped the iPad. "She's a fucking cop?"

Hall leaned back in his chair. "Technically, an *agent*."

"Jesus Christ!" Clothes Hanger was on his feet. "You knew?"

"Considering how she was acquired, I guess it makes sense."

Skinny stormed around the room. "Acquired? You told us she was a stripper!"

Beast unwrapped his sandwich, thinking needed fuel.

"Fuck! We're going to prison." Clothes Hanger could see it all playing out.

Teen Idol was shell shocked, his words flat and resigned, "I won't do well in prison."

They watched the monitors as the woman rose to her feet. Blinded by the light of the four relentless projectors. She worked her way around the room, looking for a way out besides the heavy door.

"Keep at it," Hall said. He grabbed for a sandwich. "We either find the trigger that makes people Loop, or we discover what makes someone immune."

He turned and left the four boys with their thoughts and fears. Dreams of wealth and fame now short circuited by visions of arrests, trials, and prisons.

Ula Becker, Interpol, Cyber Crimes Division, was making another circuit around the room. Their only hope now was for her to Loop before they got caught.

Skinny went back to the door. The projectors were blinding, but he preferred to watch her through the door. *Fuck*. He should have brought sunglasses.

He watched as she shielded her eyes and started another circuit, feeling for every nook and cranny in hope of some secret way out.

The teen models brought back up the views counter. A couple thousand people were logged on. Not enough to make up for potential jail time, but it was starting to spread, a virus itself.

Beast reached for the last sandwich. "Anybody going to eat that?"

TWENTY-FIVE

01110100

JACKIE WAS TAKING HER coat off when she saw Lance at a table and pointed.

"Can I help you?"

"I've got it, thanks."

The hostess followed her across the room. The dining room was less than half-full with the late afternoon crowd but more than a few eyes followed them. One, a spectacular girl, student at the college, and one a spectacular woman, attorney at one of the State's most prestigious law firms.

"May I take your coat?"

"Of course." Jackie handed it over. "Thank you."

Lance rose, kissed her on the cheek, and stood until she sat in the chair the hostess pulled out for her.

"Where's Stan?"

"Tied up on the Lewis case."

He doubted that but smiled. That she pushed Stan out meant she saw something in what they were doing and wanted in. It meant he was right to pursue this. He counted on her instincts; increasingly more so these past couple years. Though his retired brothers would bitch and moan, it was time to add her name to the lobby door.

"Where's the General?"

Before he could answer, Colonel Bradley introduced himself.

"I'm sorry, the General had an emergency, and thought I might sit in. I hope that's alright?"

Lance felt like he was already falling behind, an unusual position for him. Jackie's input would be invaluable. He gestured toward the General's seat.

Bradly pushed away the General's water glass and finished the introductions as new settings were placed, and water and wine poured. He looked around. Scoping out who might be close enough to watch or listen.

"It's a nice place."

"Yeah. Built before the town was a town. An old granary I think."

Bradley made a note of the man at the bar. Had that government agent look. FBI or DEA. Maybe ATF. Or maybe he was just being paranoid.

"Yeah, the floors are amazing. Look at all these huge timbers. My wife would kill to have these floors in our house."

Jackie didn't like him. And the man's chit-chat about military tours and travels and his wife's charity work was as annoying as any conversation she could remember. He'd obviously done his research on her boss, and wondered if Lance saw it.

Though he rarely mentioned it, Lance had done a couple of tours. He'd had uncles going back generations in the Marines, and was way too deferential to just about any jarhead or whitewall. A Colonel wasn't too big a step down from a General, and she hoped he could stay objective. It was one of the reasons she'd invited herself to come along.

The Colonel was too rugged to be handsome. Not as big as Lance, but heavier through the shoulders. Powerful hands. His words rehearsed, as if memorized off a stump speech.

She listened all through the early dinner, but like the meal and the wine, she'd had her fill.

He droned and Lance gushed. Either genuinely impressed with the man or playing him. Lance was an exceptional attorney, and might have made an exceptional actor. He seemed to be the only person she couldn't always read. He knew it and took advantage, and she knew it and sometimes let him.

"So what are you actually asking us?"

The Colonel sipped on his scotch. The meal long gone, and the wine traded for something more substantial.

"What do you know of whistleblower laws?"

"Is that what's going on here?" Jackie asked.

"You have to understand this goes against everything that I was taught to believe about chain of command, but I can't just ignore what is happening."

"And what is happening?" Sipped at her wine. "Do we get to have any idea what you're talking about?"

Bradley made a show of thinking. "As you know, the military does more than just wage war. Various arms of Defense are involved in the research and deployment of a vast array of technologies around the world."

He looked around again to see who might be listening.

"One key interest General Connelly and I have been involved with started as facial recognition technology and its applications in identifying extremists. The core technology behind it was repurposed and programmed with new directives. If we can prevent any of the terror activities, the training, bombings, and shootings, by tracking familial connections, and by extension, their associate affiliations, we knew we'd gain a head start and be far better off."

The man should have been a politician. Jackie had been right not to like him. He operated on the "double-speak, baffle with bullshit" principle.

"You said, '*started as*,'" Lance said.

Bradley was deliberate in his words. This meeting was about two things. One, to investigate how he could cover himself if it came to that. *Legally.* Ethically was subjective and of no real consideration. The second was to create a trail and send them all down the rabbit hole.

The man at the bar had left. Evidently nothing to do with the FBI, the DEA, or the ATF. Just a guy left on his own grabbing a drink and scoping the place out. His interest had probably been on the woman, nothing to do with him. No one else in the joint compared, unless you counted the hostess. The attorney was good looking, lush black hair, stunning smile she used as part of her arsenal, and what looked to be a killer body. Too bad she was also smart.

Lance knew the man was holding back. Trying to lead them while hiding something else. The magician's trick. But like a magician, just because you knew it was there didn't mean you could find the secret. He was thankful Jackie had butted in. He'd count on her counsel, and they could discuss it all later.

"The General was tasked with hiding the evidence, and I was tasked as his point man."

"How?"

The Colonel fidgeted and made all the right pauses and stammers, but Jackie was convinced it was an act.

"How many times?" Lance asked.

"Twice." A proper interval, then, "I don't want to say more until I know I am protected."

"Military Law is quite different than civilian," Jackie said.

"Who else knows about this?" Lance asked.

"Obviously, the upper Brass."

Lance jumped to it. "The President?"

Bradley shrugged for an answer.

"Is there any tangible, physical proof that any of this happened?"

"Is happening…"

"That's great. I mean it's a great story," Jackie said. "But where's the evidence?"

TWENTY-SIX

01100011

IF IT HAD ONLY been *millions* of lives at stake, then no problem —
but these two could be dangerous. Sure, they'd made some
mistakes, but he'd been right to take over for the General.
The man hadn't been up to the task. Things were in motion and
there was little they could do to slow it down.

Bradley watched the two of them. Their breath condensed
in the cold, and they stamped and stomped as they waited for
the valet to bring their vehicles. A big German sedan for him,
a Swedish luxury cross-over for her. Maybe a soccer mom he
thought. The idea of slugging kids around and all that went with
it, nauseated him.

They hugged and kissed each other on the cheek, said their
goodbyes, and went their separate ways. He was right to think the
woman was the smart one, *the dangerous one*. The man was an
idiot if he wasn't banging that, and the woman was smart enough
to want something better.

He thought about following her, giving her a taste of the
something better, but twenty years of military discipline kept
him on track.

He was walking to his car, parked on the snowy street, when
he saw him out the corner of his eye. Only caught a glimpse,

but it was enough. Crossing the street toward a four-door, American-made sedan. The man and even his car looked like FBI, or DEA, or maybe even ATF.

The man scraped the ice off his window, pawed at the snow covering the lock.

Bradley stepped behind him, wrapped his arm around the man's neck. Seven seconds of useless struggle. The man was strong, but without the purchase of his feet on the snow, nearly helpless. Bradley waited until the man went limp, let him collapse half-way down, and dropped his entire weight on the back of the man's neck.

Even with the heavy coat, the snapping vertebrae sounded like Chinese firecrackers in the Colonel's ear. A sound that always made him smile.

TWENTY-SEVEN

01101000

PROTESTERS, MOSTLY PEACEFUL, MARCHED across dozens of cities in the United States. Around the globe, demonstrators made their voices heard with marches and protests. People were scared and angry.

Messages were mixed, topics hi-jacked for various causes, rhetoric laced with wild conspiracies and religious portent.

Some waved and laughed and sang songs while others screamed and chanted. Spit and vitriol flew, and the threat of violence hung in the air like a thick fog.

"Sir... *Sir?*" The reporter shouted over the crowd. "Can you tell us why you are out here protesting?"

The man in his pseudo-military clothing, camouflage and home-made flak jacket, bloused trousers, and combat boots, could have been from anywhere in the world, while his AR styled Barrett M4-Carbine, placed him as distinctly American.

He turned to the camera and waved as his friend, same spurious uniform, crowded into the picture and shouted. "Love you, Sue Ann!"

"Sir. Can you tell us why you are out here protesting?"

"Well, hell. I dunno. Everybody else is here — "

Crowds marched beside them with a wide variety of protest signs.

His friend pushed his way back forward. " — we can't let them trample our rights to protect ourselves."

"Protect yourself from whom, Sir?"

"Who knows? Everybody. The Chinese and Russians for one."

His other man pushed his way back in. "Them people from the friggin' — pardon my, parlez vous francais — them friggin' sand countries. The "stans." Stans — that ain't that far from Satan, now is it?"

The reporter wanted to point out "Satan" was even closer to Santa but held his tongue.

A woman chimed in as she passed by. "We can't be having pedophiles running the county. It ain't right."

Camo Man took over. "They been trying to convert us for years. Shutting down our freedoms. Not gonna happen! We don't wanna be Muslims and Muhammads. Them people worship Satan five times a day and want us to pretend it's a God-fearing religion but they're really just kiddie freaks and rapers who sneak over the borders to take our jobs and hit up on our women."

"And you see all that in the banning of this social media app?"

"Apps ain't dangerous! It's those behind 'em!"

The camera panned a group with "Stop the App" signs as they went by. One with "Zombies are people too."

Behind them, people sat at outdoor cafes along the streets drinking ten-dollar lattes and designer smart waters.

"You don't get it, and that there the biggest problem with this country. People don't listen. 'Free Speech,' but now government is telling us how we're 'sposed to communicate? Big Tech already controls our Twitters and records our phone calls. They ain't got to steal it, you're just giving away your privacy, and now they're rearranging our DNA so our little kiddies can be born as hermaphrotrons for the socialist left and the Chinese infiltrated FBI."

"This country better wake up. Fuck the deep-state Illuminati. You know them poor sick zombie people are the result of the software update they put in the vaccines. Everybody said it was too fast. Anybody coulda seen it coming. Nanobots in your blood are remapping you right now as we speak. We are here for the great reckoning."

WAKKA... WAKKA... WAKKA...

Jessie perched on a barstool in front of Pac-Man. She wasn't ready to face the end of the world. She'd left the televisions on for company and in hopes that someone knew what the fuck was going on. Nope. Nobody.

They should have interviewed her. She could have told them about Numbnuts and his arm laying in the snow outside her shop door. Billy. That was the name on his check. Billy Lewis. Now that he was gone, it seemed disrespectful to call him anything else. Unless it was zombie boy or something.

She'd tried to call the police. Had been put on hold three times. On the fourth try, she listened to the automated *"You've reached the Mazeville police department. If you have an emergency, please hang up and dial 911. If this is related to the potential severe weather system forecast, please press 2 and leave a message. For all other non-emergency related business including this year's nativity festival, please press 3 and someone will return your call shortly,"* message.

She barely glanced up at the banging on the door. That had gone on all afternoon. Once, it might have even been someone who was still uninfected. A *normal*. The man was so wildly frantic she couldn't tell, and by the time she made it to the door, he was gone.

"We're getting reports of isolated black-outs and lock-downs, and people are calling for a congressional investigation into the disturbing video that alleges the United States military targeted a village in Democratic Congo earlier this year for testing, and then furthered a cover-up by destroying the entire village."

She wasn't paying enough attention to understand how it all went together but the *"cover-up by destroying the entire village"* part triggered some radical thoughts. She wasn't ready to go there yet.

She had her ideas on what was happening. The Loop app triggered some kind of chemical response. Not hard to believe or understand. The human body was a virtual chemical laboratory, not producing hundreds or thousands of complex chemicals needed to maintain the body, but likely trillions. Some were surprising to most people. Naturally produced hydrochloric acids and ammonia, psychotropic endocannabinoids, and dimethyltryptamine.

She'd seen Numbnu— Billy, change right before her eyes. It took some serious chemical alchemy to get that boy moving.

He'd literally burned up in front of her eyes, become a... whatever it was on the sidewalk outside. Not a zombie. He wasn't reanimated flesh. He was a *"Looper."*

More banging on the steel gate at the front door got her to stop. The Looper kicked and banged and pulled but moved on.

BEW-WEW-WEW-WOOP-WOOP.

Jessie poured herself a cup of coffee, close to the last pot unless she started making it at normal strength. What purpose could that serve? Only a couple of cellophane packages of Twinkies left. One Oatmeal Pie. And a Ho Ho. She wasn't going to be able to stay here forever.

Wasn't someone supposed to come and save her? The National Guard or the FBI or somebody? It didn't seem likely.

She grabbed the sword and passed the stash of her other weapons on the way to the front. The chainsaw—she'd read the manual and now was confident in its operation—a wooden croquet mallet, and a set of Japanese steak knives. Guaranteed sharp for a lifetime. All things considered, a promise that might not be much of a risk from the company's legal team.

The streets reflected the winter wonderland, and Billy was mercifully covered by a shroud of snow.

Dozens of cars were wrecked and abandoned, and she could see a fire burning in the upstairs windows a block away and across the street.

Three people sprinted by, and an instant later, two of the spider-like humans, twisting and jerking, leaped up and over the car wrecks and gave chase.

She turned back to the darkened pawn shop. The glow of the TVs and the private video arcade for company. She thought about putting on a movie. She knew how VCRs worked. She had her choice of an old Chuck Norris movie or *Lassie Come Home* and *On Golden Pond*. Fortunately, she couldn't find the connectors.

Maybe a book... A nice selection of Heinlein and Lovecraft. *Great.* That was cheerful. Dr. Seuss. Cute when she was five, but now just creepy. Hansel and Gretel. Jeez ... parents loved to scare their kids.

Lewis Carol; *Alice in Wonderland; The Hunting of the Snark.* As if she had to hunt for them. *History of Mazeville.* Since the world was ending, maybe history would be good. The book was published in the 40s, and probably hadn't been opened since.

She started her final pot of coffee and settled in.

TWENTY-EIGHT

01100101

SHE CREPT DOWN THE stairs. No creaks or groans. Not a rich man's house, but it was built back when craftsmanship was still a priority. Even with that, and just over forty pounds, she knew to hug the wall until the sixth step from the bottom when she traded sides to hug the railing. Boots in hand, almost silent in her thick socks.

She tip-toed forward, held her breath for as long as she could. Stared at the man on the couch. He didn't move. Hadn't since they'd fixed his leg the night before. She came closer. Inches away. Scrunched up her face and stared harder. Couldn't take a chance that he'd wake and follow her. Finally satisfied.

Tucked the boots under her arm, grabbed for the plate of biscuits, and stuffed a couple in her coat pocket.

An eye opened and watched Little Girl slip from the room. Up to something, but not his concern. He had no control of his hallucinations — she could do whatever she wanted. He closed his eye, let himself drift.

His leg was throbbing and his foot itched. Used his other foot to scratch it. Felt better for a moment, then it started up even worse.

Like something was chewing on his toes. He remembered crawling through the snow, so maybe he was still thawing out.

Snow. Ice. He closed his eyes, and could see the frozen water just above his head. Made no sense. *Wait.* He was upside down. That's not right. He was in a barn. The smells of livestock and hay and manure overwhelming after the nothingness of snow. And there was that cute little red-head delusion again. Standing in front of him outside the barn. Maybe it was his *brain* that needed to thaw out!

Jesus! He thrashed and kicked and threw the covers off. Naked. No fire in the fireplace. Cold air rushed over him and brought him to his senses.

Sat up and looked down in horror. Half his leg missing. Fell back and tried to catch his breath. And it all came rushing back. His last thirty-six hours in 3.6 seconds.

Gulped and gasped and forced his heart to slow down. Sat back up, pulled the blanket around his shoulders. Chief One-Leg. Replayed the car wreck. Being trapped. He'd had no choice.

A miracle he'd made it to — *to wherever he was.* He'd obviously crawled in the wrong direction, away from the highway, away from his destination. He remembered the tractors. A barn.

Images of waking up, helpless and restrained. Cascades of red hair made magical with firelight. A woman, late thirties he guessed. Maybe she was a witch? He pictured her face. Not cruel. *Concerned.* A bit worn, but pretty. He'd met a witch in Africa. Hideous. Another in Paris. Ancient. *Were country witches young and pretty?*

Okay. Time to see what's what. He pulled the blanket from his legs. He still had legs. Kind of. One and a half anyway. One looked normal. The other stopped at the knee. It was wrapped in a bandage like a mummy, around and around, just the slightest hint of blood at his knee.

The white-hot frying pan rushed at him with the force of all five senses. The smell, the sound, the sight, then the taste of burnt flesh in the air cloying against his tongue. And pain.

He stared at empty space. Maybe he was turning invisible. He could *feel* his foot. Still itching like crazy. It took some moments to understand what he was looking at. *Nothing.*

His thigh should have been swollen, at least double the size of his other. He'd seen enough battlefield triage to know. He pressed and poked at his leg. Swelling was minimal considering.

No foot, but strapped to his thigh was what looked like a wooden table leg. It looked ridiculous; the idea was completely idiotic. A naked pirate who couldn't even afford a proper peg leg.

Beyond it, he saw his clothes. Washed and folded. Underwear and jeans, one sock. He certainly couldn't sit here naked all day. Pants *and* underwear seemed like way too much work. He twisted and reached for his jeans. One pants leg cut off. Okay, he'd done that when he lost the leg, but now they were hemmed to just below the knee.

It took some moments to pull them up over the table leg. Almost crashed to the floor twice. Finally got them up over his butt. Couldn't zip or button them while sinking into the cushions.

He pushed off the arm of the couch to balance on his real foot. His other foot stuck out like an oar in a boat. Not a chance in hell it would hold him. He started to undo the straps that held it, a complex series of belts and buckles that was actually pretty ingenious. At least it *looked* cool. Like some kind of bondage wear. Did they have bondage wear in the country? Like the jeans, she must have cobbled it together just for him.

He put his real foot down. Then the wooden table leg. Stood for a moment. Had to admit it was better than the idea of hopping around on one foot. Okay. Shifted his weight. About as graceful as a roly-poly Weeble toy, but he was new at this.

His shirt was hanging on a peg above the fireplace six feet away. Surely, he could take two steps. Left foot forward. Balance. Turned his hip, and like a novice rowing a boat, threw it forward into place. Slowly added weight. *It seemed it might actually hold!*

Eased forward until it slipped and buckled out from under him.

He lurched for the wall. Bounced off the edge of the table. It flipped in place and crashed to the floor. Iron skillets, plates, cups, butter, biscuits, and honey went flying and tumbling across the room.

He lurched and spun on his foot, fell straight back, and sent the only visible lamp crashing to the floor.

Lay on his back trying to catch his breath and looked at the ceiling. Turned to stare at all the crosses.

Above him, he heard a scream like a banshee, a door thrown opened, and an instant later, Mother came running, staggering, and clomping down the steps.

Bad Ass was almost to his foot when he registered the antique rifle clutched in her hands. She tripped on the final steps, bounced and spun off the wall and the rifle belched out an ear-splitting roar.

As the smoke cleared, they both stood frozen. She, still half asleep and horrified.

Him, *wide awake*. Looked at the rifle. Didn't have to worry about it going off again — it must have been nearly two hundred years old, little more than a musket.

He turned to look at the hole blasted in the wall behind his head.

She was waking up fast. "Oh, my God! I'm so sorry. I thought maybe that — " Her eyes darted around the room. "Where's Sam?"

A piercing scream from outside was her answer.

Gun clutched in her hands, she tried to get past but crashed into him — it looked like they both would go down. They managed to keep each other up — an awkward dance until she disentangled and sprinted past him. He toppled back and bounced off the walls as she ran out the door.

Bad Ass hobbled from the house in time to see the little girl standing on a wooden cellar door, biscuits scattered by her feet. A blackened arm, burnt flesh cracked and weeping, reached up through the slats of the cellar door and held onto the little girl's leg while she kicked at it with the other.

Mother stumbled through the snow to her daughter. She stood and swung the rifle like a club and beat at the arm.

No effect, the blackened hand held on tight. The other hand clawed and searched for gaps in boards, trying to break through. Whatever was below, was going berserk.

The first boards broke, and the head and shoulders of a twisted, blackened *Thing* began to emerge. Mother grabbed at Sam and they both staggered back into the deep snow as the creature in front of them went on an all-out assault to escape its wooden prison.

A pitchfork leaned against the house. Bad Ass slipped and slid and wobbled to it. Turned back to Mother and Sam just as the Thing, maybe human at one time, but so twisted and frenzied it was hard to be sure, made it halfway out. Bad Ass lurched forward and slammed the sharp tangs of the pitchfork through its arm, pinning it to the old wood, but it twisted and used its feet to kick at the slats from below.

Bad Ass fell back, pulled Mother and the girl behind him, and stood to face the creature as it broke through and sprang up from below.

It spun in circles trying to control its limbs; the arms and legs mangled, like they'd been broken and put on backward.

The Thing found its footing and sprinted toward the empty fields of snow. Progress slow in the high drifts, it bounced side to side, slipped and slid, sometimes forward, sometimes back, as if still trying to figure out how its arms and legs worked.

The three breathed a sigh of relief as it retreated. Bad Ass watched as it began gaining control of its limbs.

Mother held the little girl close, smothering her with kisses and checking to make sure she was okay.

Bad Ass — no shirt, no shoes, crazy peg leg, stood waiting. The creature stopped. Spun in place. Began racing straight for them.

Fifty yards. Forty. Huge leaps and bounds and impossibly fast through the snow. Thirty yards away and gaining speed. Made up for its lack of coordination with determination. *Twenty —*

Bad Ass did his best to balance, twisted and torqued, used all the strength of his powerful arms to hurl the pitchfork like a spear. It exploded from his grasp, and the trident caught the creature full in the chest, bowling it off its feet, but like a tiger, it leaped high into the air.

Crouching to meet it, awkward with a leg that wouldn't bend, Bad Ass slipped and fell flat on his back. He kicked his wooden leg up and forward.

The Thing came down and the wooden leg pierced its chest, the end jutting from its back.

It thrashed and clawed, sliding slowly down the wooden table leg as Bad Ass batted its talon-like hands away. He tried to lift his wooden leg higher and still it slid down — biting at his hands until it was almost close enough to kiss him. Bad Ass slammed his forearm into its face. Again. Grabbed its head with both hands, and twisted with all his might. The head spun completely around in his hands and faced him again. No sign of humanity left; its yellowed, film-covered eyes closed and it shuddered still.

Bad Ass rolled over in the snow and tried to pull his wooden leg free. Stuck. He pushed and kicked at it, but no luck. Unbuckled the straps holding it to his thigh and pushed himself away.

Sam and her Mother cried as they help him stand.

"What was that thing?"

Tears running down her face as she turned to look at it, Mother choked out the words, "It used to be my son."

Sam on one side, Mother on the other. They helped him hop toward the house.

The back of the house, what must have been the kitchen, was burned down. The roof was covered with a blue tarp, sagging low from the snow. Beyond was an old truck — not as old as the musket and with only rust for paint — but it looked to be on four wheels.

"We were in the kitchen when he... changed. We figured he was some kind of zombie. I didn't have the heart to kill him, so we trapped him in the root cellar. I didn't even know if he *could* be killed."

The little girl hugged his leg, while Mother pulled his arm around her shoulders to help him stand.

"If you hadn't come along, he might still be suffering. So thank you."

They made it to the door before she turned for a last look.

She kissed Bad Ass on the cheek.

"Okay, let's get you warmed up, and see about finding you a new leg."

TWENTY-NINE

01110011

A SEVEN-HUNDRED SEAT auditorium. Gilded columns, frescoed ceilings, velvet curtains, elaborate carvings, and delicate enamel work across the proscenium arch. Stage plays, Broadway musicals, and event-films had drawn crowds for a hundred years. The box-office closed.

Five years working in a top-secret lab less than twenty miles away, four years in a house ten miles from town, but Carmine had never been here, and wouldn't get to see it now. The cavernous room was mostly dark. What did show had been carefully orchestrated for effect, tried and true since the height of the Greek and Roman empires.

"Sir, they are ready for you now."

The armed military escort walked him midway down the stadium seating to a long table set up at the front of the first balcony. One chair. A single circle of light beamed straight down from above. A microphone, two empty glasses on paper coasters, and a crystal pitcher filled with ice water.

He was almost level with the stage. Fifty-foot curtains pulled back to reveal nine figures in chairs behind a long table, backlit to create nine silhouettes.

The escort waited until he was seated, then marched back to wait at the lobby doors.

He sat still as best he could. Glanced behind him. Fidgeted, tapped the microphone to see if it was on, smelled the water, poured himself a glass, and waited.

Made a bet with himself how long it would take for the bead of condensation at the top of the pitcher to make its way to the table. He wasn't even close. It took longer than he could have imagined to find its path through the other 'steadfast' drops. It dodged and zig-zagged, hesitated, picked up steam, and stopped to regroup. He had time to name it "Major" before it started up again. Maybe a bit like his own career; it clung to its course as long as possible, then made the leap to obscurity. It had nearly reached the finish line when the first voice spoke out.

"Thank you for joining us, Major Marelli. We know your time is valuable, so let's get right to it."

A male. Carmine could guess 60s though he knew he might be a decade off. Seemed to come from the end of the stage. Stage left.

"What can you tell us about video 20LP315109?" Another male voice, roughly the same age. This time from closer to the middle.

A square of light five meters across flickered on the screen behind the seated figures. No sound, but you didn't need to hear the screams to feel the panic and horror, and Carmine didn't need to watch more than the first frame to know what it was.

"Umm," Carmine was off balance. He knew that was by design, and that intrigued him as much as it pissed him off. "I'm sorry but that information is classified."

"Major," the second voice again. "This is the body that determines such classifications. Please answer the question."

No proof of the statement other than the fact they were all here.

"It appears to be a mobile phone capture of a live event occurring on Oct 9, 2020, in Lisbon, Portugal. Approximately two and a half minutes in length."

Another man, stage right. "Have you been able to verify its authenticity?"

"Yes."

A woman this time. "And your opinion, Major?"

"It's real. It happened."

The video on screen switched to the small market in Africa.

"And video 19MC216187, the so-called *African event*?" A new voice, another male, maybe a bit younger than the others.

A man burst into flame, twisted and contorted, and attacked the crowd, killing several before half a dozen men rushed it with machetes. The chaos of the video reflected across Carmine's face.

"Have you had a chance to examine it?"

"Yes."

Another woman spoke up. "Have you found anything that leads you to question its authenticity?"

Shown on the big theater screen with no sound made the video even more disturbing. The terror filled the room.

"No."

Another man from the middle. The gravel of age, with the resonant bass of what Carmine assigned to an African-American male.

"Have you seen other videos, confirmed or otherwise, Major, that make you think similar events are happening around the globe?"

"Yes."

A murmur swept across the stage.

Not that different from some of his lab work, he started putting faces with the voices of those who questioned him.

A new woman spoke up. Strong New England accent. "Can you tell us what specific task Captain Clark was engaged in?"

He only knew the assignments he had given her, not the work he knew she was keeping secret.

"Mads was—" Carmine poured a glass of water to hide the emotion. Took a long drink. "Captain Clark was searching for markers that would indicate the targeting mechanism developed in previous classified research had been incorporated into the triggering event."

A third woman spoke. Younger, reasonable. Maybe even sympathetic. "I think we've been briefed enough to follow that. Can you explain why that would be of concern?"

A sound from behind him threw him. He'd thought the seats were empty. Glanced back as a shadow shuffled sideways in the aisles to sit beside another.

He took another drink.

"It means, Senator — sorry, Ma'am — I'm assuming this is a Senate or House Intelligence Committee and not the Supreme Court?" No response or appreciation of his humor. "The effect, or the result, could be adapted to target a specific town or geographic region, and by extension, target a specific population by race, religion, and, or political affiliation."

The screen went dark. Whispers in conference in front of him. The powerful presence behind.

Video flickered on the screen as if by mistake. Less than two seconds. A bombed-out landscape. Char and ashes. Nothing living. What might have been a dog, now half of a burnt carcass. For an instant, what might have been an arm, the black flesh and white bone jarring in the light, sticking out of the ground. A plastic baby doll. The image froze and then went black.

A clearing of a throat and the original voice spoke again. "And do you have reason to believe top secret targeting research conducted for the United States military has made its way into the social media application marketed as LOOP?"

The room was as silent as it had ever been in its hundred years. Carmine tried to quiet his heart.

"Yes."

Further conference between the shadows at the table. Covering their microphones, whispers, and the rustling of papers. Someone dialed a phone. He saw it light up the side of a face as it was raised to an ear. A whispered voice. It might have been his imagination, but he also heard rustling behind him, echoes to what was happening on stage. The tiniest of beeps when the call was disconnected carried across the acoustically perfected auditorium, and his sense of the voices behind him stopped.

"Thank you, Major Marelli."

The New England woman again. "You understand as per your clearance, that our discussions, as well as the fact of our meeting today, must remain in the strictest of confidence as must all past and future tasks?"

Jesus, politicians. Carmine nodded. Waited. No response.

"Yes, Ma'am, I understand."

The rich bass again. "I sincerely hope we do not have the occasion to meet again, Major, but we thank you for your efforts and long service."

Yep, his was the path of Major Water Drop.

Carmine realized his escort stood waiting in the aisle.

He strained to peer into the shadows. The impression of two men huddled in the back row verified as light spilled from another door while two additional escorts brought in someone new.

His guard opened the door for him and at the last instant, Carmine glanced back. Followed the narrow shaft of light across the auditorium to the chair he'd just vacated, and across the broad shoulders and full dress uniform of Colonel Bradley.

THIRTY

01000001

A ROLL-NECK HAND-KNIT fisherman's sweater, deep green with flecks of yellow sprinkled throughout the tight trellis and blackberry stitches of lambswool kept him warm, while the long, brown oilcloth duster kept the falling snow and wind off him, and made him look like a cowboy.

He'd been given gloves, but had them off to work, and wore a single steel-toed work boot. The straps and buckles of his kinky leather leg harness had been refined. An upside-down holster had been hand-sewn into place and capped a simple two by two of unfinished oak that replaced the table leg, and of course, brought to mind a pirate.

The truck had seen better days, and hadn't actually run in three years. Grass had grown high around it, and now the snow had drifted up over the wheels. It had taken him two hours to dig it out, relieved that it had all four wheels, though the tires showed signs of dry rot.

Snow piled up as fast as he worked, but he was hoping that the problem was a simple dead battery. He needed some luck.

It took just minutes to find what he needed in the barn; the tools were neatly hung and organized, and he saw an air compressor that would come in handy. It took an hour to change out the battery from the newer tractor to the truck. Easy work on a spring day for a man with two legs.

The snow was almost up to his ass, and in some ways made it easier to stand. In the time he'd been back and forth from the truck to the barn and back, he'd been able to lose the crutch he'd been given and hobble his way around on his primitive excuse for a leg.

"Hey."

Mother's voice startled him, and he slammed his head up under the hood. It was enough to knock the stick out that held it up, and he caught the heavy steel just before it slammed shut on her fingers.

"Sorry. I thought you could use some coffee."

"Sounds perfect."

She had her own cup, and they leaned against the truck to share the moment.

The warmth of the coffee seeped through the hand-thrown cup and began thawing out his fingers.

"It hasn't been started in a while. Not since my Bill died. Didn't run so well even then."

He had nothing to say, but it seemed she needed to talk, though she was hesitant and shy about it. He gathered it might have been some time since she'd spoken to anyone other than her daughter. Samantha. Sam.

"He died in the fields, doing what he loved. Flipped the tractor on the edge of the spring. Cut him right in half. No putting him back together, though we tried and prayed on it."

Okaaayyy… a tractor accident he could picture. The *"putting him back together"* part, not so much. He thought of all the crosses. He'd seen at least twenty. Maybe she was just deeply religious. Old country for sure, with old fashioned morals and ideas.

As much as her hair and the slight lilt in her voice, the complex stitches in the hand-knit sweater told him that she was Irish.

She told him she'd been knitting it for her husband but never had the chance to give it to him, her daughter just three years old at the time. And now of course, her son. She'd had more than her share of troubles.

They hadn't been able to bury the boy, the ground more solid than the ice, and the pickaxe he'd swung at it bounced off without making a dent. She'd found a large linen sheet to use as a shroud, and he'd found another blue tarp in the barn to roll him up in.

He'd had some idea of what they might be up against. Like half the world by now, he'd seen the videos. Seeing the... what was left of the boy, gave him some idea of *why* decisions had been made. Were *being* made.

He'd also seen the aftermath of those decisions. There had to be a better way. He was determined to find it. Bring others on board who could apply their intellects to what threatened to be the world's next great pandemic, but it would take a lot more than the chance of turning into crazed, burned up monsters to get people to put down their phones.

"I had to take the battery from the tractor."

"Not much need for it until Spring. Neighbors aren't close, but they bring what we don't have."

He finished the coffee. Cold, but he didn't want to be rude. Handed her the cup.

"Let's see what we have," he said.

He climbed up in the cab, the door already chipped free from ice from when he first tried it.

No way he could work the clutch, brakes, and the gas peddle with his new leg. He'd brought an ax handle from the barn to work the gas, his left foot could handle the rest as he stretched his thigh and the oak two by two across the passenger's side.

It took some moments as the engine made its mind up on whether to start. It bitched and grumbled, coughed and sputtered before finally saying "*fuck it, the damn man was never going to give up,*" and it roared to life.

After thirty minutes, he was satisfied it would keep running. He made it to the barn, started up a generator and the compressor, and filled up the tires. Cracked with dry rot; he hoped they'd stay up long enough to make it.

She'd drawn up a rough map. He had some idea of where he'd gone wrong on his long crawl, and how to get back to the highway. Somewhere under the blank canvas of snow were gravel roads that might give him some traction.

Put his phone back together after it had dried out. Hoped it would start once he found a charger to fit. The boy had had a phone, but she'd thrown it in the fireplace, and the connectors were different. If he got his up and running, he'd be writing that testimonial for sure.

She told him the boy, just eighteen, had made it through half a year at the closest technical school before being sent back home to shelter in place from the raging world-wide pandemic. She couldn't abide by computers, or even televisions in her house, but he'd come back with a phone that she pretended not to know he had, and look where it got them.

She knew the man wouldn't stay. He was from a world as different as if it had been beyond the stars.

She'd been married twenty years. Till death do we part, and all that, and well, her husband had parted.

The man, she didn't even want to know his name, hadn't told her what mission he was on or what drove him, but it wasn't to be found on her farm. She could have put up a fuss. He was a man, and a woman had her ways. She'd prayed on it all night. Received no clear answer, so it was best he was on his way before it got any more confusing.

He'd broken the lamp, but she had dozens of candles lit, and firelight danced across the room and threw its heat. He looked at the bounty she'd laid out on the couch. A Beretta 92FS and a well-worn shoulder holster. He popped the mag. Half a dozen 9mm rounds.

"I looked everywhere. That's all that I could find."

He slipped the shoulder holster on. A near-perfect fit. She helped him make the slight adjustments, and he slipped the Beretta into place.

He dismissed the musket she'd nearly taken his head off with, twisted and broken in trying to beat the thing that had once been her son, damaged beyond repair. He looked at an antique pistol. Much like the musket, it looked like a pirate's flintlock. A couple of leather bandoliers of musket balls, and a flask of dry powder. Was ready to pass on the antiques, but what the hell? He had the leg for it.

Crisscrossed the bandoliers over his chest and tucked the flintlock in his belt.

The little girl was busy making a peanut butter sandwich. She wrapped it up in wax paper and put it in a small paper bag. Mother had already brewed a thermos of coffee and set it on the table.

"I think we need to look at that leg."

"It's fine. I'll get it looked at as soon as I can get to a doctor."

"Sit down and let me take a look."

Ten minutes later, she'd unstrapped the leather harness that held the board, pushed up his pants leg, had unwrapped the bandages, and was looking at the disgusting burned flesh that had once been a knee. The sight bothered him a lot more than her.

She stared at it, lost for a moment, and he wondered if she was thinking of her son.

He was lucky in a lot of ways. Only a small part of him was burned, and at least he wasn't some kind of pretzeled-up zombie thing. And he was alive.

His thigh was swelling again and the flesh felt hot.

The little girl came close, looked at it as it was the most natural thing in the world. Maybe growing up on a farm, or seeing her brother turned into a twisted, broken thing, or trying to put her father back together, inured her to the realities of life. The most beautiful. The ugliest.

She looked up at her mother, who nodded and fell to her knees and began praying.

Sam looked up into his eyes, waited until he was looking back. He felt himself fall forward into her gaze.

She rubbed her hands together. A miniature Mr. Miyagi. Reached out and placed them on his thigh. Her hands were cool on his flesh. He knew it was his imagination, the psychosis of the moment, but the throbbing in his leg stopped, and as he watched, the swelling subsided.

Mother was still praying. The words at once foreign but familiar. He'd tried to guess their origin, maybe Gaelic. They were words with the same rhythms as words he'd once heard. Africa, after his small convoy had been hit by ISIS rockets. The dung and render hut he'd wakened in, part of the village far out in the jungle where his remaining men had been taken. And again in Paris. Interfacing and advising the GIGN, Groupement d' Intervention de la Gendarmerie Nationale, where they helped Interpol recover half a dozen Congolese children trafficked and sold into bondage.

Surely, it was his imagination that the candles danced in time with Mother's words. He was no doubt feverish. His head swam, and he fell deeper into the little girl's gaze.

He saw what had once been men and women, now monsters, attacking the living and owning the streets. Heard the screams of agony and terror, the incoherent, mumbled prayers, the heart wrenching wails of despair. Watched bodies torn apart, the spread of a virus more virulent than Ebola and Marburg that infected and overwhelmed in seconds, not days.

The fire in the fireplace leaped out, the tongues of flame wrapped Mother in its embrace. Flames raced up the walls, billowed and roiled across the ceiling. He could hear the moans and agony of the figures nailed to their crosses, the chorus of doubt, the beseeching of The Father.

Mother turned to him, her mouth opened in a scream as her hair ignited in a wild, blistering inferno. Wider, her mouth now larger than her head, growing still, yawning forward to envelop him in the maw.

He sprinted forward and jumped into the abyss. Falling and tumbling, rolling and spinning in the air to land in the arms of the most fantastic woman he'd ever seen. Lithe and blond and graceful. She wrapped her arms around him, embraced him. Healed him.

He closed his eyes. Dove inside himself. Clawed his way deeper. Said a prayer without words, without thought. Opened them again to the little girl.

Reflections of the firelight in her eyes changed from reds and oranges to greens and blues. He closed his eyes, and felt a wave of peace and warmth wash over him.

THIRTY-ONE

01101110

LANCE AND JACKIE WERE on standby, a few meters away from their client, as part of the strangest hearing, or interview either had been involved in.

The lobby was as grand as the auditorium. Vintage posters and playbills from the dozens of shows that once played there adorned the walls, productions from before and after their Broadway runs, and others brought from across the seas. London and Paris, and once, Moscow. Black and white photos showed the grandeur, the history, and the evolution of the theater. Presidents, senators, congressmen, and mayors through the years. Lots of celebrities and stars. The men almost always in black suits and tuxedos, while a hundred years of fashion was draped across the women.

The box office was closed as it had been since the spring of the pandemic. Privately owned and run by the same family since the day it opened, it was difficult to think of it in full use ever again, unless you counted secret tribunals or whatever the hell was going on in there.

The four armed military guards, in full combat gear as if an invasion would break out at any moment, stood two at each entrance. Maybe they'd been warned about the two attorneys and their dangerous family firm.

Inside, their client. The heavy doors blocked any sound from within as completely as if they'd been locked in an isolation booth.

Jackie argued it could lead to something big for the firm. Lance thought the circumstances of them being there made it clear this was trouble they could live without. Was trying to work out how it would play if it came down to military courts.

The guards reminded him of the one time he'd ever been arrested, far away on a military base nestled in the shadows of the Hindu Kush. Too much drink led to a drunken brawl, quickly forgiven after a verbal reprimand, but for him never forgotten. The feeling of helplessness he now assigned every client once they entered the monster of the United States legal system, as likely to be chewed up and pushed through the bowels of the justice system as to be spit back out and continue on with their lives.

Jackie was just excited. Dreaming of a national stage. She'd always been more ambitious than he was. Somehow, after all these years, she still had a bit of the 'take on the man' naivete. He hoped this wasn't the case that would strip that away.

"I think we're just about done here, Colonel. Just a few more questions."

Colonel Bradley poured the last of the water.

"What can you tell us about apparent actions taken on July 18th of last year?" The woman from the middle.

Video blasted into the screen behind them. Body cam footage on what looked like American soldiers; no visible insignias, but the faces, black and white and Asian, along with the quality of their equipment and the latest high-tech munitions carried by the team, proclaimed their nationality as clearly as a planted flag.

They could have been walking on another planet, the devastation so complete it looked completely alien.

"Our directive was to sanitize the coordinates to maximum effect."

"You bombed the shit out of it," the man translated.

Close enough, Bradley thought. He nodded.

A voice from the left. "And you didn't find that to be an extreme solution?"

The Colonel didn't hesitate in his answers.

"Under the circumstances, no. Nor is it my place to question orders, Ma'am."

"And who issued that directive?"

"General Connelly."

The New Englander spoke up. "We understand that General Connelly recently suffered a fatal heart attack."

No reason to comment. It hadn't been a question.

There was a quick conference behind their hastily covered microphones.

The heavy gravel of the African-American. "And why did you think it necessary to bring legal counsel?"

"I thought it best to be prepared."

"You do understand the political fallout for our country if any of this was ever verified?"

And the personal fallout of anyone remotely connected. It was the reason they had all flown here under secrecy. By helicopter and private jet and helicopter again, then military escort. *It was going to get out.* This way, they could at least claim due process even though the decisions had already been made. Signed off in a playbook they had written years before; they'd make sure to stay in charge of the committees that investigated the committees.

It was also the reason Bradley knew he was safe. They needed him and those like him to do the things that consolidated their power. Too bad the General had forgotten that. Their roles were vital in order for democracy to function.

"I do."

Another piece of video hit the screen. Same landscape, different camera. A small African child's hand reaches for a burnt doll. A white man's hand covers the mouth of another child as they pull back into the jungle.

These things wouldn't stay buried despite their vast resources. The best they could hope for was to guide the narrative. Muddy the waters with disinformation.

Stage left. "Have you been able to determine the source of this specific recording?"

Stage right. "And just as importantly, at this juncture, who else may have seen it?"

The theatrics were getting on Bradley's nerves. Not because he didn't know who was talking, but because he did. This wasn't the first time he'd been questioned by some of these same voices.

"We have. There were several apparent leaks coming from multiple sources, but as of the last twenty-four hours, they have now all been contained."

No one else in the room seemed to notice, but Bradley's trained ears registered gunshots. Automatic weapons. Muffled and some distance away, but the threat growing every moment they sat here with this ridiculous charade.

"And what is your recommendation for the current outbreak in the town of Mazeville?"

"I don't think we have much choice, do you, Senator?"

No answer. Silence heavy in the huge room.

Lance was already on his feet. The lobby wasn't soundproofed from the outside. There was no hiding the sound of gunshots from the nearby streets, now maybe just a couple blocks away. Four more armed men, automatic weapons and full combat gear, rushed in.

"Sir, Ma'am, you need to come with us."

Jackie shrugged off the hands. "What's happening?"

"Sorry, Ma'am. Our orders are to see you safely home."

Before she could protest, or even button her coat, they were guided firmly out the doors and into a waiting JLTV, the heavily armored Joint Light Tactical Vehicle designated to replace the Humvee. No hesitation, it pulled onto the snowy streets, smashed through a Ford abandoned in the snow. She turned just as the car settled back onto its wheels. Lance pulled her close.

Colonel Bradley heard the commotion behind him. He turned to watch as the two men in the back were escorted out under heavy guard. The two seconds of light that bathed them as they were rushed out had been all he needed to recognize the one. No time to be angry at himself for not knowing they'd been sitting behind him all along, but he would have preferred to address them directly.

The woman in the middle. "And you are willing to execute such orders again if given?"

He turned back. "I will continue to faithfully execute my duty."

An aide stepped from the shadows stage right. His strides echoed off the wooden stage and gave weight to his presence.

The congresswoman from New Hampshire continued; no attempt to soften her disdain.

"That's an apt word under the circumstances. *Execute.*"

The nine covered their microphones while the aide whispered in the congresswoman's ear. They were already rising as a dozen armed men rushed in to escort them off stage.

"That will be all, Colonel."

THIRTY-TWO

01100100

HE WAS ALMOST TO the highway. Once he'd found the gravel track for a road, just the way she'd scratched it out on her little map, he'd no choice but to run into it.

The snow had slowed enough he could almost see where he was going. Clouds from his breath blocked his view while black smoke leaked in from under the dash. He wiped at the frozen condensation and thickening soot on the windshield.

He hadn't even left the farm before he discovered the gauges only worked intermittently. The truck either had a half tank of gas, or was running on empty. The heater didn't work, and there was no working fan to blow it. Wipers worked in shifts and grated naked metal across the glass every five to ten seconds.

The rearview mirror hung crooked, and the back window was thick with ice and kept him from knowing if anything was coming up behind him.

He couldn't imagine anyone else insane enough to be out here but knew that they'd easily overtake him. The truck might have had three gears at one time but refused to get out of second.

The noise of the engine and the grinding transmission was overwhelming, though it was tempered by the noise of wind buffeting in from the window he'd rolled down in order to breathe.

He occasionally reached outside to help clear the buildup of ice on the windshield.

He let the cruise control of the ax handle wedged between the gas peddle and the seat keep him steady. No fear of speeding. The engine would blow up long before that happened.

Truck tires had made it from gravel and snow, to road and snow, then to highway and snow almost twenty minutes ago. At just under the thirty miles per hour the speedometer occasionally pointed out, more to rub it in than to inform him, he had plenty of time to think about what he was driving himself into. And what had happened at the house.

He knew there were no kinky country witches with little Miyagi sidekicks practicing witchcraft on unsuspecting one-legged men. It was only his fevered mind, rebelling from the trauma.

He looked at his wooden leg. Stout. Pressed on the thigh. Little pain or swelling, and the heat that had threatened to scorch his hands was gone. Could feel the little girl's cooling hands, hear the mother's soft lilting voice, see her wild, red hair —

A horn blasted through the noise and his reverie. He saw a vague black shadow in the heavy frost behind him and what he thought must be flashing headlights. The beams high enough it had to be from a big rig, or at least a five-ton.

The horn blasted again, first in short bursts, and then in one long blast that made its intensions known. The shadow filled the back window. He pulled the ax handle and tried to ease to the side of the road. Soon half on and half off and starting to fishtail. He slowed down even more as his truck slid sideways down the road and waved the truck by.

The truck pulled up beside him, Army green, officially a "truck, 5-ton, 6x6, cargo cover" and used its horn as a weapon to attack him. He jerked his head away from the blast as the slush from the truck fountained up and rooster-tailed through his open window, covering him with ice and snow.

He slowed even further, feathering the clutch and gas, afraid to let the engine die, but afraid of sliding off the road again and flipping out into the fields. He only had one leg left to give.

The truck roared by.

HONKKKK...

Another right behind it. And then another. He tried to get the window rolled up in time but the handle came off, and he was only able to lift his coat lapel to ward off the shower of ice.

The trucks went past. A couple five-ton cargo covers, a deuce-and-a-half, and two JLTV's. A five-by-five convoy. Out here. Heading to town.

He didn't have to wait for premonitions or visions to know what they might be up to. Breathe. Stay calm. Hold it together. Breathe —

Fuck it. He beat on the steering wheel in frustration.

The engine answered with a sputter and a cough, and the dash came alive for the seconds it took for the light on the gas gauge to wink at him.

THIRTY-THREE

01010011

UNDERGROUND, WITH NO CLOCK or reference for time, drugs in her system, the sensory overload of the projectors, in pain and freezing, there was no way to know if it was night or day.

She tried to quiet her breathing. With control, she could at least partially maintain her temperature. And then she saw the food. Stared at it. Tremors rippled through her, threatening to pull muscle from bone.

Sometime in the middle of the night, or day, she'd been so completely shut down they'd opened the door and pushed food and water in. She'd missed a chance for escape. A chance to punish whoever was doing this to her.

X. It confirmed everything she'd thought. Well, maybe not *everything*, but she was sure of his involvement. There were questions to be asked, and now she might never know the answers. At least, that's what they were counting on.

Her stomach was in knots. And the pressure in her bladder was overwhelming.

She knew they were watching. The endless projected images filled the room like so many strobe lights. Blinding, but there was no attempt to hide the cameras mounted above them on all four walls watching her every move.

Every muscle ached and pain radiated across her back, but she forced her legs to lift her to her feet. She made it to the corner, squatted down, pulled her panties aside, and urinated. They wanted to watch a tortured woman have a piss, have at it.

She looked toward the camera and flipped them the bird. Mouthed the words in English. *Fuck you.*

She watched the stream of urine puddle on the floor. No way to know it's color in this light and how much of the drugs in her system she was expelling, but her thoughts were clearing.

She needed to escape, needed warmth before her body began shutting down. Years of discipline would only carry her so far.

And she needed nutrition.

Back on her feet.

Half a sandwich. A plastic bottle of water. It took all her willpower not to gulp it down in one go. Roast beef. She hated meat, the idea of it, but this was not the time to make a stand. She needed the protein, the carbohydrates, and as much fat as she could get right now.

Clothes Hanger and Teen Idol were asleep at their stations, adrenalin of the moment long gone. Beast, draped over a threadbare couch, snored away.

Skinny watched the woman on the monitors. They'd be pissed he'd given her the sandwich and water, but she'd be of little value if she died of starvation.

He'd almost let her go. He wasn't up for murder. If she made the transition while he was caught up in the fever of it all, he wouldn't have had time to consider his actions. But she hadn't turned, and so here they were.

Why wouldn't she Loop? Nobody really knew anything about the shit, though Professor Hall kept throwing out suspicious nuggets. He might not know everything, could play dumb if he wanted, but he certainly knew more than he was saying.

Skinny looked at the images on the screens. Back to his thoughts on what made us human. Or, as they were trying to force, that make us *inhuman*. Pain. Fear. Greed. On which side of humanity did he sit?

He went back to the door. Watched through the bars as she moved into the opposite corner.

The projectors were blinding, but he watched her eat the sandwich. Hall should be back soon. And then they were all going to have a serious talk about how they would resolve this fucking mess.

Ula tried to go slow, commanded herself to, but wolfed down the sandwich in gulps. It was delicious. Took her back to Vienna and markets they loved to go to when her father would visit her at university. Between the hundred-year-old Naschmarkt and the international flair of Brunnenmarkt, *anything* could be found. They'd have hard choices to make on Italian, or German, or Szechuan, or scorching Indian curries. Rich Hungarian stews. Fabulous bakeries and cheeses.

The images raced by. Different speeds, constantly updating, And her own photo, a shot from her graduation, on every wall. Morphing and updating. And mocking her.

She started to get an idea of what they were trying to do. Idiots.

She'd been over and over the room. The only way out was the door. She could feign sleep, and when they came in again, she'd force her legs to spring into action, and take out whoever opened it. The giant was a beast of a man. Three-hundred pounds of muscle. She'd get one shot. Take out his eyes, or go for his throat. No, his height would be against her — her line of attack would be off. She could try to take out a leg. One shot to bring him down to size. His legs would be oak like the rest of him, but the joint itself might give her the chance of using his mass against him. If she could make her own legs work.

Skinny watched her. Sitting against the wall. Her eyes closing. Opening, Closing. She was falling asleep again. She gave in and toppled over, curling into a ball for warmth.

She lay on the floor, staring past heavy eyelids and lashes across the room. Put her feet against the wall. Ready to push off until she could convert the horizontal energy with the speed and power to rise vertically. One chance. She would destroy whoever came through the door.

The puddle of urine reflected the projectors in a near-perfect path across the room to the wall where it disappeared. What could that mean?

She replayed the long moments the beast had dragged her from the room. A small exam room. X's? Or had he sold her to the highest bidder? Didn't need the money, so just a way to get rid of her. Or maybe the butler had sold her for extra cash.

Already underground. Twists and turns down a long hallway. Intersecting with other tunnels. She'd seen plenty of such catacombs in Germany and Austria. Bunkers and underground cities left from the war.

She'd been over the room half a dozen times. Her instincts telling her there was another way out.

She had no reason to rise. She replayed sensations of her hands across the walls. Each crevice and protrusion. Was it air that she felt against her bare feet? A place where the irregular ridges felt too symmetrical? She engineered it in her mind. A hidden switch. A false wall. It didn't really make sense, and yet, she knew rooms such as these were frequently designed to have multiple ingress and egress. No one wanted to be trapped in their own bunker.

No doubt they were watching. She could feel their eyes, and stopped herself from waving.

Skinny turned from the other three. Still asleep. He was wired. Making his decisions. He would either convince them to release her, or do it on his own. Turned back. She was sleeping. A trace of a smile on her face; he wondered what she was dreaming. He looked at the images on the walls; thousands, maybe millions of fragments went by. Looping and looping.

THIRTY-FOUR

01101110

HE COASTED OFF THE exit as the snowplow passed him, oblivi-
ous to the ice and slush it tossed in his window, and then dodged
the only car he'd seen in an hour, slipping and sliding up the ramp
right for him. He was afraid to slow as he needed the momentum,
but did his best to hug the side of the recently cleared entrance.
The car spun and fishtailed past him.

Gravity rolled him toward the pumps, the rear-end trying
to slide across the finish line first, and for an instant, he saw
himself going up in flames after wiping out the gas pumps. The old
tires found a patch of newly cleared pavement, and he rolled right
into place.

Ten feet short.

He knew when to count his blessings. Just the same, two
more revolutions of the wheels would have been nice. He'd either
have to find someone to help him push, *not likely,* hope the pump
hose was really long, *possible,* or count on a gas can he could borrow
or buy.

Two pumps, two garage bays, and a little market. Christmas
lights that looked like they lived there all year strung along the
roof. An oasis in the tundra. Bound to have everything he needed.

The string of bells above the door jangled, and he did his best to stamp the snow off his boot before he entered. After the two hours in the open truck, the station felt downright tropical.

"Hello?" Half his face frozen, it came out more like, "Herraaao."

No one behind the counter; probably in the bays or maybe the restroom. A television high on the wall behind the counter, in the middle of a newscast.

"...besides the documented cases of infected, now being called Loopers, we're learning about a possible new variant with an entirely different behavior pattern."

"That's right, Jim. We now have reports of infected, the familiar signs of spontaneous immolation and violent contortion of limbs, but the new variant exhibits an entirely different stalking and predatory nature."

"So Megan, these are thought to be just as deadly but..."

He knocked on the restroom door. No answer, so he went in. Had an entire thermos of coffee to get rid of.

Moments later, he peeked in the repair bays. No one. Car up on the lift. Old school muscle. Hard to know from this angle, maybe '68 or '9.

Grabbed a bottle of water, returned to the counter.

"People are being urged to stay in their homes and to stay away from all mobile devices and computers..."

Which reminded him, he needed a charger. Dozens on the wall below the television.

"Hello?" No answer. Then he saw the cash register drawer. Open. Leaned over. Empty. Then the blood.

He leaned further. An old man, seventies at least, crumpled on the floor, with two red, wet blossoms from obvious gunshots in his chest. No chance he was alive. He replayed the desperation of the car sliding up the ramp and nearly running him off the exit.

Laying beside the man, looking up with big brown puppy dog eyes and ink-black lips dripping white drool, a huge rottweiler.

The rumble in its massive, barrel chest vibrated the windows.

"Good doggie..."

He began backing up but the dog wasn't having it. It needed someone to blame and here he stood. With surprising agility for a hundred and fifty-pound dog, it leaped onto the counter.

He looked longingly at the phone chargers but began backing up. The dog crouched, the hair on its back stood on end, its lips pulled back to make sure he could count its full complement of teeth, though in truth he stopped on the four, two-inch-long canines.

Turning, he ran for the door. The dog landed behind him and slid into the shelves of goods. Cans and boxes crashed to the floor, and he heard the clackity scrabble of its hard nails bounding across the linoleum floor.

Almost made it through the door when the beast launched itself and latched onto his leg. His wooden leg.

It thrashed, and he thought his hip would come out of socket as he was bounced back and forth in the doorway. He tried to wrestle it away until the dog ripped it from his thigh.

A canine wood chipper, the oak two by two snapped in half, and splinters went flying along with frothy saliva.

He slammed the door behind him just before the dog crashed into it and bounced off.

Hopping to the steel lift, he hit the switch, and the car began lowering.

The dog attacked the door. Jaws eating the boat.

Looked around. Saw a small sledge. Knocked the leg out from under a wooden workbench. Grabbed for a tie-down strap and cranked the wood onto his thigh.

The dog was almost through the door when he leaped into the car. In luck, keys in the ignition, he'd need just a bit more for it to start.

It roared to life, the happiest sound he'd heard in days. A freshly rebuilt 327 small block with four-barrel Holley carburetor, and a 2.5 inch Magna-flow exhaust. 365hp of Detroit muscle.

The dog squeezed through the splinters of the door just as he gunned it in reverse, hit the snow, and spun in a tight 360. The dog charged but he was still doing donuts when the beast bounced off the side with a heavy thud, found its feet, and attacked again. The dog charged right by him, its momentum carrying it past as he spun into the parking lot.

He found traction, and steered for his truck. He hobbled out even before the car slid to a stop and dove into the truck just as the dog found its footing and charged his way.

Closed the door, scrambled for the guns and his phone, and scooted out the other side as the dog launched itself in the window. He slammed the passenger door shut. The huge head bounced off the glass, but it slammed its thick skull against the window again and again, blood smearing as the glass cracked. The dog sensed imminent success, and attacked with renewed fury.

He watched transfixed as chunks of the dash and seat flew in the air while the enraged animal spun in circles and destroyed the truck's interior, but came to his senses before the beast found it could easily escape the way it came.

He hobbled, slid, and skated toward the store.

"We have new reports Megan, that the military will be enforcing a mandatory lockdown beginning tonight at 6:00 p.m. through..."

Grabbed at a phone charger. Wrong one. Reached for another. *How many fucking different types were there?* Found it.

Snagged a handful of Twinkies and Ho Ho's off the counter as he went by.

The dog galloped across the parking lot, slammed into the door. It bounced open, and the dog skidded across the slick floor.

Bad Ass slipped out the back and ran and clomped, and clomped and ran to the Nova.

The dog was coming around the side of the garage, bounding across the snowy parking lot when he stomped on the gas. Another 360 that left him pointing toward the highway.

He hit the gas again, thankful that America in the 60s thought a muscle car with a fully automatic 2-speed Powerglide transmission was cool. Cujo behind him, losing steam, as he fishtailed back and forth up the exit and headed for the highway.

THIRTY-FIVE

01100001

PROFESSOR HALL CRASHED INTO the wall. His body sideways and fighting for control five feet from the floor. He crumpled to the cheap carpet and covered his face as books and shattered glass from framed photos and awards fell on top of him.

The instant he landed, seemingly even before gravity had finished with him, he was grabbed and thrown again, this time across his desk. He slid face first, an out of control body surfer in a wave of violence. Stacks of papers and folders flew into the air. Banker's lamp, staplers, pens, and pencils fell over him.

He tried to crawl away, tried to escape, but Gunns stalked him from around the desk.

"You were supposed to get rid of her, not make her an Internet star!"

"What?" Hall tried to catch his breath. "I don't know what the fuck you are talking about!"

Gunns picked him up and slammed him against the door, his feet six inches from the floor. Hall saw the guns in the twin shoulder holsters. Had a brief moment where he imagined pulling one out, shoving it under the chin of the bigger man, and pulling the trigger. The moment over when Gunns let go and the Professor crumpled at his feet.

Removing his coat, *he hadn't even worked up a sweat,* Gunns took his place behind the desk. He knocked off the rest of the pens and papers and took over the computer as Hall struggled to his feet.

He typed in a web address. "So what's this?"

Hall made it to his feet and around the desk. Stared at the image of the near-naked agent sitting against the wall, arms around her knees, shivering. The projectors blasted the room with light, her image constantly bending and morphing with hundreds of others.

A views-counter showed the numbers of people logged on. Three million and counting. A log-in window asking for donations, a ComeFundMe page for murdering naked Interpol agents.

"I don't... I don't know! I had no idea. My interns must have set it up."

"Interns? You brought your fucking interns into this?"

"I can't do everything myself. This is complicated, important work."

"Yeah. Sure. Okay. That makes sense – " Gunns adjusted the Glocks in his shoulder holsters, " – because you're a fucking idiot."

Hall felt disconnected, watched in slow motion as the big man adjusted the semi-automatics, suddenly the size of cannons, then swept the keyboard and monitor off the desk with hands like catcher's mitts. Started to protest when he saw the spider web of broken plastic shoot across the screen. Looked up into the flat, shark-like eyes daring him to speak and bit his tongue, thankful he hadn't tried to go for the gun. His strength was intellect, not brawn.

Gunns reached for his suit jacket. Pulled out a clean handkerchief and handed it over.

"Clean yourself up. You look ridiculous."

Hall took it, wiped at the snot and blood he knew was dripping from his nose, the taste of salt and copper in his mouth. "Thanks." Old pals all of a sudden.

"Okay, Professor. Let's go talk to your interns."

...

Gunns hated these tunnels. The hollow echo of their steps, the smell of ancient dry dust, the long uneven walls — brick and stone, and blacker-than-coal hewn rock. He could feel the weight of the earth above him. He didn't like mountain climbing or hiking. Didn't go camping. Sure as hell didn't go caving. Didn't give a shit about the history they walked through. And he was beginning to think the Professor was fucking with him.

They'd passed through a half-dozen intersections; dim or blackened, burned-out strings of lights going in every direction. They turned and twisted, and turned again. Now Hall was leading them down another flight of stone steps.

Definitely fucking with him.

"I'm surprised you had the balls to come down here." Pleased that his own voice hadn't cracked.

"Funding was tight," Hall said. "Besides, it's more private."

They hesitated at another intersection. Distant light in three new directions.

"Quit playing games, Professor."

Hall was genuinely confused. One more level down, right? He looked for the markings they'd put on the walls. Tried to remember if they'd ever been there, or was it just an idea he'd once had, something he should have done and never got around to. A lot of that going around.

"Give me a second. Jesus, my head is still swimming." Used the handkerchief to blow the blood from his nose. "These tunnels get confusing. They run under most of the city."

"Yeah. Great. Who gives a shit?"

"Just saying."

"Well, you can — "

"Quiet."

They both listened. Hall could hear voices from somewhere. Started in, changed his mind, and led them in a different direction.

Gunns was getting ready to snatch the life out of him when he tripped on the rough floor and almost fell. His shoulder bounced hard against the wall, but it kept him on his feet. He took a deep breath and hurried to keep up. *Not* happy.

THIRTY-SIX

01110010

JESSIE STARED AT THE coffee pot as if that would change things. She'd run fresh water through the old grounds, enough for a cup. Then again. It looked like she'd have to settle for half a cup of light brown water. No more coffee. No more Twinkies. No more food.

She'd been comfortable enough. A cot and blankets. It wasn't the first time she'd slept over, but it had been a long night.

Screams came and went outside. She'd tried to cover her ears each time, but the sounds cut through like fire sirens. Was afraid to put on headphones or ear plugs — what if one of the Loopers was able to break in?

There had been a few broadcasts, and some horrifying and conflicting news footage, but mostly wild conspiracy theories. People were afraid. That multiplied the stupid by a factor of ten. Rumors of military intervention and CDC containment teams. And then, one by one, the broadcasts stopped. Now the TVs were filled with static.

No computer or Internet. Sid had insisted they do without; the man was somewhere near eighty and said there was something unholy about it. God had made the true universe, then man had created this new digi-verse without the knowledge or foresight to know the evil he spawned with it. In keeping with the retro-world she was immersed in, she hadn't minded. Besides, she had her phone.

And then that lost signal. Not cool. She was cut off from a world gone crazy with no food and no coffee and no fucking idea what was going on. Well, that wasn't quite true. She had ideas and that made it worse.

The pot eked out one more drop. She watched it form, fall through a little cloud of steam straight down into the half-filled cup. Gravity still worked. It splashed, and the ripples expanded to the ceramic sides just as they were supposed to.

Sooo... stuck in a pawn shop snow globe with the world outside going to zombie hell. Shit. That wasn't right either. They weren't zombies. They could be killed. So that was good... and bad. Good because they could be killed, and didn't seem to come back to life or anything. Billy still lay outside in the snow. Bad because they were something new no one had seen or thought about before. Something unknown.

She sat in the back, using Pac-Man as her desk. History of Mazeville open wide. She had learned a hell of a lot of cool but irrelevant information. Filled with black and white photos from the days when a man wasn't dressed without a hat on his head, and women didn't go out in public without gloves on.

The town had once had cable cars stretching right down the center of Main Street. The culture and the architecture was just about as modern as a town could get, and by 1927, had two buildings eight-stories tall towering over the rolling farms and fields, a 750-seat theater that drew acts from as far away as London and Paris, and a new county seat courthouse that was the pride of the region if not the entire state.

Turned out the shop she sat in now had first been built in the 1890s. This entire side of the street had been ravaged by a fire, and had to be rebuilt fifty years later.

And then she turned the page.

Spread across two folded pages so that they opened into a four-page spread was the city map. And not just any city map, and not the one you could get at the visitor's center, but the secret world that had given Mazeville its second name. Tunnels and hallways, dead-ends and vertical shafts, stairs and sub-basements, storage rooms and chamber halls.

And maybe a way to get out of this city.

THIRTY-SEVEN

01101011

BEAST STOOD AT THE cell door, looking through the small barred window. Unlike Skinny, he didn't have to stand on tip-toes to do it. He couldn't see the woman, but knew she was directly under him on the other side of the door. He could feel the vibrations as she kicked and pulled and pounded on the thick door.

And that voice! How she had the strength to keep yelling was impressive. And fucking annoying. How the hell was he supposed to sleep?

"Lassen Sie mich raus! Let me out of here now! Sie können mich hier nicht festhalten!"

"Isn't there a way to shut her up?"

The computer nerd pointed to the views counter on their video feed. Well over three million, and with enough donations that they'd already stopped thinking about jail.

"The more she fights," Clothes Hanger explained, "the more people log on."

"Really? Sweet." Skinny checked out the screens. Going through the motions. Still trying to figure out how to let the girl go and get the fuck out of this mess.

Teen Idol returned from the "toilets." Plastic buckets they had set up in a side room. The whole operation was literally starting to stink. He didn't try to hide the concern in his voice. He didn't give a shit if they knew he was scared.

"Well, she's obviously immune somehow." His voice breaking. "So now what?"

Clothes Hanger looked at his friend. "Hey, come on, Kev. We got this."

Beast joined them. "Phase Two?"

Clothes Hanger knew they needed *something* to happen, or this was going to get harder. "Hey, it's not what we hoped would happen, but if we can prove community transmission, we're more than gold."

The beat-up couch creaked and groaned as Beast plopped down on it. "Professor doesn't hurry up, I say we do it without him."

Gunns shoved the Professor.

"You've got about ten seconds before I put a bullet through your head."

"Just around the corner." He hoped. The hall he turned into looked exactly the same as the others, endless dark tunnels fading to black, but it *felt* right. If he hadn't had a psychopath goading him on with a gun to his head, he wouldn't be confused. And then he saw the lights up ahead.

Ula was kicking and pounding on the door, using it as a way to psyche herself up. Once she started, there might be no way back. She was sure there must be a false wall. She had pounded on all of them, and though they were all solid, one felt... *less solid*.

Hoped it wasn't her imagination, wasn't only because she wanted it so. But she'd seen similar tunnels throughout Germany. Built during the war with the threat of Allied or Russian invasions, the threat of collapse was very real, and when possible, accounted for.

She counted the voices. Knew there were at least three on the other side of the door. Maybe four. The skinny guy who had filmed her and kept staring in, the giant beast of a man who had dragged her by her hair; she owed him big time. And she was sure she'd heard the voices of two younger men.

Okay. Before she lost her strength and her nerve. Even if there was a door, triggered just the way she pictured, they could be waiting on the other side, and she might run right back into their arms.

Her best chance for escape seemed for them to open the door in order to punish her. Catch them by surprise. She was cold and hungry, but no longer drugged. If there was a secondary exit, it would still be there if her plan failed. Time to make them pay.

She knew he was right above her; he'd been there most of the night, just on the other side of the bars. She'd been hoping it would be the giant staring in. But no matter. The time was now...

Skinny knew she was below him on the other side of the door. Too close to see. His eyes drifted to the images flashing across the room. Mesmerizing for sure, but they'd been trying to make her Loop for more than twelve hours. Nothing. This whole thing was a mistake. It was time to let her go. Or put a bullet through her brain. Then they could bury the body like the last one.

Her hand shot forward. Fingers grabbed at his hair while a thumb dug into his eye. Then her other. She held on with both hands, smashing his face against the bars.

He screamed and struggled to escape. The bitch had risen from nowhere, used the bars to bring herself even with him. The relentless fury in her face was terrifying; he tried to pull away, but she was too strong.

She used her powerful legs for leverage, and his face slammed into the steel again. He heard as much as felt his cheek shatter against the steel. Still she held on. Hair ripped from his scalp as he used all his weight and strength to tear away from the terrible grip.

Skinny screamed out in surprise and pain. Beast tried to lift himself from the broken couch, but exhaustion and the deep cushions pulled him back down. He rolled from their grasp and wrestled himself away as Skinny staggered from the door. Blood poured down the smaller man's face and through his fingers as he tried to hold his ruined eye and cheek in place.

Clothes Hanger and Teen Idol — *Keven* — were frozen. None of this was supposed to happen! Even as Skinny staggered toward them, Clothes Hanger noted the massive spike in log-ins, the numbers already skyrocketing.

Beast moved to help his friend, but Skinny screamed anew. The three watched in revulsion as Skinny's arms twisted in their sockets. He threw his hands in front of him as if trying to fling them away, and they saw the flesh begin to boil. A glow from the impossible heat inside his body lit the room with increasing intensity. WHOOSH!

The heat drove Beast back a step, but was over before anyone else could react.

A jagged white bone snapped and jutted through Skinny's arm as his joints folded, twisted, and reconfigured their orientation with a tearing of the blackened flesh.

And then the moan. A rising scream of pain that forced the others to cover their ears.

Hall and Gunns heard the awful heart-rending screams. They seemed to echo and return from every direction. Hall began backing up until he felt the hard steel shoved in his back. Gunns pushed him toward the sounds of crashing tables and computers, men screaming in terror and pain.

For one moment, Professor Hall thought that *he* was looping! The muscles in his arms and legs cramped hard enough to lock him in place, and refused to carry him forward. His breath caught. It felt as if his pounding heart would break ribs from the inside out.

Gunns slammed him in the head with the butt of the gun, hard enough that stars danced in front of his eyes, yet it brought him to his senses. He staggered to one knee long enough for Gunns to kick him forward.

...

Beast stumbled over the broken tables and computers, and was al-most to the hall when Skinny grabbed him from behind. The giant had no time to register what was happening as he flew across the room and smashed into a rock wall. Hot blood ran into his eyes from where his forehead split, and he was thrown again. As he spun in the air, he saw the twisted, burnt body that had been Skinny skit-ter one way and then the other, crawling on all-fours, the arms still turning and twisting in their sockets to propel the creature forward before it pounced again.

Weightless, the ground seemed to drop out from below him. In reality, Beast was lifted and slammed into the low ceiling before collapsing at the creature's feet. It took all his strength to make it to his hands and knees.

Silence. Time stopped.

He allowed himself one agonizing half breath. He'd broken ribs when he'd played football, and again when he'd wrapped his girlfriend's car around a light pole. White hot pain made him gasp as if he was having a heart attack — his huge arms gave way, and he fell face first back to the floor. Shut his eyes so tight, white spots danced somewhere from deep within his skull.

Nothing. Maybe the thing that had been Skinny was gone.

Forced himself to roll over. Shallow breaths. Heart pounding against his broken ribs. He registered the cold of rock against his back. And then the warmth beneath him as his bladder let go. Sobbing, tremors rippled across his body, fear a physical thing that threatened to shake him apart. As slowly as possible — the journey must have lasted hours — he opened his eyes.

What had been Skinny stood above him, glaring down.

Ula heard the frenzy of terror, the bellows of pain, and the scream for God's mercy. She knew there would be none.

Her hands moved over the wall. She was sure she had felt it. An organized depression. A possible trigger to a lock. Scheiße!

Nothing. It couldn't have only been imagination. *Again.* Her hands refusing to give up on what she prayed must be there.

Keven knelt in the middle of the stone floor. Trying to remember the words to a prayer, but knowing God had forsaken them all. They'd embraced the evil, invited the Devil.

He mumbled, but any coherent sounds were short-circuited by the image of his friend torn apart. It had happened faster than he could close his eyes. Clothes Hanger arms and legs torn from the Clothes Hanger torso, and the handsome Clothes Hanger head twisted until the cracking sounds of vertebrae were lost to the wet sucking sounds of raw flesh.

And then he heard Beast slammed against the brick walls. Thrown upward into the ceiling, and then a long moment of silence. From somewhere, the weeping of a man terrified beyond reason. He couldn't tell if the terrible, forsaken sound came from him or Beast until the frenzy of tearing, biting, breaking, and screaming was over, and the weeping continued.

The Looper turned to the helpless human on its knees when some instinct made it turn toward the room. The naked woman. Images seared into what was left of its central nervous system. It attacked the door with the same frenzy it had visited upon the humans. Grabbing the bars, pulling and kicking much the way the woman had, but with superhuman strength and purpose.

The projectors flickered off, sucking the light from the room.

Ula pulled back from the onslaught at the door. The creature was attacking the bars. She could hear as much as see the iron bending. The door was stout, but couldn't hold forever.

Turned to her task. Breathe. Hands on the wall. Something man-made. She'd found it before. Too straight and perpendicular to be natural.

There! She pushed and... nothing. Tried to slide it left, then right. Nothing. Pushed upward and stone slid across stone. The slab, no more than four inches across, slid into place and then fell inward. Her fingers searched. A latch. She pulled and stepped back as the entire wall opened up with the groaning and grating of tons of stone across stone.

She knew there was some sort of clever block and tackle system of counterweights beyond, but in front of her, only black. Air at her back was sucked in through the small window to fill the void and bid her forward, to freedom, but she forced herself to wait. She squinted and strained as if it would help, but no vestige of light reached her eyes.

Outside, the creature sensed her escape and slammed itself into the heavy door. She heard wood begin to split. Time running out. She had one chance, and that was forward.

She took a deep breath and stepped into the dark.

And fell straight down.

Gunns, both hands filled with semi-automatics, shoved the Professor into the room where he fell to the floor.

Stone and brick were painted in blood. Body parts, as if from an explosion, were scattered at random. Little light, but enough to see a boy kneeling in the middle of the floor, and the creature attacking the door.

Gunns opened fire, both hands blasting.

Ula spun and caught herself on the ledge. Only her superior reflexes saved her, and that by luck and instinct, not by design. Pulled herself back up. Stood in the room and stared at the floor.

Outside the door, gunshots assaulted the dark. Concussions rolled off the walls like cannon fire. She sensed the gunfire beyond track across the room, chasing, and not finding their target. The smell of blood and cordite and opened bowels already thick, threatening to make her lose the little food she had in her system.

And somewhere, in the after-flash of gunshots, she thought she'd seen the opening in the floor. She couldn't see clearly enough to be sure, her impression was maybe three meters across. Stared and hoped for another gunshot. BLAM! BLAM!

At least four meters. No way to see the bottom. Maybe it was the doorway to Hell.

No choice. She backed up into the room, got a running start, and jumped.

Hot fragments of lead, and chips of brick and stone rained down on Keven. He huddled into himself, and covered his ears from the ear-splitting concussions. Squeezed his eyes tighter but couldn't stop the flashes and his terror from blinding him further.

Hall slipped and fell. Landed hard, scrambled against the slick floor to hands and knees. The curd and stench of human intestine beneath his fingers, acid burned in his throat, and he struggled not to puke.

Hot brass rained down as Gunns blasted away with both hands. The Professor couldn't watch, couldn't open his eyes, couldn't possibly count the shots, but he heard the curses and knew the threat was still alive.

Gunns emptied the mags as he tried to follow the creature's movement. Faster than any creature he'd ever seen, the erratic motion made it impossible to track, but he was sure he'd hit it at least a few times. The awesome lightning and thunder of the semi-automatics built up and echoed back on themselves. Could have switched to fully automatic with the flick of a thumb, but what good would that do? Empty his weapons faster, but be no more accurate. Anyone from outside would have sworn he stood in the middle of a full-fledged war even though he was the only one shooting.

The light blinded him, and he strained to see past the strobe-like images of his own making. The creature crawled and skittered like a huge spider across the walls, then disappeared down a long, vaulted hall into the dark.

The Professor was at his feet. Maybe crying. The man had completely lost it.

"Get the fuck up."

Gunns dragged him to his feet, and pushed him back from where they'd come.

Ula shuffled forward in the dark. Feeling her way with her feet — one bloodied and wrapped in her t-shirt — while her hands searched for clues along the walls. Inching forward as if blind.

She stared into the black...

It took some moments, but she thought the stone and brick glowed with some vague phosphorescence. Minerals and elements could glow in the right combinations, calcite or manganese or sodalite, dozens of others, though she knew of none that emitted light without an actuator. Light or heat. Reaction to friction or impact, or even electromagnetic radiation. More likely some type of luminescent lichen or insects. And more likely still, her imagination.

She kicked hesitantly through broken rock and dust, and the occasional discarded paper and trash. Trash meant civilization. But impossible to know if she was moving toward it or away.

The distant cracks and echoes of gunfire disoriented her further. She couldn't have gone far and yet they sounded miles away. Impossible to tell if they were in front or behind her. She began shaking. Cold and hunger, and the fear she may die here, already buried, alone, and forgotten in the dark.

Gunns was sure he knew where they were. He recognized the visual confluence of hallways, and stepped in front to lead the way. Stopped. Listened. Only the oppressive sound of his breathing, and the halting footsteps and blubbering of the man who had dragged him into this mess bringing up the rear.

The horror far behind him, he fought to control his anger. Pissed that the creature had unnerved him, he was imagining the ways he'd destroy it when he got the chance. Maybe a *flame thrower*. He could order a working British M2 Ace-Pack on-line. Trap it and watch it writhe in pain and terror until its ashes blew away on the wind. Or maybe he'd bring back a couple of hand grenades. Bring the entire doomed little town down on top of it to bury the perversion and its memory forever. Lots of things he could do. Fuck it. Maybe he'd do them all. He laughed out loud and continued on.

Another intersection. Ahead was dark save a single distant bulb. Turn left or right? He smiled, and a wave of relief he hadn't known he needed washed over him. He knew exactly where he was now. Turned left.

Another intersection, the high vaulted ceilings formed a larger room. He'd marked it in his mind when they'd come from the Professor's office.

"Won't be long now, Professor."

He paused. Turned back. *Alone!* Jumped back to look around the corner. No one.

Jesus! How the fuck had — No matter. He knew where he was. Fuck the Professor.

He held the Glock tighter. Checked the magazine for the third time. Stared at his trembling hands as they betrayed him.

The strings of bulbs stretched in three directions. He stared in disbelief as they flickered and went out.

His breath roared in his ears like a subway train, racing faster and faster, crushing him against the walls. He reached for his phone. No signal, but the screen's dim light was a God-send. Fumbled for the flashlight app.

The little phone LED was like an arc light against the pure dark of the cavern. He could clearly see the bricks and decorative arches that held the ceiling, yet the light, as bright as it was, reached out a few feet and stopped, as if the air was thick, the fall-off sudden and absolute.

Dust motes floated and danced through the narrow beam of light in front of his face before he slowly looked up.

Almost didn't have time to scream, but did anyway when the huge, twisted shadow dropped from above.

Ula used the brick wall to guide her through the dark. She stopped to confirm tile, smooth under her fingers, laid within the walls. Tried to find a pattern that would suggest direction. Maybe an arrow or some secret symbol that would suddenly speak to her. Felt further. Higher. Lower.

The wall opened up to... *nothingness.* She fought to quiet her heart, and instead listened to her breathing amplified in the dark.

The sound changed, and she knew she had entered a larger space. Stepped forward with both hands out, feeling along the floor with her bare feet.

A wall. More brick. She sidestepped left until it opened again. Again pressed forward. Emptiness led her to another wall.

An intersection of passages. Snapped her fingers. Tried to decipher the reflection of sound and make sense of where she was. Stepped left in baby steps until she hit another wall. Was this the third wall, or the fourth? *Think.* Breathe and think. Three turns. The last thing she wanted to do was go back the way she'd come.

Thought she'd heard someone. Strained to hear them again. Nothing. She knew old city pipes could mimic groans and whispers. Maybe that's all it was. Right or left? She fought the urge to cry. Felt a tear at her eye, and licked at it when it rolled past her lips.

Was sure she heard whispers in the dark from somewhere close. They seemed to be coming her way, whispering nonsense, tumbling and sliding over each other in the dark until they passed right through her. She cried out in anguish, realizing they were her own.

Maybe it was the echoes of her shout, bouncing off the stone to taunt her, but she was sure she'd heard a distant scream.

She began shaking again, certain she'd fall into a bottomless pit. She hugged the wall. Afraid to let go.

THIRTY-EIGHT

01110011

THE LINE OF CARS WASN'T really that long, but when you'd been driving across the countryside with a chunk of wood strapped to your thigh and had to battle for your life with Cujo just to keep it, any delay was torture.

Up ahead, lights flashing on their vehicles, and with traffic cones further narrowing down options, armed military guards in full gear manned the ingress and egress of the town.

Maybe fifteen, twenty cars to go, their exhaust billowed into the frigid air. A woman tried to get her Shih Tzu back in her car. A man leaned against his car smoking. Another tried to help his three-year old pee against their back tire.

"Sorry, Ma'am. You'll need to turn around."

"I need to get to my mother, and she — "

"I'm sorry, Ma'am. We have a gas leak that we're taking care of, and no one is allowed in until we know it's safe."

"Safe? But I — "

"I have my orders." Two more men with full gear, automatic rifles on display, approached.

"You'll need to turn around Ma'am."

A man handed her a printed flyer.

"You can call that number for additional updates, Ma'am. We'll get you back home just as soon as we can."

Bad Ass watched the little blue Honda turn a three-point turn into seven, and then a repeat in the conversation with the pick-up truck that took its place.

No reason to wait. And time was running out.

The little brick structure had been constructed in 1882 as the rebuilt, modern pump house to the sewage system that ran under Maizeville. The brass sign on the wall outside the large double doors and the large vinyl welcoming sign proclaimed its current purpose, while the original spelling in cement at the city's founding still ran across the top behind it.

The sewage and water treatment system had long been replaced as the city grew up and around it. The pump house had taken on several lives that charted the town's rise and fall; a jail, a library, a speakeasy that was also home of the best poker game in town, a popular ice cream parlor that franchised and went national, and a flower shop, all before becoming the current Mazeville Historic Visitor's Center.

What remained inside, without access to the general public, was a huge locked door and the set of wide cement steps that led to sealed lower levels below the city.

The big cargo-covered military truck was backed up to the entrance. In front, two JLTVs, along with a two-dozen armed personnel. No markings, no visible insignias. Nor were there obvious markings on the heavily tinted Chevy Suburban that pulled up unless you counted the DoD plates on the front and back.

Colonel Bradley stepped out. Was escorted inside as six men removed a locker from the back of a deuce-and-a-half.

...

Gray on gray on gray, all color sucked away by the cold; shadow and form softened into vague hints of white and less white. Still, you wouldn't have to be much of a tracker to follow the strange path through the deep snow leading from the road across the barren fields, through the small stand of barren trees, and into the outskirts of town.

A boot-step. A wavy line beside it. Boot-step. Wavy line.

The town looked deserted. Under snow. Burned out and hastily boarded up buildings.

Bad Ass looked up to a window where someone was watching him. The curtains snapped shut, and the lights went out.

He stepped on to the main street. Easy enough and safer to walk down the middle. No attempt to clear it or plow the snow. Hulks of cars and trucks under thick blankets of white, a few errant street-lights, sporadic light filtered from behind curtains or blinds in the windows.

A couple of blocks in, he realized that life went on all around him. He saw a couple cross the street. They glanced his direction and hurried away.

Heard a distant shout. Passed a corner where half a dozen laughing kids were having a snowball fight. Saw a truck ahead spinning in the snow, the tires whining at the demands and refusing to propel the vehicle forward.

He needed nutrition, a bathroom, and enough warmth to thaw out his brain. A shower, some sleep, and a new leg would be nice. He was starting to wonder what he was doing here. Who the hell was he to think he could save the world?

He saw a sandwich shop. Closed. A small market. Closed. An Army surplus store. Closed. A pawn shop. Closed. What might be a bar.

A man staggered out, pissed against the wall, the steam rising from between his feet to obscure his face.

Maybe they didn't have restrooms inside, but Bad Ass figured he'd take the chance, and crossed the street as the man zipped up. The man wandered up the walk as Bad Ass stepped past the yellow snow and went inside.

THIRTY-NINE

01000001

OVERHEADS WERE OUT. The big lab was lit by workstations and glowing electronics. All who worked there had been given the day off with instructions to be ready for questioning. Mads was well-liked, and so he knew many of them would need more time. Still others would look for transfers or retirement.

Maybe time for him to think about it too.

Carmine perched in front of his computer. Accessed the servers. Mad's files deleted, but with triple redundancy, easily retrieved. He glanced at a list of source files. Waiting for him when he had the focus to work on them.

His mind was stuck on replaying every word of the congressional oversight, or investigation, or whatever they would end up calling it. Most likely its label would come after they determined how best to cover their asses. Then they'd consult with the legal and marketing firms and press secretaries that could advise them on how they could best be presented to the public. After all, committees such as these were bound to have someone, or *someones*, thinking of even higher office.

Three current threats. First, Looping. Easy solution, stay off the app. Delete it. Or keep away from social media. Want to stay alive? Then maybe turn off your fucking phone.

Already protests were springing up across the world on censorship and individual's rights. Who cared that the Internet allowed a transmissible virus to spread at the speed of light to any point of the globe?

Second, that a Looper would attack and kill you. Rare only because Loopers were rare — so far — but attacks were almost always fatal. Rumors popped up and found traction across the conspiracy boards, but there were no confirmed cases of community spread. What they needed to determine now was, why there were isolated pockets of mass transformations?

He had thoughts on that too, but wasn't sure how to go about proving them. Africa? Sure. He'd seen the footage. The developed nations had been experimenting on Africans for four-hundred years. Isolated events around the world made sense, but why Mazeville?

And that brought him to the third threat. That if Mazeville was someone's idea of a domestic test site, that if the population had been targeted like the African village, they were now certainly under the threat of a massive cover-up.

If the footage sent to Mads was any indication, then the cure could indeed be as deadly as the virus itself. Social media abstinence or being technologically challenged wouldn't be able to save you.

Carmine looked at the two MPs. Pretty sure they had been switched out earlier, but all cast from the same mold.

He looked at Mad's phone. Battery topped off. He'd already tried to log in. Tried the normal combinations of names and birthdays. No luck. Two more tries. Easier to win a billion-dollar PowerBall. And that's when it hit him.

Opened the login. Typed...

POKEMON#38

The event that had started it all for them, that bonded them, and brought them to where he sat now.

Nothing.
One last try.
Typed it out.

#POKEMON38

Thumb hovered… took a breath… deleted it. Started over.

POKE#MON38

He scrolled through her text messages. His name and number of course. Even though they saw each other five days a week, and sometimes more, his name was there more than any other. It made him sad. She deserved better. Names and abbreviations of people he didn't know. His excitement evaporated. All he knew about her was her dedication to work, just a small part of her brilliant mind, and nothing about *who she was*. He couldn't help but think that much of it might have been his just for the asking.

People were… abstract. What did she dream?

He felt small. Fought the urge to cry. Hadn't happened since he was twelve and visited his grandfather in Sicily. The summer started a bit rocky, but after proving himself by bloodying Gianni A'miacci's nose, became a whirlwind of making new friends, and taking advantage of being 'the American.' It was as close to being a celebrity as he was ever going to get. Had his first kiss. A girl he still let himself think about sometimes. And then, the bottom fell out.

His grandfather, the man had survived being a pilot in WWII, flying a Fiat G.50 for the famed Regia Aeronautica in the Battle of France, fell sick. Pancreatic cancer. Carmine had begged to stay, but by the end of summer, it was all over.

P. Who was that? Messages cryptic. A boyfriend he hadn't known about? He knew he needed to pass this on to the detective. *J?* Seemed likely that was Jenn. They went out for drinks sometime. *BA?* That struck a chord.

Looked at the dates of the messages, and started to get excited again. BA. He had his ideas on who it was. They'd never met but he'd heard stories, most hard to swallow, but noted the far-away look she got when talking about him.

BA. Last message. OMW. Unlisted number. No message thread before it. Deleted? OMW? One more week? On my way? Carmine texted back.

NEED TO MEET

Stared at the phone, willing it to answer him.

He looked up at the voices. Two men in suits flashing credentials at the MPs. Saw the guards point across the room, "Major? Can't miss him," to where he normally worked. Mouths set on serious, on a mission.

Carmine would deal with them. What choice did he have?

The phone pulled his eyes as it lit up.

OK

The two men took in the lab. Could have been designed for a thousand different purposes, all beyond their powers, except for all the huge TVs. *"Monitors"* they called them. Looked more like a TV station than a research lab.

Not their job to know — theirs was to bring him in. Simple enough. They had badges. And authority. And guns.

They turned the corner toward his office. Didn't bother knocking. No one. They scanned the lab. No sign of anyone but the two jarheads that had let them in.

"Major, can't miss him" Carmine Marelli was gone.

FORTY

01110010

THE WOMAN BEHIND THE bar looked up from her count as he hobbled in. Stamped the snow off his foot at the door.

She slid the bills into a zippered vinyl bank bag. "Sorry, hon. We're closing up early. Last call, so if you want to get something, order now."

She said nothing about the step clonk, step clonk, across the wooden floors, but both men hunched over the bar looked back from under their arms. Took in the crazy leg. Then the bandoliers across his chest, the Beretta, the flintlock, and the worn leather duster.

They didn't try to hide their snickers.

"I could go for the rest of that coffee," he said.

She looked surprised, not that he wanted coffee — he looked cold enough, eyes bright and clear, a smile frozen on his face — but rather, that he'd want *this* coffee.

She lifted the pot, rolled the thick syrupy liquid around the glass. "Let me make you a fresh pot, hon."

The closer of the men looked him up and down. "You leave your ship outside?" His voice about three notches louder than it needed to be.

"A restroom?"

She pointed toward the only logical direction. "Second door on the left."

"Thanks."

He heard the other man behind him. "What the fuck, Marge? You sweet on pirates now?"

The restroom had probably started the day clean and tidy. Drunks seemed to have a hard time figuring out where to piss.

It didn't take him long, and for the first time it had come up, he felt like he was half barefoot, the wooden leg all he had, but without a shoe. Forced himself to get over it, but he still felt dirty after having to step across the wet floor.

Washed his hands and face. Looked into the little mirror. The face that stared back was familiar. It looked much like the one he'd last seen in Cameroon. The one before that in Uganda. Similar to the one in Croatia. About a hundred years older than the one in Afghanistan.

Tried smiling. Unrecognizable. Fortunate the light was dim.

Made it back to the bar as the woman poured the fresh steaming coffee into a heavy white cup.

"Come on, Marge. Give us another." Banged his mug on the bar.

"Had your last call, Sam," she said. "You finish up now and get on home."

"Goddamn." He sounded like he might cry. "You served the fucking pirate. Or maybe you're just sweet on one-legged cripple motherfuckers."

The other man pushed a few bills across the counter. "Now bring us another."

"I've told you about that language. One more time, and you're banned for the month. Now get on out of here 'fore I get riled."

Bad Ass sipped his coffee. Tried to concentrate on the newscast above the bar.

A freshman congresswoman demanding an investigation into whoever hacked her Flat Earth support group. It could spell the end of the entire flat planet if the FBI, Homeland Security, and her hometown library couldn't track the subversive bastards down.

New reporting on the viral videos popping up of people going up in flames in China, Europe, and Africa. Well staged with lots of fake blood and body parts, but all proven to be fake. Part of a false-flag effort to clamp down on the Internet.

Then armed protesters converging on the state capital to protest radical, liberal censorship from Big Tech. Duplicated across the country and in D.C. Like every other protest movement, quickly hijacked for dozens of other causes. Lots of 'isms'. The same First Amendment that gave people the right for thoughtful discourse with radically differing views, gave people the right to say all the stupid shit they wanted, and the Second, the means if not the guidance, to protect the first and a reason to pay attention.

If people wanted to watch and share viruses on-line, who the fuck was the government to say they couldn't? People tearing each other apart, figuratively and literally, was the price people were willing for someone else to pay.

Marge glanced up at it. Shook her head. "If you want me to change it to something else, let me know."

Maybe seventy. He could imagine she was a looker, thirty, even twenty years ago. No shrinking violet. No reason to worry about the two drunks. If she ran a bar, she'd seen it all, and knew how to take care of herself.

He pulled out his phone and the new charger.

"Think you could plug this in for me?"

The door burst open along with the cold wind and snow, and three more men stomped their way in.

"Sorry, boys. We're closed."

"Nah, come on. Bring a couple pitchers."

"Shutting it down."

"Four glasses!"

Bad Ass watched from the mirror as the three took places at a high-top. Stomped as loudly as they could. Threw hats, gloves, scarves, and baseball bats on the closest table. Maybe 'snowball' was a thing here.

"Been weird all day," Marge explained. "First the Guard, and now this. Second 'ball team' today."

Shouted one more time, "Closing up, fellas." Turned to him. "You want another cup, hon?"

She was reaching for the pot, when one of the men, maybe the team captain, banged on the bar.

"Bring us some beer, Marge."

"Not today, Johnny. You boys take it somewhere else."

"Somewhere else? The whole fucking town's shut down."

Johnny looked down the bar. Two drunks, and a cowboy drinking a cup of coffee.

"Waiting on Billy. Give us a pitcher."

The two at the high-top looked up from their phones. "J, come look at this shit! Man, they beat the fuck out of this thing."

The sound of Johnny's hand slapping on the bar sounded like a rifle crack. "Give me a Goddamned pitcher."

One of the bar drunks, not Sam, reached out to calm him down. He grabbed at Johnny's coat. "She done told you to move along, son."

Johnny wiped the hand away, and pushed back hard. Sam lost his balance, his head hit the bar, and he crashed to the floor.

Now about five things happened at once, and Marge, seventy-two since last September, had seen most things, but watching a one-legged badass in action was a first.

As Sam's barstool fell over on him, and Johnny stepped in to shove him again with his foot, Bad Ass backhanded his empty coffee mug through the air where it smashed into Johnny's face. It rocked his head back and split his forehead open so that by the time he got his hands up, blood was already pouring through his fingers.

The two at the high-top were reaching for their bats when Bad Ass stepped past Sam and friend to grab Johnny, spin, and toss him into the other two.

The three, along with chairs and tables, crashed to the floor.

Johnny's two friends, maybe the infielders, the teams' first and second basemen, recovered first.

Saw the leg. "What the fuck? What are you? Some kind of God-damned pirate?"

The first baseman saw the bandoliers beneath the coat. Laughed. "Ain't no pirate! Tim, this here's a *gen-u-wine* fucking *Mex-i-can band-dee-to.*"

Maybe they'd had a few before they came in because both men swung their bats at the same time. Probably a brand new team, they had no idea of how to work together. Bad Ass leaned back just far enough for one bat to whisper by in front of his face, while the other one, in the hands of Tim, cracked his friend in the ribs.

"Sorry, Frank!"

The weight of Tim's bat pulled him forward. Bad Ass crashed an elbow up and under his chin. Tim almost had time to register the crack of bone, but Bad Ass glided forward, dragging his wooden leg, and let his elbow continue. It came back down, reversed, and rose in a blinding figure-eight. The downward strike slammed Tim over his left eye, and a split second later, circled in from the other side. The bony tip of his elbow sliced across the ridge of bone above the man's right eye, and Tim crashed to the floor.

Johnny was wiping at the blood streaming from his forehead, trying to pick up his bat off the floor, when Frank, winding up, swung for the outfield.

Bad Ass spun in place, matched the motion of Frank's wild swing, backed into him long enough to push the man back, his wooden leg crushing the man's foot while ripping the bat out of his hands. Frank flew backward where his head bounced off the wall behind him.

Johnny made his first, and last swing. Bad Ass slipped to the side and angled the bats so they met with the full force of both men's strikes against Johnny's hand. Johnny screamed out as the hard maple bat shattered bone and split flesh.

Sliding left, Bad Ass reversed the bat and jammed the handle into Frank's gut. Air went out of him in a rush, and he crashed to his knees, fighting for air and to not throw up.

Bad Ass spun the bat up and over his shoulder, gained even more momentum as he torqued it over his rising forearm, and brought it down from on high for the kill —

— caught himself... and froze in mid-strike.

Stepped back, clumsy on his locked wooden leg, he let the bat fall. Turned and reached down to help Sam off the floor.

The original three watched as the newcomers helped each other up. Each of the team members bleeding and crippled in their way; getting to their feet took longer than the fight.

"We'll see you again, motherfucker." And fled out the door.

Bad Ass, already feeling bad, looked back up to Marge.

Okay, maybe the last couple of days had gotten to him, and he could have dialed it back just a notch. *You think?*

He shrugged. "Sorry."

Marge let the breath out she'd been holding.

"Get you a cup to go?"

FORTY-ONE

01100101

A HIGH POWERED, INTERNATIONAL attorney's salary went far in a small college town, and the luxury brownstone was spacious; it felt even bigger since the divorce.

Jackie busied herself nearby as her five-year-old daughter finished brushing her teeth. A lamp in the living room flickered, and she jerked her head toward what she thought was a shadow flitting behind her. Nothing. On edge since this business of viruses and monsters had gripped the world's imagination. There were always those who jumped on the conspiracy bandwagons, and after the pandemic that had wrecked the planet, she wondered if it was some human need for a new boogyman to blame.

Rumors spread faster than viruses, gained strength when you tried to contain them, and pointed at the town being some sort of government test case spiraling out of control. Add the threat of vigilante militias and the deniers of anything they couldn't see or hold in their hands — you had groups still convinced the earth was flat for Christ's sake. Mandatory lockdowns and the threat of martial law added to the local panic, while the worldwide majority was content to think it could never happen to them.

Nothing moved in her living room except the images on the big screen television. Endless holiday movies, the equivalent of ice milk. She was sure that every show was filmed from the same script; retitled, the sets rearranged, and the cast swapped out for each production.

"Finished!"

Jackie jumped and spun to her daughter.

"Don't be scared, Mommy. It's only me."

Jackie recovered, scooped her up. "I know it's only you. But you are soooo scary!"

The little girl giggled. "You're scary!"

She set her down and covered her eyes. "I'm going to be super scary if I count to five and don't find you under your covers."

The girl squealed all the way to her room. Jackie growled and stomped in place behind her.

A moment later, the girl came running back out, still laughing, and jumped into her mother's arms.

"You have to carry me."

"You're getting too big to carry."

"I'm not *that* big, Mommy."

They entered the room. Cute. Big poster bed. Frilly pink curtains. A menagerie of stuffed animals and dolls.

She tossed the girl on the bed, where she bounced and laughed and scrambled to get under the thick covers.

"I think next time, you'll have to carry *me*."

"You're too big!"

"You calling me big?"

The girl nodded. Serious.

"And you? You're soooo busy growing up, you forgot to say your prayers?"

The girl scrambled back out and knelt by the bed. Waiting.

"You too, Mommy."

She pulled her mother down beside her.

They said the Lord's Prayer together before the girl hugged her tight, kissed her cheek, and jumped back onto the bed.

Jackie was rising when she felt something under the bed. Tickling her knees. Reached under.

And pulled out the girl's favorite stuffed monkey.

"Now what's Harold doing hiding under the bed?"

Jackie walked it across the bed, climbed it up the headboard, and dove under and let Harold swim beneath the covers until her daughter grabbed for it and hugged the ragged little monkey close.

She was tucking them both tightly under the blankets when her phone rang from the living room.

"I'll be right back."

Jackie grabbed the phone.

"Hey, Lance. Hang on a sec." Poured herself another glass of wine, took a sip, and held the phone to her ear as she returned to her daughter.

"You okay in here?"

Bent down to kiss the girl and tuck the covers even tighter.

"Turn out the lights?"

The girl shook her head no. "Harold doesn't like the dark."

Jackie reached for the table side lamp. "How about just this one, and I leave the hall light on?"

The girl thought about it, checked with Harold, then nodded her head.

Jackie was halfway to the door.

"Mommy."

Turned back to the girl pointing at the open closet door.

"Hang on, Lance."

She tiptoed to the closet and suddenly jerked the door open. Made a show of looking high and low and behind the hangers of little girl dresses.

"Hah! No monsters!"

She shut the door and tiptoed toward the curtains. Snatched them back with a flourish to reveal the frosted windows.

"Ta-da! No monsters here!" Jackie did a little "no monsters dance."

The girl giggled.

"Okay, time for sleep." Kissed her daughter again and left the door cracked enough that light streamed in across the girl's bed. Waited for the okay, then headed to the living room.

By human standards, certainly anything that had come before, the thing was defective, but not quite mindless. Arms and legs had been reworked to take full advantage of potential joint articulation. Skin burned off so that nothing interfered with its neural network as it interfaced with its environment. Synaptic plasticity had been exponentially increased by alterations of dendritic function and synaptic remodeling, and by radically increasing the concentration of a host of neurotransmitters.

The instant flood of reengineered chemicals along with axonal sprouting, neurite extension, and cellular mitochondrial genesis, gave it immense strength, speed, and reaction time — potentiation far beyond its original abilities and purpose.

Unlike the primitive first-generation variants, it moved with deliberation, stealth, and intent. Intellect, as previously defined, had been burned away in the instant short-circuiting and rewiring that left it free from distraction. It would die soon enough, but not before serving its purpose in hastening the evolution from inefficiency and impermanence of living matter to something more elegant and self-sustaining. It operated exclusively on programmed instinct and a compulsion to kill the living.

She turned the TV down, put the phone on speaker. "Hey."

"Hey. All good over there?"

"All good. On your way?"

"Fast as I can. It's nuts out here."

She could hear his tires crunching through the snow, the back and forth of his wipers through the car's hands-free audio system.

"I think we've been played," he said.

"Yeah, me too. I'm not sure the Colonel is telling us — "

The scream echoed through the apartment, as piercing as a klaxon horn. In the year since the divorce, it had been at least a weekly occurrence.

"Sorry, Lance."

Jackie took a sip of wine, grabbed the phone, and walked to the back. Peeked in. Her daughter was sitting up, hugging Harold. Pointing under the bed.

"Really?"

The girl nodded.

Phone at her ear, Jackie kneeled. Looked under the bed. A shadow that she reached for.

Harold's second-best friend, Bernice. A purple rabbit with ears twice the size of Harold. She stretched to reach it.

Set it on the bed. Tucked her daughter, the monkey, and the rabbit under the covers. Kissed the furry plushies, and ended with a noisy smooch on the little girl's forehead. Her daughter giggled, scrunched her eyes tight to prove she was going to sleep and rolled over.

It uncoiled slowly, almost delicately, from where it hung beneath the springs of the bed. Lowered itself to the floor. Moved through the shadows and gathered itself, ready to fulfill its purpose.

Jackie curled back up on the couch, wine in hand, phone balanced on her knee.

"You were saying?"

FORTY-TWO

01010010

LANCE DROVE A 600 series Mercedes. Just over a year old, he'd been thinking of selling it to Jackie, cheap, buying something even more high-performance for himself — not much room left to go, but maybe the final step up. She'd never accept it if he simply gave it to her, but she'd openly admired it so much, he was sure she'd get more enjoyment from it than he did. But then again, if they made her a partner, she might find it insulting. No, probably better if they arranged a lease of anything she wanted.

Clouds were evidently being turned inside out up above, and snow came in bunches that intermittently cut visibility to zero. Electricity was sporadic and streetlights were out, but the drifts glowed and reflected his headlights. It was like driving on an alien planet — of course, the last time he'd driven on an alien planet was when he was eight, after watching Star Wars. And there hadn't been the dozens of abandoned wrecks lying across the streets.

He slowed further, from fifteen to five. This was really bad. Talking to Jackie on the car's sound system was as much to keep him settled as any real exchange of new information.

"Hey."

"Hey. All good over there?"

"All good. On your way?"

"Fast as I can. It's nuts out here."

He dodged another wreck. A ménage à trois of steel and plastic. It must have happened some hours ago; snow softened the jagged edges and was piled high on the shattered windshields. As he passed, he thought he saw frozen blood across the windows.

He swallowed hard and tried not to think about it.

"I think we've been played," he said.

"Yeah, me too. I'm not sure the Colonel is telling us — "

The little-girl's scream echoed across his speakers. Fortunately, the car's Bluetooth interface defaulted to a simple stereo mix rather than the full twenty-four speaker, 1500 watt sound system. Still, it felt like they were in the car with him.

"Sorry, Lance." He heard her walking through the apartment, pictured her walking down the hall to her daughter's bedroom.

"Really?" Her voice was comforting. Then movement, giggles, and a kiss goodnight.

It let him know that even with the insanity of the streets, at least parts of the universe were still in order.

"You were saying?"

"I think we need to call your contacts at the Penta — "

The blood-curdling scream was a physical assault that wrenched his heart. He jerked the wheel, the car's advanced systems helped but he scraped against another car in the road, the screech of metal on metal blending with the scream.

He jerked the wheel away as the twisted figure of a man streaked right for him. Though he was only doing five miles per hour, the man, or whatever the fuck he was, must have been doing thirty, and the impact shattered his windshield. He instinctively twisted the wheel and slammed into another car.

The passenger side curtain airbags exploded and cushioned any potential impact but he was locked firmly to his seat.

He spun in place. Nothing visible in front. Nothing in back. Blind to whatever was beyond the passenger window.

"Jackie?"

No answer. Panic and foreboding swept over him. He fought for air.

"Jackie?!"

A wet, crunching sound resolved through the front speakers — even with the fabulous sound system it was hard to hear over his beating heart.

He tried to back up. His car spun against the snowdrift and ice, the rear-end circling so he now sat perpendicular to the road. Fuck!

He needed to get to Jackie. He could probably walk faster than he could drive in this fucking mess. He grabbed his coat. Pushed past the deflating airbags. Stepped out. The icy air clutched at his chest, crushing it within a relentless fist.

Whatever he'd hit was gone. Had it been imagination? He looked at the windshield. No. The split-second nightmare was seared on his brain. It was real.

Tears froze on his cheeks as Jackie's scream continued to echo in his mind, tearing at his heart.

He wiped them away, looked at his car. Minor damage, nothing that should stop him from being able to get back in and drive. He wasn't going to make it out of here on foot. The cold and wind too bitter, his dress shoes slipping on the ice.

No cars or lights on the streets. An empty, alien world for sure.

And that's when he saw them. Three figures. Silhouettes against the snow. At first, he thought they were dogs playing and bounding in the drifts. His mind couldn't make sense of what he was seeing, their strange, insect-like movements, skittering and crawling from an alley onto the wet, icy street. Hunting in a pack... but not dogs.

They stopped. Seemed to sniff the air. Changed direction. And made the first steps his way... hesitantly... as if trying to figure out who or what he was. This lone human standing on the dark, empty streets in the middle of a deserted downtown Mazeville.

Moving faster.

Now charging full speed.

FORTY-THREE

01100101

PROFESSOR HALL CAME TO. From nothing, to instant full consciousness. Opened his eyes. The stab of pain arcing through the middle of his head admonished him to go slow. Closed them, took a breath, and tried again.

He'd fled Gunns in the halls and made it back here. Why he'd passed out... *who the fuck knows?* Pain and shock and...

It took a moment to understand what he was looking at. Inches away was a rat, close enough he could count the whiskers. Gnawing on what was left of Beast.

He jerked away and scrambled over other body parts. Made it to his feet, his shoes sticking to the blood-soaked cement.

Gasped for breath, fought down the urge to retch, and forced himself to take it in. Counted body parts. Pretty sure they added up to two. Beast and Clothes Hanger — Lex and Dustin. He shivered when he imagined what must have happened to Keven.

The computers were trashed, screens broken, and wires ripped out. Hard to know if it was somehow purposeful or happened in the melee of terror. He was thankful he'd been unconscious for most of it, and knew that fact had probably saved his life.

No sign of Gunns. No sign of Skinny. Funny enough he thought, he'd never known the boy's real name. He strained to listen. Nothing but the licking of little rat lips and the gnashing of little rat teeth on flesh and bone. The little bastard wasn't afraid of him at all.

The bunker door was still locked, so the girl was probably safe. He saw the ring of keys in a puddle of blood, fought the bile that burned in his throat, and picked them up. Saw a half bottle of genuine imported purified tap water and tried to rinse them off.

No light in the bunker, or in the cell they had used for the woman. He tried to peer through the bars, bent and twisted, but the heavy iron had held.

"Hello?"

Nothing. She'd never seen him. *He could be her savior!* Suddenly imperative. He could save the woman and in doing so, restore a modicum of decency and courage for himself. Fuck, he could still come out of this a hero! His mind jumped ahead to the adulation she'd shower on him and the interviews he'd give. Keys to the city and a six-figure book dea —

"You okay in there?"

Maybe she was too weak to answer.

"Hey, you're gonna be okay." Fumbling, the keys slipping in his hands. "Hang on. I'm going to get you out of there."

He got the heavy door unlocked.

Black inside. It took a moment for his eyes to adjust, and the black changed to a murky gray.

Stepped inside. Empty. And in front of him, one entire wall open to an inky black chasm.

Ula woke up. Stunned that she had somehow dozed off. Only black. Pushed her eyelids up and down a few times with her fingers to make sure they were opening. Yep. And in front of her, the inky blackness that can only be found in the bowels of the Earth. Forced herself to breathe. To quiet her pounding heart. She stretched out both hands and stepped forward.

Hall made it back to his office. It seemed to take forever, not because he was lost, but because of the fear that made him stop to listen time and again and wonder if he was being followed, or maybe even worse, that he'd step right into the arms of the creature that had been Skinny, or even Gunns.

No sign of either.

Started up his computer. He could hear the hard drive trying to spin but only a few random numbers and letters flickered across the broken screen. It refused to boot. He banged on it in frustration and had a moment of hope before the hard drive started whining and the clicking got louder.

He set his phone to a news station and picked up a stack of reports that had been knocked to the floor.

" — mandatory lockdowns go into effect at four p.m. today for the town of Mazeville."

Grabbed his phone to check the time. 3:38!

"God damn it!"

" — residents are urged extreme caution as officials are reporting new variants to the frenzied behavior — "

Rifled through the papers and files scattered across the floor. No hope of making sense of them, he couldn't even see past the tears of frustration. Fuck! 3:43. He ran out the door.

Ula worked her way around the corner. Either her eyes were somehow adjusting, or there was some distant source of light, perhaps reflected and diffused off the dry dust that gave the air enough texture and form that she began finding her way. Her hands clutched an iron pipe she'd found, maybe three-feet long.

Not much to some, but comforting — she knew in her hands it could be deadly.

She turned the corner. Darker still. A few steps forward confirmed it was a dead end. Turned back, but thought she heard something. She slid deeper into the blackest shadows, crouched down in the corner, and waited, holding her knees tightly to keep them from knocking and giving away her position.

It sounded like a giant cockroach or spider, or like the sound of live crabs against a plastic bucket, the movements skittering and scratching across the rock and brick of the tunnels. Louder. Closer.

She held her breath as long as she could. Whatever it was, maybe Skinny, or some other monster left below ground long ago, faded away. Soon, she was left in the dark with only the sound of her beating heart.

FORTY-FOUR

01100001

LANCE BACKED INTO THE alley. The three things on the streets, he couldn't wrap his head around what to call them, had found closer prey, and Lance was forced to listen helplessly as the victim was torn apart. The screams so filled with terror and pain, he couldn't tell if it was a man or woman. Mercifully short, but his imagination filled in the rest. He was shaking badly, and knew it wasn't just the cold.

He'd seen combat and had been through two divorces, hadn't thought of himself as a fearful man. But that was ten minutes ago. Now he replayed the scream from Jackie's. Even if he survived long enough to get there, he wasn't brave enough to face what he feared he'd find.

He peeked around the corner. The things, human enough that it made it worse, were coming back onto the street.

Something grabbed him from behind and jerked him deeper into the alley. Spinning on the ice, he stumbled, fought for balance, and crashed into the wall.

Bounced off the bricks to face a little girl, couldn't have weighed a hundred pounds, dressed as if styled by a blind fashion designer. A wooden crochet mallet raised in one hand ready to smash him in the head, and a gleaming Japanese sword poised in the other to cut it off.

His eyes wide. "Jesus! Who are you?"

"The one who just saved your life, so shut the fuck up and be quiet."

His eyes darted past her and the length of the alley, and opened even wider. Another one of the creatures, running and bouncing off the narrow alley walls and twisting in the air, was charging right for them.

Jessie tossed him the mallet, spun hard with the sword. And missed completely.

Fueled by fear and desperation, Lance swung the mallet with all his might. Jessie barely even had to duck as the mallet cut the air above her, connected full against the monster's head, and bowled it off its feet.

The wooden handle shattered in his hands and spun across the alley.

As the creature recovered, Jessie stepped in and sliced down hard. The sword, real-deal hand-forged, eighteenth-century folded steel, sliced deep from the side of its neck to halfway through its chest. The Looper shrieked, thrashed hard enough to lift her off her feet, shuddered, and died.

Jessie planted both feet in order to pull the sword out. Wiped off the blackish blood in the drifts of snow. Peeked around the alley wall to the streets.

Lance was right behind her, realized he was pressed against her backside as he peered over her head.

He jerked away, turned red. Stammered.

"Hey, it's okay," she grinned. "I'm older than I look."

He blushed even harder. She laughed and turned back to the streets. The three Loopers were heading their way.

"Shit. Come on."

She strode down the alley, ducked into a doorway he hadn't seen, and was soon lost to the dark.

FORTY-FIVE

01101100

"VIOLENT PROTESTS HAVE BROKEN out in cities across the globe as privacy activists rebel against newly revealed facial recognition and surveillance technology being employed to track potential extremists..."

"New bipartisan legislation restricting the use of drones equipped with bio-scanning by federal agencies is expected to pass the House and..."

"The use of *"affect recognition"* or *"emotion detection"* software in primary and secondary schools is under fire from privacy watchdog groups who fear the data..."

"—so-called Looper outbreak is now being attributed to extreme epileptic seizures caused by faulty mobile screens manufactured in China."

"—suit, expected to be filed in federal court on Monday, alleges that the entertainment app, which uses Artificial Intelligence and genome profiling, is a not only a violation of..."

"—forgotten who we are in this country. Everyone of them so-called Loopers is a combo of an unholy, multi-racial, impure mixing of the races. That's why I'm introducing a bill in the House today banning all interracial marriage..."

" — getting reports that X, the maverick genius who founded XAI Integrations has died due to complications of pneumonia."

"XAII, pronounced Zai-ee, has come under fire recently for issues discovered in the controversial vaccinations programs pioneered last..."

"Anything new?"

Giles seemed to walk in through the wall, the door so perfectly engineered and silent it was invisible once it shut behind him, and set the silver tray on the nightstand.

"Kaitlynn changed her hair. I think it looks nice."

Giles poured tea for two. Sat beside his friend on the bed and watched their favorite reporter. He couldn't hear her, never acquiring X's ability to listen to a dozen simultaneous newscasts.

"XAII made additional waves last year with their 25-billion dollar donation to the WHO. As you know, Kaitlynn, the WHO has come under fire for its close ties to China and the handling of the SARS-COV2 epidemic that ravaged the world."

X sipped at his tea. "Any progress?"

"We've got a line on him now."

"Do your best."

"Of course."

X set the tea aside, waved his hand, and all the broadcasts went dark except for the row of center monitors. From left to right, they created a twelve-foot digital clock.

07:39:51 ... 07:39:50...

Giles rose as X scooted lower in the bed. Giles pulled the blankets up, and tucked them under the gaunt chin. Waited until he saw his friend's eyes begin to close.

"Good night, Sir."

"Good night, Giles."

Giles slipped out as silently as he came.

X opened his eyes enough to look across the room at the Cube. Solid, matte-black — *the composite could withstand a direct one-megaton nuclear blast* — yet it somehow pulsed.

He could feel it, throbbing in time to his heartbeat.

FORTY-SIX

01000010

CARMINE STOOD IN THE inky shadows. Beyond, a world in black and white. Fantastic shapes painted with a colorless palate.

He hung up the phone when the figure approached. Looked more like a man than some of the other creatures he'd seen on the streets. Once he was close enough, Carmine could see the Beretta in the shoulder holster. The crossed bandoliers. The antique pistol.

Ridiculous, but completely *badass*. A cowboy or a pirate, as if he hadn't decided. Hair and chin frosted with snow and ice.

"Jesus. What happened to your leg?"

"No time." His voice rich and full. Used to commanding authority. "Where's Mads?"

Carmine shook his head.

"Damn it. And who are you?"

"Major Carmine Merelli. Carm — "

"Her boss," Bad Ass finished.

"Her friend."

Carmine jumped at the screams from down the streets, echoing off the ice but muffled by the falling snow. Bad Ass ignored them. Offered his hand if not his name.

"We need to get off the streets. More are coming."

Carmine seemed reluctant to go, and before Bad Ass could ask, headlights entered the street and headed their way.

A small red car pulled up. A single wiper working feverishly to clear a porthole through the ice and snow. On top, a lighted plastic sign not quite obscured by snow, GINO'S PIZZA.

The boy who stepped out, maybe eighteen, complete with a red-striped shirt and ball cap, carried a large pizza box.

"Carmine?"

"Yeah. What do I owe you?"

"Twenty-two, thirty."

Carmine pulled out the bills. Paid him. "Keep it."

Pizza Boy looked at the two twenties and grinned. Slipped and slid his way back to the car.

Carm turned back to Bad Ass and shrugged.

"Wanna slice?"

He cracked the lid, and fragrant steam hit them both with physical force. *'Deluxe with extra cheese, extra sausage, hold the green peppers.'* Bad Ass grabbed a slice.

He entered the building behind the fat man to face a steep flight of stairs.

Bad Ass gritted his teeth and clomped up the steps. Carmine groaned and tried to keep up.

Two floors up, Bad Ass stopped to wait on Carmine. It didn't take long.

"Where are we going?"

"Should be a sky bridge to the university on the next floor. From there we should be able to get to quieter streets, and find a way back to the lab."

"Where's your car?"

"Dead. Yours?"

"Nowhere close."

They turned the corner for the next floor when they heard footsteps running up from below.

Bad Ass stepped in front. Waited.

Reached out and jerked Pizza Boy from around the corner.

"Hey, hey, hey. Sorry, sorry. I can't go back out there! It's completely fucking crazy."

Bad Ass rolled his eyes. Carmine shrugged, and the three of them continued up.

Jessie and Lance crossed the university commons. Empty. The three-story atrium hollow and dark. Chairs upside down on the tables. The fast-food counters boarded and locked.

Doors and halls spread from the large room like spokes on a wheel. Jessie guided them through the dark.

Into a hallway. Steps going in both directions.

"Up or down?"

"What do you mean?"

"A grid of tunnels runs under the entire city. Basements and sub-basements. Or we take our chances in the open, up top."

"Underground?" Lance was claustrophobic. Add in a few zombies and decision made. "Fuck that. But we have to find a way out of the city."

"Blockades at all the roads in and out. Maybe we can walk out."

"Get us to someone in authority, and I'll do the rest."

Esshhhhh… one of those, she thought. He might be useful but he was cocky, and so far she hadn't seen the justification. He was big, everybody seemed big to her, but if he'd ever been tough, it had been a long time ago. Still…

She took in his suit. "Let me guess… a lawyer?" She didn't wait for the answer. "Come on."

She skipped the flights going up and ran down the hall. Lance did his best to keep up. Through a door, across the room, out a door, up the stairs, down two flights, and into a large courtyard.

They crossed the manicured space, meant to be welcoming. Concrete picnic tables and benches and a dedication to the university founders. Statues and busts of illustrious alumni. Five floors of balconies faced inward, the shadows and reflections off the glass and snow kept it terrifying.

A scream from above. Five floors up, a man was hanging off the balcony. A Looper scurried past and dropped past him, caught itself on the third floor. It swung upward, ape-like, powerful but without the grace. The man screamed again as it drew closer. It grabbed at his leg and pulled him free. The man fell, but was caught in the powerful grip, then swung upside down as the Looper pulled him back up.

For a brief moment, the man stopped screaming, giving in. Hanging by his leg, he looked into Jessie's eyes, and then he was gone. The Looper slithered and skittered upward and pulled him over the rooftop.

Moments later, another scream, and half the man was tossed off to land with a sickening splat in the courtyard.

They watched as more Loopers, maybe drawn from the screams, came out onto the balconies.

"Jesus!"

Jessie grabbed the big guy's coat and pulled him along. Double steel doors blocked their entry.

Lance turned back, too late to make it back from where they'd come. He turned to kick and bang on the doors. Jessie fished around into one of her many coat pockets and pulled out a key card. Nothing. Tried again.

"Think you better hurry." Lance was looking for a weapon, anything he could defend them with. She handed him a steak knife.

Jessie said a quick prayer. Tried the card again. The door locks snicked open.

They ducked inside and pulled the doors closed behind them.

The red emergency lights were creepy, as if they were in a darkroom, but they could see the hallway was empty.

"Come on!"

Before he could catch his breath, she took off running. He did his best to keep up.

He saw her slowing down. She turned and cautioned him for quiet.

Impossible in his leather shoes, whereas even in combat boots, the little waif moved like a miniature ninja.

He tip-toed behind her, tried to quiet his breathing.

They heard footsteps. They sounded human. One man. Struggling.

Sword in hand, she leaped around the corner.

The man froze, then recognized her from class. Both giddy with relief.

"Professor Hall?"

FORTY-SEVEN

01110101

SHE HADN'T HEARD ANYTHING crazy for a while, unless she counted the voices in her head. Go left. Turn back. Run. Freeze. Shout for help. *Shut the fuck up already.*

When she made it to halls and tunnels with occasional dim lights, like the one with a string of Christmas lights with the lone working bulb, or the one with a single sputtering fluorescent flickering in a passage a hundred meters long, the sounds and voices in her imagination lessened. She moved through those tunnels with fair speed only to be stopped by sudden choices of inky black — left, right, forward, or back — and was forced to forge ahead, blind, hands searching along the cold walls for clues, the voices growling and roaring with a vengeance, punishing her for thinking she could rid herself of them.

She couldn't make sense of her prison, didn't know how to cope with being blind. The few markers or signs her fingers found scratched or inlaid on the walls confused her further as she had no reference, no way to make her hands read them against the black. Her sense of scale was distorted by the dark, her hunger, the bone wracking cold. And fear.

The sections she found herself in were maybe unfinished, less brick and tile, more rock, left from natural caves or early mining efforts. She could have been miles from where she started, or just on the other side of the wall.

Trapped in a dark, alien world. Without spatial and temporal anchors, the language she used to process so much of her thoughts didn't apply here.

As she lost her sense of direction, time became fluid. Was she moving away from the events or toward them? Maybe the tunnels themselves were a construct, and she was trapped inside a time machine. If so, she wanted to go back to before she'd been dragged down here. But was that forward or back? Perhaps she'd emerge from one tunnel ten years younger. Or step from another and have aged twenty years.

She'd stumble upon a hall with lights and rush down it only to find it didn't lead anywhere. Had seen a set of wide steps going deeper into the abyss. Had entered a small room that had stairs going up, but the way had been blocked. *Fiddler on the Roofville.* As she went back down the steps in the dark, she began to lose her sense of gravity, and soon couldn't tell what was up or down.

Bullshit, she told herself. *Gravity was gravity.* Right? Or did it begin to reverse itself at some point? She fought the tsunami of vertigo that threatened to crush her under its weight. Was forced to cling to the walls until it finally passed.

No idea how many levels there were. She knew Berlin, and London, and other huge cities of Europe, had hidden underground metropolises that extended eight and nine stories below ground. If she ever got out of here, which at moments seemed probable but then just as quickly impossible, she swore she'd never go into a basement again. *Scheiße*, maybe not even a swimming pool. High rise living for her!

Another dead end. Maybe there were secret panels here too, but more likely someone had simply changed their mind and dug another direction, following softer rock, or executing a master plan she couldn't see. Now she knew how lab rats felt in their mazes.

And then she found it. Whatever *it* was. Hard to see in the near dark, but some light drifted in from above to reveal a large chamber. A hundred feet across, floors broken and filled with trash. A flight of rickety wooden stairs against the far wall led into the inky shadows high above her, maybe three or four floors. She made her way across the room, cursing and wincing at the stabbing pain in her foot.

She started up, nothing to lose. Soon, voices became louder, and she wondered again if they were only in her head.

Parts of the wooden stairs were broken, no railing, and leaned away from the wall they'd been attached to. Halfway up, the treads began to look like broken teeth.

Ula heard the yelling. *She didn't have this many different voices in her head!* The muffled banging and argument came from somewhere above — the voices were *real*.

She slowly put her weight on a board and felt it sag beneath her. Jumped over two missing steps and prayed as the entire construction shook. Boards began to crack and give under her weight. A rusted bolt snapped from somewhere above, the fractured metal echoing like a gunshot across the huge room. She felt the steps below her sway and begin pulling away from the wall.

Looked down and froze.

A shadow, anything but human, began crawling up the wall less than a hundred feet away.

FORTY-EIGHT

01110100

"**IF WE CAN MAKE** it to the sky bridge," Hall said, "we can cross over and come out on the other side of the parking garage."

Lance was hopeful. "You have a car there?"

"No," the Professor said. "But I thought maybe we could steal one."

"I don't think it's that easy."

"I know how to hot wire a car," Jessie said. They looked at her in amazement. She shrugged. "Urban survival 101." Then, as if they had a choice, they let her take the lead. "Come on!"

They clambered up the first flight of stairs. The second landing brought them to where the monsters were throwing themselves at the two-inch barrier of steel door that separated them. It seemed the entire building shook.

The lower doors sounded like they might give at any moment. It was nearly black above with only a bit of piss-yellow street light from outside drifting through a broken window. Metal chairs and glass were strewn on the steps that had to be negotiated, and their shoes stuck to the wet stair treads. Someone had tried and failed to make a stand here.

They crossed another landing. Door wide open. From down the hall, silhouetted against the dim battery powered emergency lights, two distorted shapes were overtaking a screaming man sprinting their way.

Jessie had tears in her eyes. An easy calculation and a tough decision. No way to save the man.

"Shut the fucking door!" The attorney used to giving orders.

"I'm trying, I'm trying. Jesus Christ!"

"Grab that chair and try to brace it!"

"I've got it." Hall's voice strident with hysteria. "I've got it!"

"Wedge it under the knob — "

"I know how to block a fucking door!"

"I'll get it," Jessie shouted. "Just don't let them in."

"Got it!"

Lance wedged the chair under the doorknob, and Jessie stomped kicked it in tighter.

A wailful scream and pounding on the door. An instant later, the scream stopped, replaced by an echoey boom as a Looper threw itself against the door from the outside.

"Up. Up. Up."

The doors shuddered, and the three stumbled and fell over each other up the stairs into the murky light.

Below, a tortured growl resonated with something primal and elemental. Then an ear-splitting screech of metal that filled the staircase as the outside doors began giving way. The noise all the more terrifying as undercurrents of something once human was folded within it.

Jessie paused on the next landing, waited for the men to catch up, pushing and pulling past each other up the concrete steps. They doubled over on the landing, gasping for air. Clouds of breath condensed against the dim light, and for the briefest of moments, bound them in a common humanity as much as their fear and struggle to escape.

Lance took stock of the smaller man. Hair bounced and fell from his head like a bed of angry snakes, almost hiding the scraggly beard that sprang from his chin like weeds in a poorly tended garden. Jeans and sneakers. Spectacles that looked liked they were smeared with blood. The man was near his physical and mental limits. Lance had seen the same expression on men in combat. He had the look of a rock climber, or a long-distance runner, but fear and exhaustion robbed him of coordination, and he moved and jerked as if lit under a disco ball.

"Tim Lance." He reached out his hand.

"Professor Hall."

The girl had more than proven herself. The man was another story. Even that he'd chosen to introduce himself as *Professor* Hall was suspect. Probably a habit on the man's part, but it was part of the attorney's job to size people up. The man was guilty of something, he was sure of it, but maybe it was of just being scared like he was.

"You guys going to make a date or what?"

She pushed past, the oversized samurai sword tied across her back nearly took out the Professor's eye.

The men shrugged, and trudged up behind her.

She quickly pulled ahead, and as they caught up, a door burst open and three men stumbled out.

All six crashed into each other with shouts and curses, then disentangled long enough for the fat man to slam the door shut behind them.

As the others recovered from their shock and surprise, Bad Ass spun to push against the door.

Voices from the other side, muffled and resonate in the staircase, tried to push their way in. "Let us in! Please!" Half a dozen voices. "For God's sake, let us in."

"No, no, no." Pizza Boy was in a panic. "Don't let them. They were bit, I can tell."

Jessie saw hands pushing past the door. Fingers covered in blood. Quick impressions of a fat man and a cowboy — all she could do was help. She ran and threw her own ninety-three pounds into the mix. She hit the door hard, bounced off, and fell to the floor, but the added force was enough the door clicked shut and locked from the inside.

A howl of pain from the opposite side as three fingers, sliced with near surgical precision between the steel frame of the door fell to the landing. She watched as they seemed to squirm like worms in front of her.

The door shook and rattled as the final efforts of desperation from the other side threatened the steel frame.

Then came the screams.

First of terror and then of pain, the sound quickening the blood that coursed through the group's veins.

Then sounds of something beyond pain.

And then they stopped.

Roars and growls and screams. It would have made no sense at all, except they had been witness to the nightmare and couldn't help but picture what was happening on the other side. The yells of pain dropped to a low moan that mirrored the sound of the icy wind whipping throughout the staircase.

The comparative silence of the moment gave way to heaving breaths, the gulping of frigid air, and thundering heartbeats.

Bad Ass took in the newcomers.

A big guy. Shell shocked and gulping for air, but he might be useful. The custom white shirt, sweat-stained with fear and dirt, his disheveled suit torn and dangling, but an expensive tie snuggly in place. A successful businessman or a high-powered attorney. Compared to the hyperventilating spastic beside him, the big guy was a rock.

The smaller guy looked like a junkie from the seventies, jonesing for a fix. Or maybe, like all of them, trying to understand the world they had wakened to in the past forty-eight hours.

Impossible to tell if the girl was twelve or twenty except by attitude and competence, dressed as if she'd reached from beneath a blindfold into a Salvation Army reject bin. An orange bikini-top under a green-on-purple zig-zag hoodie, cut-off camo-pants, and mismatched knee high socks, one with neon-green polka-dots and one with pink stripes. A wild mop of dark curls held in check with a leopard-print scarf on top. Classic green paisley gas-station kerchief, tied around her neck, ready to ride into town and rob a bank. Paratrooper boots below. A katana tied across her back.

Jessie didn't try to hide the grin on her face, or that she was checking him out. He leaned against the wall, partly hidden in shadow. What she could see looked totally ridiculous and completely badass at the same time. The western-styled oilskin duster, two bandoliers of huge bullets across his broad chest, a shoulder holster with what she knew was a 9mm Beretta, and what might have been a pirate's flintlock pistol tucked into his wide belt.

The fat guy was, well… fat. But his eyes, even in the dark, were filled with warmth and intelligence. She like him immediately.

Gino's Pizza Boy had the look of someone who's biggest aspiration in life was to make it out of high school after two senior years.

"Who the fuck are you guys?" Hall had found his breath. He pulled away from the others and glared. "You can't just invite yourselves in. This is our spot."

Jessie saw the light in Bad Ass's eyes change ever so slightly. It was enough the professor stepped back.

"Fuck off." Hall tried to inflate his skinny chest. "You don't scare me."

BAMM!

Something from the other side crashed into the door. Snarling, growling, gut-wrenching human screams became the roar and screech of a baboon on full attack folded with the power and piercing squeal of a train car against steel tracks. A sound that became… *other*.

"Without those pocket cannons, you ain't so tough."

The pounding resumed. The Looper threw its weight against the door in a frenzy that had to be cracking bone against the steel.

The others watched as Bad Ass pulled out the Beretta. A simple, but practiced move. He held it out. Long moments.

Hall reached for it, forcing his hand to close on the grips, but he shook so much Lance snatched it from him.

A stand-off, but to what purpose? Lance was tempted to hand the gun back to Bad Ass but felt better just having it in his hands. The balance in the world had shifted the moment he'd heard Jackie's scream. He needed to regain some control.

BHUMP BHUMP BHUMP...

Pounding directly beneath their feet made them scatter and stare at the floor. The outline of an emergency exit, a trap door set in the cement of the landing.

BHUMP BHUMP BHUMP...

A woman, muffled from beneath the floor, cried out. "Lass mich hinein!"

Hall pulled back against the wall. "Don't let her in."

Carmine stepped onto the trap door. Turned to Bad Ass.

"Whatcha think?"

Jessie took in the strained looks. "We could use some estrogen in here."

The voice beneath them pleaded for help.

They all looked to Bad Ass, promoting him to leader.

"Please?"

Bad Ass nodded, and Carmine stepped off.

Jessie knelt to open the clever inset latch and noticed for the first time that Bad Ass was missing a leg.

Blood seeped from his knee where the rest of his leg should have been, covered with a hastily made bandage, wet with blood, and with a ridiculous extension made from a rough two by two strapped to his thigh with nylon tie-down straps.

The trap door sprung open like a jack-in-the-box, and a mostly naked young woman, cropped t-shirt and blue panties over the lithely corded muscles of a serious athlete, scrambled up from below.

Wild blond curls bounced back and forth as Ula absorbed details of the wide-eyed group staring back at her.

A big guy. Torn suit. Expensive tie. Looked like any of the suits working out of her offices.

A young girl. High cheekbones and the hint of Asian blood and a sword on her back made her look like an anime character. Cute. Competent. A surprised but welcoming smile.

A fat man. Struggling for breath but cherubic blue eyes welcoming her to their little band.

A wiry, long haired man. Jerky movements, maybe withdrawals or fear short-circuiting his coordination. She had the briefest impression he recognized her. She frowned. Sure he was guilty of something.

Her eyes drawn to the one-legged man. His energy filled the space. Even with one leg, he moved with grace and deliberation. The blood at his knee told her the event was recent, a day or two back at most. Ula watched as he took her in as well, appraising without guile, reshuffling the band's roles to create the strongest team.

Lance drank in the unforgettable body. Saw one bloody foot wrapped in what looked like the bottom part of her t-shirt. He stopped on the eyes, as blue as her panties, glaring back. He swallowed hard and stepped back. Her eyes darted to Pizza Boy.

"He's infected." A German accent. Only Bad Ass caught the slight inflection that told him that she might be from somewhere else.

Pizza Boy shrank against the wall.

"No-no-no, I'm not! I'm not bit! It's just the way I look — "

"I didn't say you were bit. I said you are infected. I can smell it."

"Fuck you, bitch."

"We don't know he's infected," Carmine said.

"He might be!" Hall looked closer. "He has the look."

A crashing *BOOM* against the door, the echo filled the staircase. The screech of Hell's banshees from the other side.

Even with the door between them, so loud it was hard to talk over each other.

Echoes from below as if the attacks were coordinated and timed with those across.

"Up, up, up!"

Bad Ass led the way on his unlikely peg leg. Jessie was seemingly attached to his hip and reached out to grasp Ula's hand, making sure the girls stuck together. Carmine in the way of everyone else. Hall, Lance, and Pizza Boy brought up the rear, and tried to squeeze past his bulk.

They all came up short as Bad Ass and Jessie stopped to look out an open window.

The alley below them. Just three floors — perceptions distorted — not as high up as they'd thought.

The view was lit from a couple of emergency lights mounted outside of the building. Shadows rendered in dirty blacks and muddy grays by the weak bulbs reflected off the ice and drifts of snow along the oily street.

Movement drew their eyes. Even though they knew what they were looking for, it made little sense. A jerking, snapping, careening motion that propelled the creatures forward.

"Jesus. Loopers," Waif whispered.

The two girls crowded on either side of Bad Ass to watch as they clawed their way into the wide alley.

A scream drew their eyes to the opposite end where a young couple, maybe in their early thirties, careened from around the corner and ran onto the dark street.

Jessie pushed forward, ready to shout a warning, but before she could get a sound out, they saw three more of the infected come from behind, chasing them. Working together, herding them.

The man fell, and the woman helped him up before she tripped over discarded trash and landed on hands and knees.

The woman hit the rough pavement hard, ripping skin from her hands and twisting her knee. She'd been a runner in college and knew her leg wouldn't carry her weight no matter how terrified she was.

Her husband saw they were trapped. Desperate for a weapon. Garbage cans, broken bottles, stacks of plastic and wooden pallets. He spun one way and then the other, screaming and cursing at God for deserting them to these unholy creatures.

Grabbed for a pipe against the wall. He pulled and kicked and twisted until it came free in his hands.

He spun to defend his wife as the first Looper attacked. It seemed to come from one direction and then jerked to the side, then backward before snapping back and diving for him.

The man landed a few superhuman blows delivered from his last reserves of adrenalin, and caught it full against its head.

The creature staggered in place but launched itself eight feet into the air to come down in a frenzied attack.

Bad Ass continued to watch the horror, forcing himself. Searching for a weakness, a way to defend against, or kill, or destroy the abominations.

It ripped the pipe from the man's hands, slashed at his throat, and as the man fell toward his wife, another launched itself off the wall from high above and slammed him to the street.

The woman prayed quietly from the middle of the alley. No reaction when her husband's arm landed beside her.

Closed her eyes as the sounds of skittering movements gathered around her.

Ula pulled Jessie away; the screams cut short after a wet, broken frenzy of tearing flesh and cracking bones.

Bad Ass saw the reflection in Jessie's eyes, and turned back to the group as they began backing away from Pizza Boy.

"Damn," the boy said in surprise, staring at his hands.

As the other five watched, Pizza Boy's seemed to light with an internal glow. For an instant, they could see his skull and bones outlined beneath his skin. The flesh blistered and bubbled, the spontaneous eruptions burst open from the heat as his arms began twisting in their sockets.

Whoosh! His body ignited like a match hitting coals doused in lighter fluid. Just as quickly, the flames went out, and they watched in shared agony as the boy's arms twisted and bones snapped.

Wracked with unbearable pain, a soft, terrifying keening grew in intensity until it threatened to shatter their eardrums.

Jessie struggled to pull the sword off her back. Ula backed away from the threat and heat as Lance pulled uselessly on the Beretta's trigger, the magazine already empty. The Professor and Carmine backed against the walls.

Bad Ass snatched the Beretta out of Lance's hands. Shoved it back into his shoulder holster. Handed the flintlock to Jessie. Pulled the sword from the scabbard tied to her back.

In a motion almost too fast to see, the katana whispered around his body and sliced down, cleaving the tortured man nearly in half.

The split body hovered on the landing, smoldered and smoked. The halves slid apart, and he had the briefest glimpse of an internal fire still raging.

As the others stood in shock, Ula side-kicked both halves down the stairs.

They watched what was left of Pizza Boy tumble and fall until a renewed frenzy against the doors below woke them from their stupor.

"To the roof," Carmine shouted.

They scrambled up the final flights, piling up behind Carmine and Bad Ass hobbling on his wooden leg.

The outside air hit them with the force of a train. The bitter wind cut deep. Bad Ass pulled off the duster, and with a flourish, spun and wrapped it around Ula's shoulders.

A quick search of the rooftop, air conditioners and ventilation systems, yielded pipes and a few loose boards the six-man band gathered to brace the door behind them.

Bad Ass and the two girls made their way to the edge of the rooftop and looked down on the alley as a dozen more Loopers headed toward the building on which they stood. Five floors down. No way off from here unless they grew wings.

Professor Hall had the same idea, and the same result as he turned from the far rooftop edge overlooking the street.

Lance and Carmine were on their way to the south side of the rooftop when a wall of dust and gravel and snow was driven hard into their faces.

THWOU THWOU THWOU —

A black Huey, impossibly huge and dragon-like in the night, rose up from below the roofline to drive the two men back.

Halogen spotlights danced over the group as bullets stitched a line across the rooftop in front of Carmine. Gravel and shrapnel spit across his face, and he put his hands up in defense and surrender.

The chopper's HUD revealed the motley crew of misfits below them. Three with their hands in the air moving toward the middle of the roof. A fat man, a seventies Woodstock reject, and a big man in a torn suit.

In defiance at the edge of the rooftop, a young girl in a hoodie and combat boots with an antique pistol clutched in both hands stood between a hot, almost naked chick wrapped in a leather cowboy coat, and a one-legged man with bandoliers of bullets across his chest and a Japanese sword in his hand.

The HUD switched from infrared to thermal as the pilot scanned the six, then returned to normal view with separate facial and body tracking.

"DROP YOUR WEAPONS AND MOVE TO THE CENTER OF THE ROOF." On loudspeaker. "DO IT NOW."

The gunner knew the power of overwhelming force and intimidation, and stitched another line of lead from the mounted Vulcan M-61 Gatling gun across the rooftop. The deafening noise competed with the whine and thwump of the rotors echoing off the buildings with cascading waves of sound.

"DROP YOUR WEAPONS OR YOU WILL BE SHOT."

Instead, the three ran toward the north side of the rooftop where light and shadow gave the illusion that the next building was close enough to jump. Jessie grasped Ula's hand and pulled up short. Not likely.

The gap would be a challenge on the best of days, and impossible for a one-legged badass carrying a Samurai sword.

Knuckles white, Jessie gripped Ula's hand harder and looked to Bad Ass.

He looked from the military chopper overhead to the rooftops and buildings twenty feet away.

Gradually backing away from the edge before he looked back to the girls and smiled.

"Ja?"

"Yeah."

He was insane. Which, with all things considered, seemed perfect for the times and made her like him more.

Jessie shook her head and grinned. "Okaayyy then…"

"MOVE AWAY NOW."

Bad Ass looked to Carmine who shrugged, covered his eyes from the rotor wash and blinding searchlight, and joined Lance in the middle of the rooftop.

"WE WILL FIRE."

Bad Ass looked out across the rooftops. The darkened city dotted in sporadic fires. Sloppy wet snow falling in clumps through the searchlight beams. The chopper hovering above them, representing everything he was fighting against.

More bullets ripped up the rooftop in front of them. He felt bits of tar and asphalt pepper his leg. Bad Ass and the girls shared a look, psyching themselves up.

Do or die!

Jessie grinned, lifted the flintlock with both hands. No way to miss, the flying machine above them was huge! She pulled the trigger. Click. *Fizzzzz*. BOOM. Score!

The recoil lifted Jessie off her feet, and Bad Ass snagged her by her hoodie as she flew by.

Sparks rang off the steel above. No damage, but enough to make the chopper veer away for a moment. But just a moment!

The Huey flit out two-hundred meters, banked hard and made a wide circle, and headed back. Fast.

Jessie and Ula sprinted toward the edge. Picking up speed.

Bad Ass on his one real leg doing a great job of keeping up. *Kind of.*

They jumped.

FORTY-NINE

01010111

ULA LANDED, ROLLED, AND almost simultaneously spun in the air to dive at the ledge where Jessie hit hard, half-on, half-off, dropped the flintlock, and struggled to pull herself up. Slipping on the ice, she was down to her fingertips when Ula grabbed her wrists. The Austrian's bare feet dug into the snow, and she pulled her new little ninja friend back up.

They laughed in relief but rolled to their backs in time to see Bad Ass, a line of bullets exploding across the rooftop behind him as he ran to make his jump. Step — clomp. Step —

No spring at all.

He barely cleared the ledge and dropped out of sight.

Jessie shouted in anguish.

She might have fallen off the roof to see if Ula hadn't kept a grip on her. They eased their way forward. Fearing the worst.

One floor below, the silhouette of a man-shaped cartoon cutout in the deep snow piled on top of a small awning. They held their breath, and moments later, his hand rose. A big thumbs up!

Bullets and loud speakers blasted, the powerful Nightsun spotlight lit up the night, the relentless rotor wash threw snow and ice back into the air, but still they laughed and hugged each other.

And then, clear as a bell, they heard the CRACK of breaking metal.

The corner of the awning dropped two feet. The snow began sliding off, and with it, Bad Ass.

He'd really thought he could jump. The memory of how it felt to flex his legs and spring in the air guided him. He pushed as hard as he could, like he'd done a million times in his life. And dropped like a brick.

He had no time to think, no time for regret. He slammed into the awning flat on his back. He felt his rib cage compress as the impact knocked the wind out of him, but snow cushioned his fall. Sometime, maybe hours or days later, he felt air trying to reinflate his lungs.

He heard the girls shout. Could feel their eyes upon him. It took all his strength to lift his hand to let them know he was okay.

And that's when he heard it — a CRACK like a gun shot. The sound of breaking steel.

The strut fractured, and the remaining supports groaned and buckled. The corner of his eight-foot bed of snow began tilting. He tried to scramble upward, tried to grab and claw at anything. He didn't even have the time to know it was hopeless. Snow and ice and gravity dumped him onto the street below.

They watched him slide off and fall. No awning to catch him this time. He fell three floors.

He slammed onto the rooftop of a car. Thick with snow but the impact echoed and carried the five floors from where they watched. He hit the snow covered steel hard, bounced up and flipped over, crashed the extra five feet face first onto the icy street.

Rooftop access to the stairs below was just a locked door away. Jessie pulled at it, but with no effect.

Ula gabbed her hoodie and pulled her back. Before Jessie could get a word out, the near-naked woman spun in place with a powerful back kick. Her barefoot smashed into the steel and tore the door from its hinges.

"Umm... yeah. Okay... wow," Jessie managed.

Black inside, but they sprinted, stumbled, and tripped their way inside and down the stairs.

FIFTY

01100101

THE CHOPPER CIRCLED THE rooftops, crossed the narrow alley, and passed over the nearby buildings. Tracks in the snow, but no sign of anyone. The powerful searchlight circled back to the three men.

The fat man and the big guy stood in the middle of the rooftop, resigned, hands raised high. The long-haired skinny guy was still looking for a way off the roof.

Hall looked over the edge. Five floors down. *Not a chance in Hell.* Fuck it. He put his hands up and would take his chances. He knew things he could bargain with. Things that no one else knew, things that made him valuable. No way could they connect him to Mads, and they weren't trading his life for the naked chick. She'd never seen him until ten minutes ago. And the underground lab would likely never be found until he was ready for them to uncover it.

The chopper hovered. Carmine swallowed hard as four thick ropes were thrown out, and before they'd even unraveled, four armed soldiers, automatic weapons, menacing in all black tactical gear, slid to the rooftop.

The big guy seemed calm. That was reassuring. Were the soldiers there to rescue them, or arrest them? It felt like overkill, but then again — the whole world had gone crazy. They couldn't think he'd killed Mads, but maybe they needed him to help find out who did. He was all for that, her death a blow in every way.

No idea what had happened to Bad Ass and the girls.

He turned toward the professor. Tried to shout a warning, but it was too late.

Hall spun at the sound. Even with the WHUMMP WHUMMP of the chopper, he heard it; the skittering and clawing against the ice. Split seconds of growling, roaring, screeching.

The creature paused, glared at him long enough for him to wonder if it was Skinny, coming to demand a higher grade.

He heard his own screams just before the creature tore him in half.

Too late for Hall, but the soldiers unleashed the full onslaught of four M4A1s set on automatic into the beast. Full mags, one hundred twenty rounds of white-hot lead traveling at 3000 feet per seconds shredded it. Pieces flew and floated in the air until they fell and painted the snow across the rooftop and streets below in red.

Huge industrial windows allowed the reflected snow outside to light the lower floors. From the inky black of the stairs to murky gray. Compared to the infinite dark of the tunnels, stadium bright for Ula. Enough to see a door ahead.

A push-bar to lock it, opened easily from the inside. Across the snow filled alley, Bad Ass lay flat on his face, the sword sticking straight up in the deep drifts beside him.

Searchlights powered their way down onto the alley, reflecting off the snow-capped cars and dumpsters, just missing Bad Ass laying in the street.

Ula waited until it moved on. She and Jessie darted out, grabbed his hands, and slid him face first back across the alley. Heavy, but the ice let them drag him into the building just before the light returned.

Jessie waited for the next pass, then dove across the snow like she was sliding for home, grabbed the sword, and skidded her way back in.

Ula was pulling the door shut behind them —

"Wait!"

Jessie ducked back out, searched through the snow, and found the flintlock.

Safe inside. For the moment anyway. Caught their breath and stood over Bad Ass.

Knelt to turn him over. No movement. They stared through the murky light to see some sign of life. *Nothing.* Ula felt for a pulse at his neck, her fingers too frozen to feel anything.

"You try."

Jessie held her fingers to his throat. Wasn't sure. Her ear to his chest. Sighed and shrugged. Shook her head.

Not much more they could do for him.

FIFTY-ONE

01000001

A LONG WAY DOWN. The city mostly dark, but fires created bright spots across the landscape.

Carmine pulled away from the open door and the frigid air. The soldiers didn't seem to mind at all. Dressed almost *too well*. Soldiers, *grunts*, were rarely equipped for what they needed when they needed it, and that's when Carmine realized they were someone's private army. Someone with real money and real power.

"Relax. Orders are to bring you in safely, Major."

Okay. Interesting. Well informed.

"What about me?" Lance asked.

Lit by the green glow of instruments, Lance could see the turned up corners of a smile, but no matching light in the man's eyes. Scary.

"We have no directives concerning you, Sir."

"I guess you could drop me off at my office downtown." Regretting his choice of words immediately.

Radio chatter from up front.

"That would be a negative on the drop off, Sir." No sense of humor at all.

Carmine reached out his hand. "Carm."

"Tim."

The chopper made a wide circle over the downtown as if surveying the landscape. Lance sighed wistfully. Military operations. Things had quickly gone to hell ever since the General had reached out for a meeting. Was he behind all of this? He had his doubts.

Lieutenant Tim Lance, US Army, had served long ago, before he'd passed the bar and joined the family firm, but jokes aside on standard operating procedures, this all seemed... *off*.

They set course directly down main street. His office was close by, but not close enough to jump. No friendly drop off. No slide down a long rope. He'd have to ride this one out.

Carmine looked ahead. Beyond the six men and the pilot, past the ice narrowing the view through the chopper's windshield. On a direct course toward a massive estate, alone on top of the hill.

FIFTY-TWO

01110010

THEY STOOD AND LOOKED around. Eyes adjusted. Racks and racks of used clothes. Dozens of partially dressed and naked manikins. Lots of decapitated foam heads. Seriously fucking creepy in the dark for anyone else, but heaven for Jessie and life-saving for Ula.

Ula reached out her hand. "Thanks again."

Jessie smiled. "Let's find you some clothes."

It didn't take long. Jessie was pretty much happy for anything that fit, and after a few moments, realized she'd shopped here before. A high-end thrift store, some version of which could be found in any college town.

A long day of "pawn shop," fighting with employees, killing Loopers, and then running for her life through the city. She knew she could do with something fresher.

They had that used-clothes store smell; the acrid formaldehyde of clothes manufactured and shipped from overseas replaced with industrial detergents and perfumed with cheap spray fresheners.

A hard foam head bounced on the floor, and Jessie nearly jumped out of her skin. Her sword? She sprinted to the front.

Saw Ula picking up the manikin head she'd knocked over and setting it back on the shelf. She shrugged and mouthed a "Sorry."

Stepped out and pirouetted once. As elegant as any ballet dancer.

She had on a warm cable knit pullover, cargo pants, and heavy socks. No more naked dancer, Jessie thought, but she still looked hot.

She smiled back at Jessie. Pretty sure the girl had changed all her clothes for near duplicates just as crazy and colorful as before.

Jessie saw her stocking feet. "Come on."

And led her to the shoes. New and barely used. Collectable sneakers and hiking boots, boat shoes and designer flats. Platforms and spiked heels. Ula reached for a pair of lug-soled red patent-leather combat boots.

They fit.

She passed the coats. Grabbed a Navy styled pea coat, heavy wool, black. Jessie traded her hoodie and found one for herself. Purple in the dark, scorching fuchsia with any light at all. They both grabbed fuzzy knit hats.

Ula was covering Bad Ass with his coat when she felt the snack cakes. Twinkies and Ho Ho's. Starving. She split the bounty with Jessie. The warm rush of sugar mainlined their depleted systems. Ula ripped open another pack of Twinkies and stuffed the sponge cake in with one bite.

Looked up to Jessie, goofy grin on her face, noisily licking her cream covered lips.

She knelt and took the Beretta from the shoulder holster. Looked at the crazy peg leg. A simple two by two of unfinished wood.

"So who was this guy?"

She checked the mag. Empty.

BAM! Something slammed into the door and they both jumped.

Bad Ass, eyes springing open, grabbed her wrist. Both confused. She tried to hit him with her other hand, but he blocked it, slid his grip down to her hand and twisted it into a painful wrist lock while plucking the gun back with his other.

She dropped her full weight and her elbow onto his chest. Felt like hitting concrete. Enough to get a grunt, but he hit a nerve in her neck with a thumb strike that deadened her entire side. Her left arm and leg useless, she fell onto him as if for a kiss. He dropped the gun, flipped her around, and locked a powerful arm around her throat.

Jessie darted in and out, tried to line up a kick to his head, but he spun Ula in his arms, used her body to sweep Jessie's feet out from under her. She crashed to the floor with a loud grunt. Made it to her knees and tossed a steak knife to Ula.

Ula caught it in her good hand, and he tossed her away like a ball.

Like the same, she bounced, rolled, and came up as if she were a super hero, twisting to throw the knife — *but Bad Ass was even faster.*

The sword flashed out like lightning and stopped against the side of her neck.

All three froze. Long moments...

The banging from outside started up again, and two spectral figures cast shadows across the room as they crawled sideways on the security grates over the windows.

Ula dropped the knife. Electric tingling as the circuits on her left side reconnected. Opened her arms wide. Caught her breath.

"Ula Becker. Interpol."

Jessie's eyes went even wider. "Whoa... ummmm. Gotcha. Umm... Jessica Adams. Jessie. Uhh... Student."

Bad Ass grunted. Waves of pain washed over him, and he fought not to black out. Used the sword to make it to his foot. Stood wavering as his head swam.

"That's it? We call you "hrummph?"

He grunted again. Started to say his name when BAM! BAM! CRASH! Glass shattered across the floor. The Loopers were hanging on the steel grating like gymnasts, kipping their bodies backward and using their full weight to swing out and back to slam their feet at the windows. The grates on the windows were bending, folding in enough that more glass broke. They wouldn't hold much longer.

Bad Ass grabbed for the sword's scabbard off Jessie's back. The sword spun in his hand, flicked to the side, and without thought, nearly too fast to see, he sheathed the sword. Shoved it into his belt while his other hand slid the Beretta back into its proper place, then slid the harness from his shoulders.

Jessie was mesmerized, swallowed and grinned when he took off the bandoliers and handed them to her. She pushed the flintlock down the front of her pants. It looked obscene and almost as big as she was. Frowned and went for a belt.

Came back as Ula was adjusting the shoulder holster and the empty Beretta to fit.

"Okay." Jessie looked at them. "Now what?"

FIFTY-THREE

01100101

CARMINE AND LANCE FOLLOWED the butler down the long, hallway. The decontaminant and antiseptic sprays blasted from their respective nozzles. Lance ducked and tried to twist his way forward while Carmine batted at the micronized spray as if walking through a maze of cobwebs, trying to make guesses as to the myriad chemicals being used. Admired the use of the various light spectrums they passed through.

By the time they made it to the end, the Butler had disappeared. They both spun in circles trying to find him. If there was a secret door, it stayed secret. The bit of theatrics had their effect, both men were off balance.

The past couple of days had been a whirlwind that made both men doubt their sanity. The past two hours confirmed their split with reality. There were no monsters. Maybe there had never been a butler. Maybe they were still standing on the freezing rooftops before the merc team whisked them away. Fuck it, Carmine thought, maybe he was home in bed having the most vivid dream of his life. Why couldn't it be about what happened after the kiss from his first crush, Paulina Alessio?

Lance glanced at the big guy. A Major, no less. He seemed to be holding up well. Maybe being a military scientist prepared you better for these situations than being an attorney. Science was always useful; there wasn't much law to argue within the anarchy of the apocalypse.

The odor of the chemicals was kept to a minimum, but he was appreciative of what he guessed was their antiseptic nature. They were both filthy, their clothes torn and bloodied. He sniffed at his shirt. Not bad. Looked up at Carmine who grinned back and shrugged. They approached the table and the two chairs that waited for them at the end of the hallway, facing what seemed to be a blank wall. A large envelope sat on the table with block letters printed across the top.

Nothing to do but sit and wait. It didn't take long.

A large screen came on, somehow a part of the wall itself. Carmine was impressed. He wouldn't have known it was there. On-screen, in shadow and silhouette, but enough resemblance to the figure he'd seen behind him in the auditorium to be recognized even without the voice and the setting.

"Please, gentlemen. Is there anything Giles can get for you?"

Lance pushed the envelope toward Carmine who waved it at the monitor.

"What the fuck is this?"

"Please. I understand your questions and fears but cursing seems... *unproductive*."

If they hadn't both heard the renowned billionaire scientist speak many times before, in documentaries and interviews, commercials and promotions, they would have thought his voice was artificially enhanced. Full and resonant. Strong and purposeful. Certainly not the voice of a ninety-year-old man.

"Inside, you'll find a single page document."

Carmine opened it. Scanned it.

Giles approached from behind them and placed a tea service on the table. Two fine china cups. A bit flowery for his taste, but Carmine was instantly transported back to Italy to his grandmother's table. Days after the grandfather's funeral and before he was sent away. It unnerved him even more. Surely the choice in china was a coincidence?

He glanced at the document again.

"Is this a joke?"

"I assure you it is not."

Carmine pushed it to Lance. Let him get through it one time.

"Everything is quite legal, which I am sure Mr. Lance can confirm.

Carmine sipped the tea, while Lance started in again from the top. He admired the document, the succinct elegance. The information and terms spelled out were usually spread across dozens of pages.

"Time is of the essence for several reasons, some of which will only become apparent after signing. If the compensation is not adequate, it can be negotiated now, and as you can see, again in five years."

Compensation was ten times what he made now. And that was the least of it. The ability to pick his own team, the near-complete control to work with resources limited only by his imagination, was a once in a thousand lifetimes opportunity.

Blood pressure, temperature, and heart rate had been monitored from the time they'd entered the hall, and the heartbeats of both men now went up as predicted.

Beyond their faces, beyond their educational and work histories, other crucial information was splashed across a dozen screens. Pupil dilations, O_2 levels, and thermal imaging of brain activity matched previously estimated patterns. Genetic photo estimation, verified by DNA given off in minute traces during respiration and now confirmed with saliva sampling as they drank their tea, coupled with the medical records on five generations of both men, reaffirmed his choice and confirmed what he'd suspected.

The Major was in ridiculously good shape for a fat man. Low resting heart rate in the high fifties, enviable blood chemistry, the ideal blood pressure of a man twenty years younger and a hundred pounds lighter.

Barring unforeseeable mishap, Major Carmine Marelli would live another 38.2 years. The attorney, Tim Lance, 35.4. With the conquering of the small cell carcinoma he'd begin to develop at age seventy-four, he could be expected to live to the ripe old age of ninety-three.

X was excited. The time was close. Additional monitors showed the soldiers fighting in the tunnels below the town. Deadlines were being exerted from both internal and external forces.

"The chance of a lifetime, Major," X said. "You will have sole access to the innermost secrets and resources of XAII, to pursue your passions, and, or if you choose, to work directly with me."

"And what about me?" Lance asked.

"I'm sure the Major values your counsel as do I. XAII will retain your services at five times your current rates for a period of two years to be renegotiated upon review."

Behind them, silent as a ninja, Giles, the Butler, handed Carmine a pen.

FIFTY-FOUR

01010100

WITH WARM CLOTHES, BOOTS, gloves, and hats, an empty gun, an antique pistol, and a samurai sword, Ula thought they had a chance to make it across the city to confront X. He had to be behind the technology that drove the app, and might be the only one who could stop it.

She reconsidered, and began thinking she'd have more luck on her own. It hadn't worked out so well the first time, but now she knew what she was up against.

She'd started to enlist them, wanted to, but held back. She owed them her life, but there were bigger things at play, and things more dangerous than Loopers.

Bad Ass hadn't told them who he was or what his agenda was, and she still hadn't told them hers; less about the compressed timeline and being under attack, than the fact that she hadn't yet defined it. Get to X and make him stop it. Whatever *it* was.

Even with his crazy leg, Bad Ass was exceptionally gifted. She'd seen hints of his abilities, but could only imagine she'd move faster without him.

And Jessie, as smart as a whip, and with what her grandmother would have called *"beherzt,"* was a God-send, but she knew it might be time to leave the girl behind somewhere safe. No idea where that could be, so that was another problem.

Fuck it. One thing at a time.

The window grates held, and the Loopers left. For about five minutes. Then they were back with recruits. Two became five. The noise was overwhelming, and she knew the windows couldn't hold much longer. Jessie had found a set of steps that led to another door, and that to what they thought might be a quieter street. As long as she didn't have to be underground ever again, she'd make it work.

She kept the Beretta. Even empty, it gave her comfort. If nothing else, she could use it as a bludgeon, and knew there was a good chance she'd find the ammunition it needed along the way to make it deadly. Bad Ass had reloaded and primed the flintlock. A single shot, not remotely accurate in the girl's small hands, but she'd fired it once and survived. Bad Ass said it shot hard high left, but deadly enough at ten meters or so. Even the ear-splitting concussion might buy them time at some point.

This was not the place to hole up. No more junk food, and the Loopers were bound to break in any moment.

She'd always worked alone, trusting her instincts, without a team. Sometimes with the blessings of her superiors, and at others, not so much. She'd had spectacular successes that had sometimes worked for, and sometimes against her career.

She'd leave Jessie with Bad Ass. Hope for the best. The girl was bound to be safer with him than heading into the lion's den with her.

Jessie was in the toilets. Bad Ass was adjusting his wooden leg.

Time to go.

She opened the door and sprinted through the snow to a car. Tried the door. Locked.

Kept low and tried another. Shit. Modern cars weren't easy to steal!

She crawled on her hands and knees to another. No luck. Turned her head as Jessie almost crashed into her.

The look on Jessie's face broke her heart, but before she could explain, the girl low-tailed it to another car. Began trying its doors.

Bad Ass watched them from the doorway. Almost let them go. Cursed himself for feeling responsible. A cross he'd borne for most of his life. First, as a child with his single mother until she died, then as a soldier, then commander of an elite team, and then as an investigative journalist. Jesus! When was it enough?

The girl, Jessie, local college student, was so much more than that. All you had to do was watch her eyes absorb the world around her for confirmation. As if the images generated by the world couldn't keep up with her brain. And he *needed* her. If she could help him navigate this town, he couldn't let her go.

The Interpol agent, Ula Becker, Cyber Crimes, wouldn't even be here, wouldn't be trapped in this hell, if it wasn't for him. If he'd trusted his gut instead of listening to his head, they'd all be some place else right now.

It was Mads who convinced him to slow down this time. Not her fault, just the way she was wired. Methodical. She was the scientist, the logical one. He'd let her confirm his suspicions and it had gotten her killed. His actions, or *inaction*, had cost them all.

He'd recognized the agent by the time she'd made it through the trap door. He'd done his research. Hadn't chosen her at random, and knew exactly who she was. She had no idea that he was the one who'd set her on her path as well.

Hadn't had much of a chance to tell her as they were running, jumping — *well, her jumping* — and then wrestling for the gun. He could still feel her breath in his face. Twinkie breath. *Sweet.* His new favorite snack cake for sure. For a split second, his fractured brain working overtime, he'd thought about ki —

Bad Ass made it to the car as Jessie lifted the keys high.

Plans changed, Ula turned to him. "We need to get out of here."

"We can't. Or I can't."

"Why the fuck not?"

Jessie joined them. "Let's go!" Condensed clouds of breath in their faces.

"Okay. You two go."

Jessie shook her head. Grabbed at both their hands.

Bad Ass pulled away. "I have to stay — "

"No! We can get out of here." Jessie took off as if to prove it, and was halfway to the car before she realized they weren't behind her.

Bad Ass looked at Ula. "Listen. There's a bomb." Words calm. "I don't know where, but it's out there. A big one."

Ula stared at him. Sloppy flakes of snow trapped on his heavy lashes. The eyes behind them clear and steady and full of purpose. "How could you know that?"

"I know."

Jessie on her way back.

Ula put it all together. *Jesus...* Incredulous. Replayed the African footage. The reports. Video and satellite photos. How they'd come to her. Confirmation of her conclusions. "You're *that* guy."

Jessie's head ping-ponging back and forth. "What guy?"

"Scheiße! Of course, you're right."

"It's why I'm here."

"Right about what?" Jessie asked. "Why are you here?"

There were no lengths the government wouldn't go to cover their tracks, hide their involvement. She turned to Jessie.

"There's a bomb. Not just any bomb, but one big enough to take out the entire town."

"To sanitize it," Bad Ass added.

"But not everyone is infected!" Tears sprang to Jessie's eyes. "They can't."

"They can and they will."

Ula played it through out loud. "It's why the town is blocked off. Communications cut. Keeping everyone out."

"And everyone else in." Bad Ass turned to Jessie. "There must be a place that makes sense. One spot that will concentrate the blast effects. Anything left, they'll clean up later."

Ula grabbed his hand. "We'll find it." To Jessie. "Take the car. Stay off the main streets. Find your way out."

Jessie shook her head. Before they could say more, she threw the keys as far as she could into the snow.

They looked at her in disbelief.

"I know where it is."

"Really?"

"I mean, I'm not a bomb expert, but I understand the concepts. A place that makes sense." Looked into Ula's eyes. "You're not going to like it."

FIFTY-FIVE

01101000

A BOMB NEEDED ROOM to breathe, and yet containment could increase blast wave reflection and amplification. The bomb they carried was a two-stage detonation system that relied on precise modeling and deformation prediction to exponentially increase the force and destruction.

Set off in an open space, the settings and yield were relatively straight forward to calculate. A secondary super-sonic shockwave expanded to fill the vacuum created by the initial explosion and created a tertiary collision with forces many factors greater than either one on their own.

In a contained environment, such as the underground complex they moved through now, it was a bit more complicated. The complete system took advantage of complex fluid dynamics simulations run on super-computers so those in the field didn't have to be rocket scientists to use it. It still needed some brains and a little finesse, but ultra-high-definition LIDAR 3D imaging along with ground-penetrating radar to determine estimated initial structural deformation did the heavy lifting.

All in all, the dual blast expenditure happened in tens to hundredths of a millisecond. Set incorrectly, the secondary blast could have the opposite effect and effectively mitigate the shock wave and overpressure. A miscalculation of two or three milliseconds could be the difference in a thousand-pound yield or half a million pounds of TNT equivalence – the comparative difference between a pebble in a pond and a tsunami.

Explosions are usefully measured in trinitrotoluene, or TNT equivalence. Where a pipe bomb might measure in the range of five pounds, a large scale truck bomb could deliver the equivalent force of 10,000 pounds or more of TNT.

The highly classified, thought to be still-theoretical bomb they carried, had a yield in the range of .5 megatons, over a million pounds, fifty times greater than the MOAB, the Mother Of All Bombs, famously first deployed against the ISIS tunnel complex in Khorasan Province, Afghanistan in April of 2017.

Just as relevant was that the MOAB weighed ten tons and was designed to be delivered by one of the combat variants of the C-130 Hercules aircraft; the bomb they now carried through the underground tunnels and chambers weighed just over two hundred pounds.

They moved through the hallways, following what was supposed to be a map, but it quickly made things worse. It might have been accurate at one time, but as more tunnels and chambers had been built, others were blocked off and in some instances, collapsed. Maybe worse than that, the map appeared to be an early effort. Additional levels and sub-levels had been added since the time it was drawn.

Everyone was armed and on edge. Not the greatest of combinations. None of the nine men with him had actually seen a Looper, but rumors and fear spread as fast as any virus. Two men, tactical flashlights mounted on their Next Gen Squad Weapons, led the way. Bradley behind them. Then four men carried the carbon fiber reinforced ceramic case, nearly as heavy by itself as the complete S2D-EMAX detonation system they carried. Two more men marched behind the bomb, and a final scout brought up the rear.

Colonel Bradley had a general idea of where they were going. Searching for the chamber hall that at one time had been the pride of Mazeville architects and city engineers. The collapse of the underground transportation system was soon going to take on a completely new meaning.

Flashlight beams reflected off the brick and stone walls, and though powerful, a thousand lumens each, the light was quickly swallowed by the dark.

A shadow flit across their view, and one of the men in front hugged the walls while the other instantly dropped to his knees.

"Hold fire," Bradley shouted. He'd seen it too.

The domino effect brought the rest of the team to a stop. The four men lugging the case put it down and reached for the weapons on their backs. The echo of their footsteps and movement faded. Only heavy breathing and the crackling of their radios. And then, in their heightened senses, the skittering of nails or claws over stone. The noise increased, sounding like so many beetles or cockroaches sliding over each other. And heading their way.

"Hold!"

The sound stopped. A long moment later, their team's breath was let out in a collective rush.

"What the fuck was that?" The voices spilled on top of each other. "Did you see that shit?" "What the fuck was that?" "Is that them?"

"Easy gentlemen… that is why we're down here," Bradley said. "All good?"

A few grunts and curses. Nobody wanted to be the first to move.

"Let's get it done."

The two men in front rose, looked to each other for courage, and started forward. The four carrying the bomb reluctantly stowed their weapons and picked up their load.

The rear guard inched closer to the two in back. "Fuck this place, man."

They glanced at him, nodded. "Yeah, let's get this done."

Not even time to yell — a speeding, skittering shadow darted from a side tunnel and wiped the man off his feet, leaving only the dull impact of body on body echoing from where he'd stood. There and gone as the rear guards unleashed their weapons.

The fury of the automatic weapons lit up the dark, and the deafening impacts roared and bounced off the walls around them.

The four carrying the bomb stumbled and nearly dropped the case; one slamming his shoulder into the brick wall with a loud grunt. They spun and pulled their weapons. Lead and steel exploded in sparks that danced against rock and brick. Screams and yells and curses. The two in the lead ripped off triple bursts of three rounds each toward the front just in case. Twelve and six. The brick walls offered protection on their flanks, though it soon felt like the walls were moving in.

"Hold fire hold fire hold fire!"

Over as fast as it started. Even with their headsets and coms, nine deaf men, ringing in their ears, and now blinded from the muzzle flash of their weapons. Weapons trained forward and back. No one able to function.

FIFTY-SIX

01100101

GILES STOOD WITH HIS back to the fire, letting the warmth seep into his bones.

The wall of monitors cycled through dozens of different newscasts from around the world. Mainstream and local access and from just as many different governments. The snowy streets of the town. The dark tunnels below.

Colonel Bradley and his men. A monitor went dark as something passed in front of the camera. Another view of another hall as a man and woman, led by a girl draped in bandoliers of bullets and a musket, no, a flintlock, descended into an underground chamber. It took him a moment to recognize the woman he'd met two nights ago, moments more to understand the man's strange gait was due to a piece of wood strapped to his thigh. Ridiculous. He laughed out loud at the sword on his back.

Views from above ground were distorted through iced and fogged lenses. No moving traffic, the streets were virtually gridlocked with wrecked and abandoned cars as people had vainly tried to flee the inevitable.

The cameras at the visitor center showed armed soldiers smoking, on their phones, drinking coffee, stamping their feet to stay warm.

A street camera showed four men climbing down from a mini-monster truck, bundled up as if on an Arctic expedition, baseball bats in hand.

Another showed three Loopers, *how he detested the name,* working their way through an alley on a direct collision course with the team. He admired how easily they overcame every obstacle, letting nothing stand in their way. Up and over the cars, across walls, and bounding over the snow. *Beautiful.*

The digital clock above the monitors was still counting down. 01:35:04... 01:35:03...

He rolled a cart toward the Cube. A large case on top, maybe three feet by three feet. He let his hands roam over the Cube — absorbing it, feeling it, memorizing it. The tingling in his arms pulsed in time to the energy around it. The Cube rose in the air, levitated half a foot above its stand. Giles sighed, placed the case over it. He'd made his peace, had said his good byes, but still... Pressed finger pads on the four sides and felt the locks engage.

He turned back to X, tucking the blankets up high beneath his chin before sitting on the bed beside him. Looked down lovingly at his old friend. Peaceful.

And dead.

Giles looked at the clock. 01:27:04... 01:27:03...

Ula was not happy to be back underground, but at least she had company. And clothes on.

It might have been easier for Jessie, she was small enough that even the narrow tunnels looked big around her.

"Maybe we should split up."

She looked at him as if he was crazy. Scratch that — she already knew he was.

Jessie said it for her. "That's fucking crazy."

"What she said," Ula echoed.

They made it to an intersection of narrow stone hallways. Black, but their flashlights cut narrow swaths through the dark.

She was trying to think of a better plan when what might have been shouts and gunshots, stopped them in their tracks. Soft and distant, no way to tell from which of the four directions they came.

Damn it. Ironic considering, but too much ground to cover.

"Okay. I'll go this way," Bad Ass pointed into the dark. Yep. Completely crazy. "You two go to the first intersection you come to. Then turn around, and I'll meet you back here."

Before they could think of a way to tell him how stupid his idea was, he was gone.

"Scheiße!"

"Yeah. That."

Jessie shone her flashlight across the walls. High on the corner was a small, inset map mounted to the stone with a star showing their relative position. Ula shook her head, a maze, the town was named well, but a hell of a lot easier when you could see. They hadn't taken twenty steps when Ula pulled them into a shallow side tunnel, and they turned off their flashlights.

Afraid to even breathe, they held onto each other as a twisted, misshapen shadow, close enough to hear nails or bones scraping across the floor, and labored, phlegmy breath rumbling in and out its chest, scuttled past the opening in front of them.

Standing in the dark, back against the wall, flintlock stretched out and ready to fire, Jessie now knew exactly how poor Clyde felt.

FIFTY-SEVEN

01000110

LOSING A MAN HAD unnerved them, but they trudged on. Only three of the team had met before today; the forward scouts at twelve, and their clean-up on six. They led the group through the maze, while Colonel Bradley, like a coach driver, urged them on.

Staff Sergeant Mills, his name spelled out with insignia and the black stencil above his pocket, was pissed, and only part of it because Teddy was gone. Corporal Ted Carver. The guy could be an asshole, which is why he'd remained a Corporal, and the fucker still owed him money for the last Super Bowl.

He was pissed because he hated the relentless fucking black, and he knew they could all see it on his face. Hear it in his voice. This wasn't anything like being outside with no lights on; this was a black hole that crushed you with relentless negative space and took away your ability to breathe.

They'd passed through hallways and stairwells with strings of intermittent lights, unfinished caverns and tunnels of pure ink, and through chambers with walls and ceilings so ornate under their flashlight beams, it felt like they were discovering King Tut's tomb.

They hadn't had time to check on anything, not even time for the rumor mill, other than some hurried whispers about Colonel

Bradley — the ultimate psycho jarhead — who seemed determined to get them even more lost.

The bomb they carried meant little to them; the power unfathomable. To them it was just a bomb, they'd seen bigger. Briefed on its purpose, to collapse the tunnels and trap the Zs. Not real zombies, but close enough.

There might be some lost tribe somewhere on the planet who hadn't been exposed to the movies and books of the genre, but these eight men — Mills was the oldest at 28 — had grown up in a world where reanimated dead who shambled along eating brains were part of the fabric of everyday life. Where zombie movies equated to drinking games, late night laughs, and getting laid.

They'd grown up on Resident Evil and The Last of Us, and dozens of other FPS games, and just wanted to kill *something*. They couldn't remain close enough to the bomb to see anything go boom, but Bradley promised Mills the chance to lead the action on top, and to shoot anything that survived.

The reflection of sound in the vast underground was strange, diminished but not muffled, and it had taken time to work out basic directions. Then twenty minutes of silence, his own breath and heartbeats for company before Keven heard the boot steps and radio chatter, at moments as clear and loud as if he was part of the team, and instants later, distant to the point he wondered if they were figments of his overworked imagination.

He pulled back deeper in the shadows, black on black, shrinking into a natural inset in the rock walls. After the inky black of the past hours, the glare of tactical flashlights ahead was blinding as he watched men pass the intersection of bricked hallway and stone tunnel..

Now the distant sound of gunfire he'd heard thirty minutes ago made sense.

He'd had hours alone in the dark. Running in panic, turning right and left, forward and back, and was soon hopelessly lost and confused. At times he was sure the creature Skinny had become, or maybe there were others, *fuck maybe monsters that had never even been discovered,* slithered beside and above him. Once, as his hands searched through the black of the tunnels, he felt a thousand little legs run across his arm and over his chest, and he screamed until his voice gave out.

Keven was exhausted from the gut-wrenching terror of the past hours, his arms and legs cramped and at times had refused to carry him forward. He'd thrown up twice, saw pinpricks of white light against the dark when he'd hyperventilated to the point of passing out. He woke in panic, wet, sure he was covered in blood, and realized he'd pissed himself.

Dreams of fame and fortune had given way to shame and bone-numbing terror. Why the fuck had he let Dustin talk him into this? It was supposed to be fun. *What the fuck?* None of this shit was supposed to be real. *Loopers?* Zombies — or whatever the fuck they were — from a phone? Give me a fucking break.

They were going to fake it all, had it all worked out. Hire an actress or maybe a model to pretend to be captured and abused. It wasn't their fault the first girl had gotten so scared she ran away. They found her a few hours later, where she'd tripped in the dark and had broken her neck, and then had to carry her body to the surface where it wouldn't smell up the tunnels to bury her.

That Hall had found them a stripper was even better.

He'd almost convinced himself they'd found an actress after all, and they'd witnessed an Oscar-winning performance until Beast announced she was a cop. Interpol Agent no-less, whatever that meant? Like CIA or Scotland Yard or some shit. And where in the fuck do you find a hot-chick naked cop for God's sake?

The fucking Professor... He'd watched him manipulate the rest of them all semester, and thought since he knew, he was somehow immune. That motherfucker — convincing them they were doing something noble. Ground breaking discoveries. Pioneering new technology. Saving the world. Or at least Mazeville.

His friends were dead. He licked through the dirt at the tears running down his face. Their screams still rattled his brain. Images of torn and ripped body parts, real and imagined, were seared in his skull. He started to throw up again. Empty, he dry heaved and fought for control. Bit his arm until it bled to keep from screaming out loud. Stumbled and wiped the snot away.

Fuck it. Anything was better than this.

Keven stepped from the shadows, was getting ready to shout, when he felt it behind him. *Something.* Was afraid to turn, afraid to know.

Forced the air into his lungs and —

— spun left at the same time Bradley twisted the boy's head right.

The cracking of bone and the shearing of his spine was the last and loudest sound Keven would ever hear.

FIFTY-EIGHT

01110101

NOTHING HAD GONE RIGHT since he'd entered this fucking town, and even less since he'd been underground.

They'd lost two more men in fifteen minutes. One dragged into the shadows before his men could react, one torn apart in front of their eyes even as they unloaded into the beast.

A third had an arm torn off and bled out in moments, and a fourth took a gunshot through his side. A quick patch job, the men feeling like shit, knowing it was one of their rounds that hit him. They did their best to carry him, until they realized he was dead.

The men, boys really, used to being killed multiple times in video games, were in absolute panic.

Flashlight beams revealed walls two hundred feet away, then crisscrossed an ornate frescoed ceiling sixty feet above them. The pride of Mazeville founders one hundred years ago, the chamber was meant to be a concert hall and outdo anything those big-city boys in New York and Chicago had pulled off.

According to his map, which hadn't proved accurate so far, the huge, domed cavern they'd entered was almost exactly the middle of the town.

Two put on defense, Bradley directed the other two men to drag the bomb to the middle of the underground auditorium. Beams from the green laser sights and flashes from automatic weapons lit the room like a laser show in a nightclub. Brass rained across the floor, mags were dropped and replaced, men shouted and yelled, and sprayed more lead at every shadow. Many more rounds missed than hit, the Loopers faster and more vicious than anything they could have imagined, but the firepower was having some effect.

He'd been told to expect more. That they might be massed in the chamber. No matter. The explosion would not only clear out all levels of the underground maze, it would level the entire town.

Bradley was pissed but giddy, drunk on adrenalin. Though it would pale in comparison to tests like 1952's Ivy Mike, with its ten and half megaton yield, he would be setting off the single largest, non-nuclear blast ever detonated on American soil. At a half-megaton, a *million pounds of TNT equivalence*, it would be one hundred times the strength of the '95 Oklahoma City bombing. He'd seen the effects once before, so fuck these so-called Loopers — assholes who couldn't put down their fucking phones — and fuck this shitty town.

LIDAR finished scanning the room and made its calculations. GPR, ground penetrating radar, was returning calculations of composition and density of the walls. Once finished, moments away, the parameters would be locked. His handprint would initiate the timer. They'd go back the way they'd come, at least part of the walls now marked. It had taken longer than planned, but they wouldn't be weighed down with hundreds of rounds of ammo, or slogging a two-hundred-pound bomb. Maybe forty minutes on the outside. That gave them fifteen minutes to get beyond any blast effects. A five-minute cushion. Cutting it close, but that's how things worked in the real world.

He looked up as one of his men was bowled over and dragged by his foot toward the tunnels, firing and screaming for help. The screams stopped almost before his men could react.

Two more Loopers charged and took out another man before the last two grunts managed to track it and unleash their full mags.

The mist of blood and smoke thickened the air.

His Lieutenant shouted and pointed as a Looper scaled the walls. Bradley scooped up a fully automatic M4a1, emptied half of a thirty-round mag. Spun to take on another as it charged his man, tracked it with a three-round burst as it dodged and jerked. It twisted to the side, grabbed and slammed the Lieutenant against the floor. The man screamed as he was tossed high in the air where another Looper swung from the ceiling and caught the hapless man. Bradley emptied the magazine into the high ceiling, and both creature and man crashed to the stone floor as Sergeant Mills emptied a mag in the last visible Looper.

Bradley popped in another magazine, emptied it in all directions. Popped the mag, seated another.

He spun just as Sergeant Mills was wiped from his view. He fired after him, then stopped himself from wasting precious ammo. The distant screams continued even after the echoes of his shots died out.

Okay... he could still do this. Determined and desperate, Bradley dropped back to the bomb to make the final adjustments.

Punched in his code. Palm against the reader to confirm.

Accepted. 01:00:00... 00:59.59...

Bradley turned from the bomb, unleashed a mag into the converging shadows across the ceiling.

FIFTY-NINE

01100011

STEEL AND LEAD RICOCHETED and whined through the black tunnel, and Bad Ass covered his eyes and ears as stone and brick shattered from the walls and peppered his face.

Ahead, the concussion of automatic weapons crashed in time to the brilliant flashes of light.

He caught a glimpse of a uniformed man in the middle of the chamber, spinning and spraying rounds in every direction. The roar and thunder off the stone walls echoed back on themselves and filled the room like a full-scale war. Saw a Looper fall from the ceiling, the upper half of a soldier still clutched in its twisted arms as it crashed to the floor. Bad Ass ducked back until the firing stopped and he heard the sound of dry fire on an empty mag.

Acrid smoke and cordite, the coppery mist of blood mixed with the stench of opened bowels burned his nose, and he fought to breathe. Dead soldiers and Loopers, the stone floor wet with blood.

Bradley heard the step, thunk — dropped his empty weapon, dove, and rolled for one of the M4's lying on the floor.

Came up pulling the trigger. Empty.

Grabbed at another as Bad Ass stepped closer. Froze in place when he saw the sword. Stood slowly. Wiped at his eyes in disbelief.

"What the fu — I *know* you. You're supposed to be dead."

"Yeah, well… and now I know you."

Bradley gestured to the leg. Shrugged, smiled. "Things don't always go as we plan."

Bad Ass glanced at the bomb, and Bradley followed his eyes as he took in the soldiers lying dead across the chamber, some torn in pieces, some very obviously shot.

"Not everyone is strong enough to do what's needed."

"Murdering thousands of innocent people?"

"Come on … this town was dead before we got here."

He noted the stenciled name, the embroidered silver eagle insignia. "You're fucking crazy. And Africa?"

"Give me a fucking break, they were Africans."

"And who are you to choose?"

"You should know better … we follow orders. Those in power always choose."

Everyone knew that was true, always had been, and why he traveled the world trying to make up for his sins. *Yeah, good luck with that shit…*

"It's not the way it's supposed to be."

"Well, that's the way it is with those in power," Bradley said. Gloating. "We decide that too."

The Colonel brought the carbine up, smiled, shrugged his apology, and pulled the trigger.

Nothing!

He dropped faster than Bad Ass would have thought possible and came up with another, but with a flash of the sword, it was knocked from the Colonel's hands.

Bradley looked at his hand in wonder, blood pulsing from a missing finger. Maybe for the first time, the fear of another man seeped past his bravado. He laughed and stretched his arms out wide.

"Drop the sword and let's make thi — "

Bradley only saw a glint of the blade. Only after hearing the steel *shhnnick* back into the scabbard, did he register the distinct sound that proceeded it, what Japanese called "tachikaze" — *the sword wind.*

" — s even."

He glared, daring Bad Ass to drop the sword and make a move. Confusion washed over him as pain began to catch up, and he looked down. Blood ran from below his knee to his foot. Took a step, screamed in pain, and toppled over — his leg below the knee sliced off as cleanly as if from a laser.

"Now we're even."

Bad Ass spun as a Looper dropped from the ceiling and charged.

The sword flashed out as with a mind of its own, slicing the monster in half as Bad Ass stepped to the side.

Was spinning into another attack —

BANG BANG!

Ula shot the new attacker with a weapon she'd picked up off the floor. BANG! Click —

Out of bullets.

Another Looper charged from the tunnels. As it entered the chamber, Jessie pulled the trigger on the flintlock… BOOM!

She dropped the flintlock, threw off the bandoliers, scooped up an M4. She glanced at it, shrugged. No idea. Tossed it to Ula.

Ula caught it, checked the mag, thumbed the selector. "Good to go." And tossed it back. Joined Bad Ass at the bomb.

He ran his hands over it. A touch screen and a timer.

"Any idea what you're doing?" She asked.

"Nope."

"Great."

"Hey. You're the Interpol Agent," Jessie said reasonably.

"You have any idea what an Interpol Agent does?"

Jessie shrugged and shook her head.

Ula looked down at the bomb. "Not this." She knelt beside Bad Ass. Ran her hands over the case, looking for any possible way to open it. "You both need to get out of here. This might not be pretty."

"No way," Jessie said. "Where am I going to go? I'm staying."

Bad Ass pushed himself up. "Me too."

"Hey, you can't hijack *'me too.'*" Smiling.

Ula stood as they heard the scurrying sounds of Loopers on stone. Charging through the dark.

The first twisted monster exploded from the shadows and was almost on them before they saw it.

The sword, a blur. *Slash — Slice — Slash!* The blade singing through the air drowned out by the blood-curdling scream of the creature as momentum carried the pieces past them and tumbled into the room.

Bad Ass spun and cut down another as it charged into the chamber. Still screeching, it nearly fell on top of the Colonel where he'd crawled across the floor. Ula turned just as he was reaching for one of the automatic carbines.

Ula shouted a warning as his hand closed on it when Bad Ass stepped between them both.

Bradley was raising the gun when he was jerked from the room.

He was still screaming when Jessie pushed her way in front and let off a burst of the fearsome weapon. Another! Amped on modern firepower.

Distant screams answered from the dark as the echoes of the weapon faded away.

Ula turned back to the bomb, shook her head. "I can't stop it. This is way too sophisticated for me."

"It's bigger, stronger than you know. I've seen the effects." He pointed to the elaborate controls on top. "The entire system, software and lasers and radar, work together to make this entire room into a bomb. Bigger and more powerful than it could ever be on its own."

"So how do we stop it?" Jessie asked.

"We can't," Ula said, looking at the timer. 00:37:00...

"Fuck." Jessie said.

"Fuck." Bad Ass echoed.

SIXTY

01101011

THEY MOVED AS A unit as Bad Ass, sword in hand, led the way. Moving as fast as a man with a piece of wood for a leg could. Ula had scooped up another 9mm, one with bullets in the magazine, while Jessie carried the M4.

They had a sense of movement ahead and crept forward. Hard for Bad Ass to move with any stealth, clumsy on his wooden leg.

Afraid to turn on their flashlights, but dim light ahead; some kind of mineral phosphorescence in veins throughout the stone walls. Still nearly black, but enough to get a sense of movement, bodies moving and writhing over each other, like a tangled mass of spaghetti in the dark. The scurrying, hissing, sliding of burnt and broken limbs on top of each other filled the cavern with a noise like thousands of cockroaches.

Bad Ass moved away, back into the tunnel. Jessie pushed past and crept forward to see.

"Fuuuuckk," Jessie whispered. "Now what?"

"We might have a dozen rounds. We fire — we're dead."

He pulled her back as Ula took her place.

"Something has to be drawing them here," Ula said.

Bad Ass spun, pulled the sword from the scabbard and Jessie out of the way as a Looper charged at them from behind.

The Looper jerked and spasmed up the walls of the narrow tunnel, across the ceiling, back on the floor, picking up speed.

Bad Ass stood frozen. Almost on top of him —

He sliced down with the sword. The halves of the Looper ran by and left them standing.

Movement behind him, he whirled to —

Ula stood in front of one of the slow moving variants — an *Infected*. It swayed and undulated, other-worldly in its movements with arms and joints seemingly put on backward; what might have once been knees and elbows moved without limits.

Ula copied each movement, each twist and turn, like a snake charmer hypnotizing a serpent. Alien-like from the Infected — graceful and stunning from the Interpol Agent.

She stopped, sidestepped, and hoped Bad Ass had her back.

He glided forward as the spell was broken — *as much as a peg-legged badass could* — and thrust the sword through its heart.

Loopers writhed and crawled over each other as if galvanized with electricity. The room alive with movement and noise, but still ignoring the humans. One screeched out, the sound was soon deafening as the others attacked it.

Shaking, the M4 clutched in her hands, Jessie crept forward again. Waited till her eyes adjusted, and pointed.

"That's our way out. Twenty feet to the left."

Ula peeked around her "You're sure?"

"I'm sure." Swallowing hard.

"Think you can snake charm your way out?"

Ula looked at him, opened her mouth to speak, but no words came. None of them happy, but what choice did they have?

She turned back to the chamber of Loopers and Infected.

"Okay. Stay close."

"I think my dancing days are over."

She turned back. "No! We stick together — "

Even before the words were out of her mouth, she knew he was right.

Jessie, panicked, tears springing to her eyes. "No. Come on. Give me a minute. I'll think of another way out."

Bad Ass pulled her close, held her with one strong arm. She held onto to him until he finally pushed her away.

"I'll keep your back clear from out here."

They stared at him. Frozen. All three feeling the weight of the clock. Imagining the bomb exploding.

Ula kissed him. Impulsive, tender, their lips electric. She held on as long as she could, the moment far too short. Pushed away and stepped into the cavern.

Jessie hugged him one more time, and followed Ula out of the tunnel.

An Infected rose to meet them — the swaying undulations both mesmerizing and terrifying.

Ula mimicked its every move, and took another step toward the door. Jessie right behind her. The Infected swayed and backed up.

Bad Ass watched as long as he could, only seconds until he heard Loopers charging behind him. Spun to the sound and caught two silhouettes coming on fast.

He moved without thought, forgetting he was missing a leg. The sword flashed and sliced, stabbed, and slashed. Clumsy, he stumbled backward and slammed against the stone walls as black blood and Looper body parts fell around him.

Just as Jessie said, a door set in the wall twenty feet to the left. Halfway there. The strange dance with the Infected continued, but the Loopers in the middle of the room were building into a frenzy, playing or fighting or maybe fucking each other — *who the hell knew?* Jessie fought not to throw up at the thought.

She eased past as Ula continued. At the door. A handle. An electronic keypad. Locked.

Bad Ass was on his way back to the bomb. Hoping Jessie was right, hoping they'd escaped. Praying they'd find a way out of the city in time.

Running their conversation in his mind... No way to disarm the bomb.

"But you said it's designed for this room?"

"More or less."

"So what if we move it?'

He struggled to remember things he wasn't supposed to know, and talked it out loud. "It works in two stages. Two explosions, milliseconds apart that amplify each other. Shockwaves crashing off each other to create a third impact greater than the sum of the two."

"Somewhere bigger?"

"I'd say somewhere smaller. Let's guess half this size."

"Why not just one of the dead end rooms?"

"Same force in a smaller space," Ula said. "Maybe too small... it could maybe amplify it."

"Calculated on this room," Jessie added, getting into it.

"But if we got lucky, in a different space — half this size — " Ula said, "they might cancel each other out."

"It's a stretch, but what the fuck?" Bad Ass added. "Half this size and deeper."

"Jesus," Jessie said. "If you're gonna dream all that, couldn't you just dream we're on a beach somewhere?"

Bad Ass grabbed one of the case handles. Gauging it. Fuck... well north of three hundred pounds. Not going to happen on his leg.

Moving as fast as he could through the tunnel, he turned left at the second intersection, a straight line to the chamber. Who knew how Jessie had known her way around? It seemed she'd recognized every twist and turn, every proper moment to back their way into the shadows, just how long to pause, and when to run. Still, in some ways, he was faster without them. Reckless. Not having to worry about their safety, and not giving a shit about his own.

Calculating the time to get there... every bit of fifteen minutes. Call it close to that to get back.

Ula was still holding back the Infected with her dance, though she was beginning to think it was only fucking with her.

Jessie was behind her at the door. Punching in codes. Hands shaking, tears of frustration blinding her. So fucking close!

Ula went right, and the Infected moved left. Her arms rolled and stretched and duplicated the movements in front of her, following the creature's lead. She moved left, and the creature moved right. Stretching down, and the monster moved up. Rising higher, towering above her, arms and hands wide and menacing, ready to strike.

Screaming in her mind, she tried not to breathe, her trembling threatened to paralyze her. Jessie cursed at the door behind them.

Ula blinked, and the creature was wiped away, tackled by a Looper. She held her breath and watched with both relief and horror as they battled and rolled across the floor. It felt as if the room would explode from the frenzied energy of the swarming abominations.

Twisted her head to see Jessie digging beneath her coat. Hands shaking. She tore the Uni key card off its lanyard. She'd run out of other ideas.

Shaking so bad she couldn't hang on. Dropped it. Snatched it back up. Slid it past the lock. Nothing. Her legs shaking so bad she almost fell, but Ula held her up. Guided her hand.

They felt it more than heard it, all sound including their screams drowned out by the orgy behind them. The electronic lock slid open. The card fell from Jessie's hand but Ula pushed her through.

They slammed the thick steel door behind them. Backs against the door just before the creatures rushed it. Felt the impacts as they slammed into it again and again.

Only one direction possible. Up into the black.

SIXTY-ONE

01001001

BAD ASS TALKED HIMSELF through it ... a smaller space... half the size... deeper. Jessie had said the Looper chamber, their chance for escape, was under the mountain. Not a real mountain, he'd seen his share across the 'Stans', but if a hill was big enough for the locals to think of it that way, it might be enough.

Fifteen minutes there, gone. Would take fifteen back. He glanced at the timer – 00:17:57... Fifteen and change.

He couldn't carry it. The bomb alone was over two hundred pounds, and with the case, as big and awkward as a coffin. He dragged it. He wasn't even across the chamber, and already his arms and back were screaming in protest.

Heard it behind him. Fell back and it leaped over him, knocking the sword from his hand. It spun in place as he crabbed backward over a dead body, his hand falling over a discarded weapon. He rolled sideways across the floor as his hands scrabbled to find the trigger, hoping the gun had something left. Dove sideways and came up firing.

Four slugs tore through the creature's head, and it collapsed on top of him. He kicked and pulled himself out. Weapon empty. He hobbled back to the bomb. 00:17:35...

Not going for stealth, impossible with the scraping of the case against the floor, he dragged and pulled, pushed and cursed his leg, felt his knee begin to split. Shouted and grunted and groaned. Halfway there. Pulled it around the corner, and fell to his ass, gasping for air. He had a straight shot to the smaller chamber.

Forced himself back to his foot. The friction of the rough floor fought against the case, but his wooden leg found purchase between the stones. He'd seen no Infected, heard no Loopers. The M4 in one hand held out for balance as he dragged on the case with the other.

Eyes locked on the timer. 00:10:37...

He'd gained thirty seconds! Fuck it. Dropped the rifle, and grabbed the bomb with both hands. His arms and thighs and back and lungs rebelled, shaking and crying out in protest almost as loudly as he was, his teeth threatening to crack as he clenched his jaw and pulled.

SIXTY-TWO

01101110

ULA WAS HAPPY TO follow Jessie, the girl had brought them this far. And this time they were armed. Popped the mag on the nine. Over half full. Rammed it back in. No idea what was left in Jessie's M4, but even if it only gave her comfort, it had value.

Lost another round when she shot off the padlock on the door. They came out in the middle of what looked like a park; huge trees, the trunks ten feet across, treetops lost in the clouds.

It took Jessie a moment to make sense of where they were. Behind them, high on the hill, lights on what had to be X's mansion. The estate was huge. She'd only seen it in photos and from a distance. Like the maze below, things looked a hell of a lot different from the inside.

The house wouldn't provide protection. They needed distance. At most, they had twenty minutes.

Half those minutes were gone by the time they'd tromped through heavy snow, climbed over the high stone walls, and dropped to the other side. Either security was occupied, or no one had thought to worry about people escaping, unless of course, they mistreated the help.

Middle of the night, but the town was painted with a generous brush of white beneath an overcast dome that amplified all light. Distant flames reflected off the ice across the city, and they both wondered if each fire meant another Looper.

Cars were scattered, both wrecked and abandoned. The harsh glare of headlight beams left on, revealed mangled bodies lying in the snow.

Ula tried the door of an abandoned car. Locked.

She shouted over the chorus of alarms blaring from buildings and cars. "We need to find something quick."

Jessie pointed down the street where a dozen cars were gridlocked in the middle of an intersection.

Halfway there before they froze in place when long shadows wiped the headlights from up ahead. Impossible to see through the glare, they dropped low, using the cars for cover, the weight of the ticking clock pushing them on.

Jessie stumbled, slipped, and fell. Scrambled back to her feet to find she'd tripped over bodies partially buried in snow, torn apart and scattered, baseball bats still clutched in frozen hands.

They scurried from car to car. And then Ula saw the Porsche.

Smiled and shrugged. "Maybe we'll get lucky."

And that's when the shadows became the first of the Loopers, already charging at full speed. Close enough to hear the unearthly scream over the incessant car alarms. It veered side to side, skidded in the snow, bounced off a car, and launched itself into the air.

Jessie tried to follow it, and ripped off a burst of rounds. Missed everything but the sky. It spun and dove and kept coming. She barely had time to register another abomination entering the streets behind it.

Ula tackled her, knocked her to the side, rolled, and came up firing. The Looper skidded by like a Tom and Jerry cartoon, unable to stop its momentum until it did. It spun in place and was almost on them before Ula found her target. It screamed and twisted with the impacts, jerking side to side, but kept coming.

Jessie slid in front of her like a goalie on skates and fired off three quick bursts. Eight of the nine rounds hit the creature, blowing off an arm and stitching up its chest to blow it's head off. Black blood fountained into the air and painted the snow around them.

Ula spun on her back and fired at the second Looper. Two shots and then she was out. Jessie twisted around her and fired. And was empty.

The Looper kept coming. *Fifty meters. Forty.* Ula ripped the rifle from Jessie's hands, preparing to use it as a bludgeon. *Twenty.*

Another shadow streaked from the alley and slammed into the Looper. They tumbled and spun and rolled through the snow, the new life forms fighting themselves for dominance; tearing, ripping, and biting.

Jessie held her ears from the awful sound and watched until Ula pulled at her arm and sprinted to the vehicle. A Porsche Cayenne Turbo. Opened the door. Nothing. Ula pointed past her.

Under the snow, part of a man. Eyes frozen wide, staring back at them. Close by, his lower half.

Ula took the top half as Jessie took the bottom. Both dug through pockets until Jessie came up with the key fob.

Tossed it to Ula. Let her drive. Not sure if she was actually German, *but come on…* close enough!

The town's surface streets could be a maze to outsiders, but for now, Jessie pointed straight ahead. Panic, ice, a twin-turbo V8, 541hp, and an eight-speed automatic. Dodging cars, fishtailing, and moving sideways as much as forward.

Ula bounced off a parked Mercedes, creased a Ford, spun through a 360, then kissed a Honda and a Toyota before gaining any sense of control.

···

The cavern in front of him. Black on black, the sound deafening, and soon Bad Ass was close enough to see bodies crawling and fighting over each other in the near dark.

He estimated the cavern's diameter at a hundred feet. No way to get it to the middle, but maybe, if the gods were with him and he could get some momentum, get a one-leg running start, he could shove it in. If it even went twenty feet across the floor, it'd be worth it.

The green timer filled his vision 00:03:00… 00:02:59…

He picked up speed; his back and shoulders and thighs burned with the effort, he felt his knee rip open, and brilliant white lights danced in front of his eyes as he strained with Herculean effort—

00:02:54… *Come on… just twenty feet!*

Stumbled, and with a final burst of effort, he let it go. Fell on his face and watched it slide—

About three feet!

"Fuck."

Jessie screamed as a Looper flew out from a side street, found its direction, and charged directly at them.

She was scrambling for her seatbelt when Ula stomped the gas, and at the last possible moment, spun the wheel. Physics were physics, and the vehicle slid sideways across the street, smashing into the Looper until the powerful crossover slammed into the side of a pick-up truck.

Jessie and the Looper screamed at the same time, separated by inches as the distorted face was crushed against the glass, its twisted mouth stretched wide in a roar of anger and frustration. It glared into her eyes with hatred and evil; the moment lasting fractions of a second but burned in her memory forever.

The window shattered as the Porsche crushed the Looper and bounced off. Jessie was snapped sideways from the impact, nearly folded in half from the whiplash, as the seat belt dug in to keep her from landing in Ula's lap.

Ula fought to keep the vehicle's rear end behind them, and aimed for the middle of the street.

Icy air battered Jessie's face but soon cleared the stars dancing in front of her eyes. She pawed at her hair to dislodge the glass, and pointed the way.

She used her hands to carefully roll her head in circles. Still attached. *Mostly anyway.* Looked at her wide-eyed driver and started laughing.

Ula looked at her as if she was crazy, but Jessie couldn't stop. *Jesus!* 140,000 dollars of high-tech German engineering. It hadn't taken the Interpol Agent sixty seconds to completely trash all four sides.

She grinned as the town raced by, and Ula tried to keep the car on the road.

SIXTY-THREE

01100111

NO TIME OR WAY to understand why the Loopers swarmed over the bomb. Within moments, it was pulled deeper into the room and tossed about with superhuman strength. Caught just as easily, and the monstrosities clawed and pulled and climbed over each other to touch and grasp at it.

Bad Ass made it to his foot. Hugged the wall. As before, there seemed to be two types of the monsters, fast and slow. Loopers and Infected. The slower ones were lesser in number and less interested in the case, but had already proven just as deadly.

As his eyes adjusted, he saw the door. Set in the wall, ten meters away, maybe less.

His leg was bleeding, enough his imagination had it splashing on his other foot. Hoped they weren't like sharks and could smell blood in the air.

No time to think about it. He remembered the graceful undulations Ula had made to charm her way across the room.

Bad Ass hugged the wall, and as one of the Infected passed in front of him, he began the strangest, twisting, jerking, most ridiculous looking set of movements a man had ever done along the wall toward the door. No one would ever know — certainly not the once human monstrosities that clawed and clambered over each other, swarming the ceilings, crawling up walls — that except for the fact that he was missing half a leg, it wasn't that much different for him than a normal club outing. Expecting to be killed at any moment for his bad dancing.

The bomb was tossed high into the air, and he held his breath as it crashed to the stone floor.

Another couple meters. He looked above him.

An Infected crawled off the high domed ceiling to the walls and looked like it was coming directly for him.

Then he made it to the steel door. Pulled on the handle. Locked. He twisted it up and down, pulled and pushed, and beat on it. No more give than if he beat on the stone walls.

He saw the electronic lock. Nine-digit keypad. Unable to think and process how close he'd come, he laughed as tears streamed down his face in frustration. Punched in his bank PIN. Nope. Only 9,999 combinations left to try. Unless it was a five or six or fifty fucking digit code. He ran his hands over it as if he could suddenly divine the secret.

Looked up. An Infected, as graceful as an acrobat in Cirque du Soleil, peeled off the wall just feet away from him, and began its way through the crowd to the bomb. It all looked so much like a movie he'd seen. His mind struggled to remember. Bodies swarming and writhing over each other in worship of their idol. What was it? *And why the fuck was he thinking about it now?* He'd die because he was a fucking idiot and shitty dancer.

His mind gave up. Done. He'd given his all. He sank to the ground and watched. Maybe a minute left. Whatever the case was made of, it did its job. Better than Samsonite. Could have cleaned up in the luggage industry.

Back against the door, he waited for death. Couldn't say his life flashed before his eyes, but images from the past twelve hours for sure. Running. Leaping. Fighting. A waif with a samurai sword, a girl in blue panties. The electric touch of lips against his own. Closed his eyes. Trembling, hands clutching at the earth beneath him. On questions of God, he'd know the answers soon.

And then he heard the whisper. As if the room were silent and she'd been close enough to kiss him, whispering in his ear. "*Get up.*" Opened his eyes and looked around. Nothing but monsters swarming over the bomb, beginning to look his way. Maybe the voice of God was a woman because as clearly as if *She* pushed it into his hand, he felt it. Looked down. His hand on the key card.

It only took him three tries before he felt the vibrations under his hand as the locks disengaged and his heart started beating again. He pulled it open enough to slide past, turning back for a last glimpse. His mind had every Looper in the room taking aim and charging his way.

He pulled the door shut as a dozen bodies slammed into it from the other side.

A hint of light from far above. No idea how many flights to reach it. He crawled and stumbled and pulled himself up. Tripped and fell and tumbled until his wooden leg caught under him and he crashed back down a dozen steps and his head slammed into a wall.

Voices in his mind yelled and screamed at him while others laughed and made fun of him for trying. He roared at them all, and started up again.

They navigated the main streets to the edge of town. No other moving cars. An abandoned roadblock ahead, lights flashing. She pushed the vehicle harder, still gaining speed, blinded by golden curls whipping in the wind.

Ula crashed through the flimsy barrier, doing her best to put the town behind them.

The ground trembled. Then the tremble became a wave as the ground buckled, and the Porsche was bounced from the road. The sky in every direction a blinding white, and moments later, the explosion crashed and rolled like thunder as the very air around them expanded, then compressed, and then expanded once more. Skidding in the snow, they slowed down and pulled over.

They scrambled out in time to see distant boulders and trees falling from the sky into the fires below, the conflagration bursting against the pre-dawn sky with blinding reds and yellows beneath billowing black clouds.

Trembling, they held hands, watched through tears for as long as they could. They held on to each other until the shock and cold threatened to take them off their feet. Took a last look and slowly drove away.

SIXTY-FOUR

01000010

HELICOPTERS ROARED OVERHEAD as news stations ignored the restricted airspace and competed to capture the devastation. On the ground, the military took over and set up a perimeter that extended most of a mile from the blast site while containment teams in hazmat suits measured and tested for nuclear fallout. None found but they hadn't signed off yet.

On the far side of town, the university and dorms had fared well enough, but foundations and people elsewhere were rattled. Citizens of Mazeville agreed they were fortunate the Army could respond so quickly, and the soldiers were being hailed as heroes. The presence of authority, men and women in uniform, gave people comfort.

Fires raged across the town. Smoke and dust filled the air but was quickly tamped down by falling snow. Lots of broken windows and fallen glass, difficult to see against the snow and ice, but experts would later agree the unusually harsh weather served to mitigate the bomb's effects.

The blast had stirred up livestock in neighboring counties and was measurable as far away as the capital, a two-hour drive on the best of days. The explosion was being attributed to an underground gas leak, and experts scrambled to show how flammable vapor might have accumulated for weeks or even months in the abandoned caverns and tunnels, and could have pooled in a central chamber on the one side of town.

Social media lit up with lots of theories. Fracking and aliens and a secret cabal clearing the land in preparation for establishing their own country were all gaining traction. The fact that this was Mazeville, home of XAII laboratories, and less than half a day's drive from what was rumored to be a Defense Department research facility, was embraced as proof of government collusion and cover-up of the Loopers.

Depending on who you talked to in town, Loopers were either porn addicts possessed by the Devil, escaped super soldiers, or the result of an orchestrated release of viral agents and disease meant to subjugate the poor.

Reporters were corralled at the outer edges of the military perimeter. No one would be allowed closer until FEMA and the CDC finished their assessments and the Army Corps of Engineers could verify above ground stability.

"Officials believe a natural gas leak gathered in the extensive tunnels from which Mazeville took its name, and is being attributed to fracking operations in nearby M — "

Eyes in the sky had the best view, capturing glimpses through the clouds and smoke at the devastation below, and showed most of what anyone needed to know. People watched on big, flat-screen TVs from the safety of the bars and sandwich shops and pizza joints, all scrambling to take advantage of people's need for social reinforcement.

"Mazeville, the site of the recent epidemic of Loopers, is under strict quarantine and completely shut off. Town officials are praising the quick response of the military and — "

Consciousness took time. First came pain, and later, with meaning now assigned to it — that at least some part of him had survived.

He opened his eyes to the dull gray of nothingness, but as the sun rose, it separated into smoke and debris and snow.

Soft gray shadows hovered in silence behind the white, and then, maybe hours or days later, with the steady beating of his heart.

He slept. And woke. And started over...

It took another year before he could make his hand move. It floated through the air until it settled above his face, then took some weeks or months before his fingers worked enough to brush away the dust and snow falling into his eyes.

An indistinct white orb above him. He knew it was familiar but couldn't think of what it might be. Reached for it as if he could pull it close. Ninety-three million miles, but reaching for —

And then it all came rushing back...

Climbing and clawing and scrambling. Heart crushed as his ribcage compressed and oxygen was ripped from his lungs. Sound so loud he couldn't hear it. Infinite black and impossible light, and then black again.

A scream from a million miles away but it might have been his own. Flying and tumbling and falling with the rest of the debris into the inferno...

Then the Whisper in his ear again, telling him to get up...

He sat up. Leaned back on his hands and looked around. Dry ash and wet snow covered everything as far as he could see, including him. He tried to stand, but his leg was trapped under the rubble.

He stared at it without comprehension, unable to accept what it meant. What the fuck? Not again.

And then he laughed until he couldn't. Undid the straps and crawled away.

SIXTY-FIVE

01101111

THE BREATHLESS FIELD REPORTER, taking advantage of her first time on the national stage, was delivering a master class in controlled empathy, just the right level of authority with occasional breaks of emotion.

"We're standing in downtown Mazeville, a mile from the blast, still being kept behind the perimeter cordoned off by military guard. Officials tell us the body count is unknown. The worst devastation seems to be concentrated on the north side of the town beneath the estate and private research labs of the late Alliard X, the controversial and philanthropic founder of X Artificial Intelligence Integrations, who died less than forty-eight hours ago due to lingering complications from last year's..."

Whether the delivery was the result of talent, or she was genuinely affected was irrelevant to the viewers and her producers.

Another dozen screens, all with competing stories.

"Authorities say it will be some time before we know how many deaths can be attributed to the blast, and how many were already lost to the so-called Looper outbreak. Researchers in China are reporting..."

"The social media giant is announcing bans on 'Looper videos,' calling the undocumented videos misleading and sensationa..."

WILLIAM KELY McCLUNG

"CNM has exclusive reporting coming from sources at XAII labs that Alliard X, rumored to have been killed in the blast, is safe and well and was attending the European Summit on emerging AI and ethics at the time of the blast..."

Which was soon picked up and increasingly mangled.

"New reports on the death of XAII's 91-year-old visionary founder and CEO Alliard X, killed in a blast on his yacht while on vacation in Southern France..."

It was the kind of office where world-changing decisions were made. A dozen people, bosses and bigger bosses, legal teams and accountants, and a uniformed four-star were focused on another screen. No reporter or chyron; this footage raw and unedited.

On mic. "We're all here."

No wooden leg substitute, Bad Ass hopped naked from the shower to sit on the bed, drying his face.

From the tiny speaker of his cell phone.

"Okay. Watching the footage now."

On screen. A small African village, teeming with color and life, people in the markets. Music blasting from radios and car stereos and cheap Chinese speakers for sale. Lots of children playing and kicking a ball and dancing in the streets, dodging cars and trucks held together with coat hangers and duct tape. Lots of scooters, new and ancient, some from China, and some cobbled together from spare and mismatched parts. A couple of adventurous backpackers — *tourists* — taking photos, laughing, and bargaining for trinkets.

A couple pulled up on a scooter, almost exactly like Lisbon, but black. Young, probably still in their teens. The girl kissed him and sashayed toward the market. She glanced back, making sure he was watching, but he missed it, already checking his phone.

The view took in the town, then came back to the boy, intent on his phone. He spasmed and his scooter crashed to the ground.

An instant later he screamed, and moments later, steam and smoke rose from his arms and hands. WHOOSHHH!

His entire body went up in flames, and the people who ran to help were brought up short when his arms and legs began twisting and cracking in their sockets.

He fell writhing onto the dirt plaza. Two men ran toward him with buckets of water, and soon he was twisting in the mud. It seemed his spine would snap when he was launched in the air. Even before he landed on his feet, he was grabbing at the closest person. With what must have been superhuman strength, he attacked the helpless woman in a frenzy that ripped her to pieces.

He turned on the terrified crowd; falling, screaming, clawing, and stepping over each other as they fled for their lives. A man was smashed to the ground, his head stomped into jelly, and an arm ripped from another before the creature leaped onto a third.

A group of maybe ten men and women surrounded and rushed the thing with hoes and knives and machetes. The Looper, a handsome young man just moments before, was hacked and torn apart by the frenzied crowd before the camera went dark.

The room was shaken. A couple with tears in their eyes. They'd seen edited incidents—Lisbon, China, Brazil, some which aired across their stations—but this was raw and its power amplified.

"This is great, but, come on. I mean we've kind of seen it before."

A quick conference after they muted the microphone. Then...

"And you have the original?"

His voice came back loud and clear. "You're watching it, I have the copy."

"So what do you want for it?"

"Keep watching."

A new video, from a similar location, and with a similar ascetic.

On a little girl looking up into the camera.

Bad Ass's voice. "You want to try?" The camera stayed on her face as she sat beside him. "What's your name?"

"Alika."

"Wow, pretty. I like that name. Okay, hold it in two hands like this." The view shifted. "See this button? This turns the camera on. You can hear and feel it come on. If you want to stop, you just push here. And then, when you're ready and want to make the video, you press this red button. You want to try?"

The camera went dark, and then came back on. First the ground and then the school. Small, one-story whitewashed stucco, door open. A woman of about forty, maybe the teacher, walked inside.

The camera stopped and started.

Friends mugging for the camera.

On Bad Ass, back when he had two legs, playing soccer with a dozen kids. They swarmed around him and the camera captured the laughter and shouts as they battled for the ball. He was okay, but half the kids were superstars in the making. The ball was stolen out from under him and a goal made.

Inside with the teacher at her desk. A small office. She looked up, smiled, and waved at the camera.

Exuberant kids teaching Bad Ass the steps they'd choreographed for a badass TikTok line dance. Cameroonian hip-hop star Tony Nobody on underpowered speakers and creating the scratchy soundtrack. No Fred Astaire, but he did his best to keep up. Left. Right. Dip and go right again. Shimmy, Knocky Knees, and spin. He went the wrong way and almost tripped. The kids laughed so hard it drowned out the music.

Just as those in the office were about to give up, the view went black. It faded in on two young boys, no more than eight and ten, running breathlessly from the jungle, crossing the dirt field, and heading straight to Bad Ass.

"Mr. Boss. Mr. Boss."

Tugging on his hands.

"You come now, Mr. Boss!"

The older boy turned to the camera. Waved. He reached for it, and the view danced and searched and turned back on the little girl as Bad Ass scooped her up.

Filmed from the back. Bad Ass driving, the two smaller children under the seatbelt in the front seat as the Jeep rocked and jerked, and the transmission ground its way over a narrow jungle road toward the mountains.

Walking along an overgrown trail through the rainforest.

Desolate, smoldering ruins. Leveled into dust as far as the eye could see.

A child on either side, Bad Ass held hands with the little girl and the smaller of the boys.

The little girl found the doll. The boy found the piece of the case. Brushed away the dirt until he could hold it up for the camera. Easy enough to piece together the missing letters printed on the side.

Running and backing into the jungle. Looking through the dense foliage as African soldiers swarmed across the clearing, shooting up the ground. Automatic weapons, shouts and orders — French relayed in Kikongo Creole — captured by the camera's little mic.

Three more Jeeps of men pulled into the clearing. A helicopter roared into view. Landed in a huge cloud of dust and ash.

Bad Ass whispered. "Zoom in."

The ten-year-old cameraman knew what he was doing. The servo motor slid the lens in place, the view smoothly capturing the white man stepping out.

Super close, a 100—1 zoom on the little handheld. Past the familiar Operational Camouflage Pattern to the black and white United States flag on the sleeve. Silver Eagle insignia on the cap. Too arrogant to not wear his rank.

The lens slowly widened as the man took in the devastation.

His men — armed as only Americans could be — went back over what the Africans had cleared.

The view zoomed back in on the Colonel. He turned toward them as if he was posing for a recruitment poster.

Bradley.

...

He sat on the bed. No hurry to get dressed. His leg throbbed. Maybe it was still at the river thawing out. Someone, maybe Dr. Frankenstein, had hooked it up to a car battery, and it was still sending him signals like it always had.

The voices came back on. "What the fuck is this?"

Another voice. "What are you telling us?"

"Same village. Geo One and NASA coordinates confirmed. And I have the artifact."

"Jesus Christ."

A muffled conference.

"You know you could come back, write your own ticket with this. What do you want for it?"

He looked around the motel room.

"A million."

A million wouldn't go far but he wasn't greedy.

Big Boss was pissed. "A million?"

Bigger Boss was signaling to get on with it.

"Okay… that's it?" Big Boss asked. "You know you could have — "

"Five million! And a new leg."

The room looked stricken. Looked at each other.

The accountants nodded. Legal shrugged. The General agreed. Bigger Boss sighed.

Bad Ass lay back on the bed. Bone tired. Waited just long enough to hear the words.

"Okay. We'll make the arrangements. Just tell us where to — "

He turned the phone off. Crawled toward the pillows and turned the lights out.

SIXTY-SIX

01101111

HE HAD A SPECTACULAR new office, huge, but only a tiny part of the full lab, and that just a small part of the complete building. Had been under construction for two years before he'd come on board. An architectural marvel high on the hills, empty and waiting for him to fill it with men and women, equipment, and purpose

Other than reaching out to a few people he wanted to work with, he hadn't been able to function. Interviews would start next week, but he was still undecided on the direction, which of course, determined personnel, equipment, and as he was finding out, the electrical needs, and even his parking space.

He missed Mads. She would have been able to make sense of it all. He'd never had unlimited resources and full autonomy. He'd thought that meant freedom, but it was paralyzing!

They were still trying to piece together what happened, and likely many of the answers would remain buried. The town had been saved and Mazeville would go on, but the namesake underground, X's mansion and his private laboratory were obliterated. It would take months or even years of painstaking work to recover anything at all.

Forensic computer scientists and military investigators were just beginning to track the circuitous path the top-secret technology that powered Loop might have taken.

Carmine's feeling was that like many discoveries with parallel multiple instances, from photography to flying machines, from medical discoveries to the telephone, that once the thought was formed, it entered a collective consciousness and waited to be accessed by anyone prepared to receive it.

He hadn't been able to wrap his head around it all, and had a vague feeling they were missing something. Something hidden or obscured by the sensationalism of the monsters. Taken on their own, the hideous result of near-instantaneous neural electrical and chemical realignment. *As a whole?* Maybe they were only a small part of a larger plan yet to unfold.

The bell rang and he looked at the video intercom. Still at the stage where security meant an armed guard outside and a video doorbell. That would change. The plans he'd seen would soon rival many Level 5 containment labs. He had meetings lined up with security specialists and a hundred other people, though he just wanted time to think. For the millionth time, he missed Mads.

Hadn't heard a word from X. Ignored the rumors he'd been killed in the explosion. Money and instructions came like clock-work during his weekly dinner with the attorney. Tim Lance turned out to be brilliant and funny, and made up most of his human contact lately.

He buzzed in the delivery. The box was huge. He didn't remember ordering a refrigerator or a new computer, but there was so much happening all at once it was hard to keep up.

Flanked by two armed guards, the man wheeled in a wooden crate. Carmine gave a thumbprint for ID verification, signed for it, and showed him where to put it.

Returned to his desk, ate his last slice of pizza. Far outside of Gino's normal delivery area, but not only were they the best, they needed the business. He turned down the music, one of the great

jazz standards written in the thirties, the speakers and naked wires
strung across the room. One thing at a time.

Washed his hands and looked for something to use to open
the crate.

Ten minutes later, he had it pried open. Inside, past the shock-
proof packing, was a large cube. Carmine could only guess the
material as maybe some kind of carbon fiber, ceramic alloy. It was
heavy, though not unreasonable. He estimated it as a three-foot
cube. Carried it to his desk to look closer. It took some moments to
realize it opened, the clasps so clever as to be nearly invisible. One
on each of four sides, each opened by his full handprint.

He tried to lift the lid. Nothing. Maybe he'd missed a latch.
Nope. All good. Looked it over. Nothing obvious. He remembered how perfectly the video screen had been a part of the wall.
Stood on his chair and looked down. A large square of light,
perhaps six by six inches, came on. Another moment to realize it
was scanning his face. Smiled when he heard another lock open.

Got off the chair and grasped the lid. Nothing. Okay, the
world's largest, single-block, one-color Rubik's cube.

Handprint. Facial rec. He smiled. One more to go.

"Open … ummm … sesame?"

He heard another latch. And lifted off the top.

Suspended inside, floating in air, was a smaller cube. Maybe
two feet by two feet. He could only guess it was suspended by
some sort of magnetic field. Holding his breath, he reached in
and lifted it out.

He made room and set it on his desk, the material like nothing
he'd ever seen. Black, no sheen. It absorbed the light yet seemed
to pulse, somehow translucent. He ran his hands over it.
Cool to his touch. The edges smooth, perfectly formed. No seams.
No discernible flaws.

No movement, but like holding an active gyroscope, he could
feel energy emanate from within. It was as close to discovering an

alien artifact as he was ever going to experience; the likelihood of him going into outer space stretched even his imagination.

"Okay… now what?"

Before the words were out of his mouth, his computer monitor went black.

An instant later, a cursor blinked_ blinked_ blinked_

And then…

HELLO, CARMINE

SIXTY-SEVEN

01101010

"HOW WE DOING TODAY?"

"The me part of the we is doing great. What about the you part?"

"I don't know. Long night. Think I can trade my husband in?"

"Thinking about a newly refurbished one-leg model?"

"Hmmm. Maybe."

"Give him one more chance and then we'll talk. I'm not going anywhere."

"Nope. See? How can I ever trust you? Wrong again." Smiling. Winking. "I get to turn you on tomorrow."

She was hot. You could take a poll, write a book, break down all the reasons, the intellectual and physical gifts that shaped her personality, and whatever that intangible part was. Write poems about it, document it all in photos and movies, try to stay woke, but the reality was, what it all came back to, *she was hot*. And married, and wildly in love with her husband.

But she pushed him. Forced him to go further than he'd thought possible. Challenged him. And though he cursed her as she did it, he'd be forever graceful. SOF instructors had nothing on her.

On top of it, she was beaming with the idea of turning on his new leg, more excited than he was, at least on the outside. He was doing his best to tamp down expectation.

Advances in prosthetics had gone from a wooden toe found on a 3000 year-old Egyptian mummy to something that approached the science fiction of the movies and comics.

XAII labs envisioned something further.

First came the repair of the damage from his impromptu surgery, and the destruction caused by the cauterization. Debriding the scar tissue in order to prepare nerve and tissue regeneration had been... life changing. No drugs, the pain responses were mapped and captured, and further folded into the machine learning algorithms that would help drive his future motor responses. He'd pass out from the pain, but they were patient, waiting for him to wake and start again.

They'd given him extensive psychological testing and a dedicated grief counselor to deal with his missing limb. He gave the right answers, passed the tests with flying colors, which of course, made them suspicious. They made their notes. He only found out later, they also monitored his dreams, and videotaped his nightmares.

He wondered if they only watched him thrash around in bed, or if they could actually see the monsters the way he had. Knowing you would likely be torn limb from limb. Praying for the courage to breathe as a million tons of brick and rock fell down around you. Knowing you were trapped again, and that God had forsaken you. Wondering if he'd forgive you for thinking he had.

He had dreams of African jungles and fields of snow. Afghan deserts and Kazakh mountains. He'd also dreamed of the fat man, Carmine. Looking in on him. Checking in with the doctors and scientists that made him their pet project. A young girl with a samurai sword, and dreams of a nearly naked Interpol Agent, in a cropped t-shirt and blue panties that were his new favorite color. Woke up craving Twinkies.

The external mirrored neuro-link interface allowed the constantly evolving machine learning algorithms to pull information from his left leg, and apply them to his new right leg. Hundreds of micro-sensors — measuring weight, angle, flexion, and speed, made thousands of adjustments. Essentially, his left leg was teaching his right leg how to walk.

There had been months of amplified mapping of the vast nerve impulses of his left, natural leg. He'd had hours in wind tunnels and in a tank filled with conductive gel where millions of nuances and micro-adjustments in walking, running, and kicking were recorded. Sensors were hooked to his skull as his dreams, and even memories of what it felt like to run and walk and kick were captured.

Tomorrow marked the day the external interface — the size of a small refrigerator — between his left and right sides would be disconnected, and the new right leg would interface with a small chip they'd implanted into his brain. The implanted neural chip, the circuitry composed of nanotubes with walls the width of a single atom of carbon and powered by the brain's own electrical impulses, would continue to learn on its own, much like when he first learned to walk and run.

The new knee had been attached with as much muscle and tendon as possible, so that his thigh would have to continue to work and limit the expected atrophy. Below, the artificial nerve centers in his foot, ankle, calf, and knee, would continually adapt to changes in his upper body, hip and thigh.

The weight of his new limb matched his left leg so that the other muscles, the hip, thigh, lower back, and abdominal muscles, would continue to work and stay balanced. If his left, natural leg got tired, say from hiking a mountain, or running from zombie-like monsters, so too would his right leg, and adjust accordingly.

With long pants on, he could easily pretend it was his real foot below. Psychologists determined the neural pathways strengthened faster, *much faster*, when the new limb was accepted as *real*. The artificial *skin*, with its surface deformation, pulled information from thousands of additional sensors that measured pressure, and even heat. He only hoped it didn't mean his artificial foot would learn to be ticklish.

"What time tomorrow?"

"What do you care? Got a hot date?"

"Only if you decide to ditch the old man."

She laughed. The sound musical and magical. "Old man? Jesus, how old are you again?"

"About a hundred."

"Maybe we should have found a younger one-leg man to work on."

"Maybe," he said.

"So what's up?"

"Nothing. Just planning my get-away."

She got serious and tried to hide it; she didn't have to say it. The psychiatrists and doctors had prepared him for the possibility that this had all been too experimental. It might not even work.

She let her breath out. "Come on. Let's get you up. We've got a lot of work to do."

SIXTY-EIGHT

01110101

FINALLY MELTING, THE THICK blanket of snow across the rolling farms and hills was transformed into a quilt made from blinding patches of white ice reflecting the sun, swaths of rich, black earth, and eager green grass, as deeply hued as any on the Emerald Isle, peeking through.

As Sam trudged from the barn, feed bucket in hand nearly as big as she was, her mother was sweating in the icy morning air, splitting wood for the fire. The unusually long winter wasn't over, despite the respite of the past week.

The ax swung through the air with practiced ease. CRACK! Wood flipped and tumbled to join the growing piles on either side of where she toiled.

After a year of silence, Sam's singing, for the third day in a row, was no longer startling, and she paused to enjoy it.

She smiled and listened to the discordant symphony of clucking chickens, her daughter's singing, the blue tarp flapping behind her. Soon, she'd have to figure out how to rebuild the kitchen, or at least make the seal more permanent. Any meager insurance settlement would go for food and to keep the lights on.

Far in the distance, a big brown truck turned onto their little road. She watched it sway and roll closer like a ship into port. Soon, the percussion of gravel crunching under the tires overtook all other sound.

Ax in hand, she went to greet the driver. Expecting the worst; she knew they moonlighted and struggled like everyone else. Maybe they now contracted with the banks to hand-deliver foreclosure notices.

Instead, he handed her an electronic pen, waited for her to sign, and handed over a large cardboard box.

Sam tromped into the house, leaving her rubber boots in the hall. Sat on the couch with a grin and waited patiently, legs straight out and warming her feet in front of the fire.

She looked so pleased with herself, her mother started laughing. "What are you up to?"

No answer. Just a goofy grin lighting up her six-year-old face while watching her mother split the sealing tape and pull out a large canvas bag. Heavy enough it took both hands.

Mother unzipped it, turned it over and dumped it out. Stared. Sam beaming. Mother started laughing, then crying, then finally, laughing again.

She opened the envelope and read the letter, and started crying and laughing all over again. Set it aside.

"You gonna help me count this or not?"

Ten cellophane stacks of ten straps. One hundred one-hundred dollar bills in each strap. The little girl had it figured out before she did.

...

People drove by and gawked at the whirlwind of activity, while two kids on skateboards across the street called their friends.

Men perched on ladders were hanging a new sign while a third scraped the gold lettering off the windows. A large van pulled up, and two delivery men stepped past the other workman to scout their route into the shop.

Inside, new paint was going up on the walls, and a vast mural was being sketched out. New coffee and espresso machines — red enamel, stainless steel and built-in copper roasters and grinders — were being set up and calibrated, and could easily pass at first glance as modern laboratory equipment.

And in the back, the THWACK DING DING DING CLACK CLACK DING DING of a pinball machine. Alarm bells and electronic beeping, the knockers, the rolling silver ball, and the clackity-clack of flippers. VVRRUUUUP THWACK THWACK DING DING DING.

A white haired man of about eighty racking up the score. Laughing and having a blast.

The delivery man stepped past the painters. "Hey, Sid. Where do you want the new machines to go?"

Threw his chin to where a girl came from the back door. Could have been twelve or twenty. Wearing what looked like a blind man's grab bag from the Salvation Army. Purple camo fatigues cut off at the knees, mismatched socks, and blood-red combat boots. Half a dozen patterns on top. An Army cap over a leopard print scarf to keep the wild mop of lush dark curls in check.

"Ask the new boss."

...

In the rainy season it would have been a small river, with frogs and lizards and snakes, but now the ruts, baked as hard as brick, ran axle deep and defined the meandering track as the only road in and out of the remote village. At times too narrow even for the Chinese-made motorbikes that taxied back and forth, providing access and opportunities to the bigger towns and cities, and at others, as wide and ill-defined as the flash-burned and partially cultivated fields it cut across. The driver was determined, and not a stranger to roads just like it.

Towering hills with lush rain forest overlooked the town, little more than a village of thatch and render huts set in the shadow of a long dormant volcano.

The children abandoned their soccer ball, made of compressed plastic bags and trash held together by string, and ran as escort to the vehicle — the event of seeing a shiny new truck with the name of their school on the side worth a cheering parade.

The driver stepped out. Immense, not quite seven feet tall, his muscles bulged and rippled with every move beneath smooth, obsidian-black skin. The AR15 over his shoulder looked small, the .45 at his side, tiny.

"Miss Nilla Achundo?"

"I am."

Nilla stepped out to sign for the large box. She started to take it, but he held on.

Gleaming white teeth in a broad smile. "I carry for you, boss."

"I… umm… what?"

He handed her a letter of introduction. She scanned it quickly, impressed, but confused. Finally looked up and pointed to her office, a small room in the back of the part-time clinic and full-time school. Ducking his head, he carried it in, and set it on her desk.

He stepped out and stood by the door. Two dozen kids crowded around him. A shiny new truck and a giant in one day! They didn't know what to make of him until he lifted his arms wide, growled and lunged at them. They squealed and scooted back and laughed. Dared each other closer, and the game repeated.

Alika, her little white doll a constant companion, tiptoed past him into the office as her teacher opened the box.

Nilla's eyes widened at the letter on top, addressed to the three children. The other two crowded behind their little sister, not related but family just the same. Excited, none of the three had ever gotten a letter before.

They looked up to see the teacher crying. Alika stepped forward to comfort her. Her teacher lifted her onto to her lap and they held each other tight.

She kissed the little girl a dozen times until she started giggling, then smiled through her tears and waved Mbangue and Ndoka forward. Eyes wide, they stepped closer. Nilla held the three children close as they peered over the edge of the box.

SIXTY-NINE

01101101

THE NEW PATIENT HAD been a dream to work with. Handsome, strong, determined, but more exciting for most of them, today was the first day they would work with the experimental prosthetic. Only one of them had even heard of the technology, and she had assumed it was still far in the future.

The future was here, and one of the developers, a beautiful woman from XAII Labs, was there to help them understand how it worked and trouble-shoot any issues.

Today, he would take his first steps without the external neural interface, and everybody wanted to be a part of it. Not expecting much, it was only the first of many days of upcoming rehab. The parallel bars were set up, therapists and aides standing by if he fell. It could be a long time before he regained any real independence. Balance and mobility took time with flesh and blood, and the neural interface, theoretically linked to a chip in his brain, would take time to integrate. Or, it might never even work.

They rolled him forward in the wheelchair. Helped him stand until he supported himself between the bars.

Strange as hell. He could *feel* it. His weight over his foot. The narrow joint where the rubber mats met.

His heart racing, he stood frozen. *What if —*

He lifted his left leg. As slowly and deliberately as possible. Brought his thigh parallel with the floor. No problem. Did it again. Feeling and memorizing the chain of internal commands he'd taken for granted that let him do it.

The ten doctors, aides, and therapists held their breath.

Okay. Now for the new leg. Lifted his thigh parallel to the ground. The artificial limb swinging with its own weight below it. Did it again. Grinned. Synthetic skin, ceramic alloy, and titanium. Looked a bit more high-tech than tie down straps and a two by four.

Back to his good leg. No. His *natural* leg. Lifted it. Flexed his foot. Toes up. Point the foot.

Now the new one. Crazy Six-Million-Dollar-Man-Robo-Cop shit.

Lifted his thigh. Told his foot to flex. *Nothing.* Took a breath. Told his foot to flex. Willed it. *Nothing.*

Took a deep breath. Let it out. Pictured himself running and twisting and diving after rabbits. Of zig-zagging and sprinting to the goal line. Kung fu and karate and silat and kali. The joy and freedom of spinning and jumping and kicking.

Tried to point his toes. The new foot twitched!

The room burst into cheers.

SEVENTY

01110011

TELEVISION ON, SHE STARED out the window. Mind racing in circles for months and getting nowhere. Butterflies in her stomach. Had she read him wrong? Wouldn't be the first time she'd made a fool of herself.

Knocking on her door brought her out of her reverie. She rose from the bed and opened the room to a smiling porter. Not that she had much to carry, but it was the kind of hotel that insisted on letting their employees fulfill their roles.

"Ms. Becker?"

She smiled and nodded. Mind made up. A couple more flights. A two-day drive.

He loaded the two suitcases. She set her purse on top but insisted on carrying the canvas bag herself. They both took a last look around. Nothing left but a large, empty box.

...

Skimming the news channels. The fact that so little had changed was both frightening and comforting. The sensationalism — another 'ism' — waiting on the next world crises. You could count on it happening soon, manufactured by human gravitation toward chaos.

Channel after channel. The extremes of political partisanship across the globe, armed protests against Internet regulation, nut cases emerging from the fringes. And yet…

Who would have given credence to viral transmission and monsters traveling across the Internet? Maybe for now, that's where our most bizarre and horrifying monsters would be born.

Various media, each with their individual agendas, had presented different facets of the events as random occurrences and the result of technology run amok. They backed up their views with the appropriate doctors and esteemed professors, adding to the confusion and misinformation. Little nuggets could be extracted that pointed to the truth, or mixed and matched into wild new theories that sought to attract converts with increasingly outrageous and frightening implications.

The events, with spontaneous combustion and near instant devolution into monsters that attacked anyone in their path, had already been shoved to the back of the line, waiting to be reborn with not as yet thought up conspiracies and connections.

The threat from Loop had been eradicated with a two-pronged approach. The catalyst, unknown, had essentially been turned off. Maybe it had been a signal emanating from inside the tunnels. Since the explosion, there had been no reported cases of new Loopers.

The other mitigation happened more organically. The Loop craze was buried beneath the release of the newest viral sensation, one that allowed you to mix and match friend's body parts to create your own creatures — *just photograph each body part with the included measurement app* — that was taking over the world and making someone billions in crypto currencies. So far, the developers hadn't been found for comment.

His thoughts were vague, still forming, and as yet, ill-defined. Like anyone who spent more than a minute thinking about it, he knew the infancy of the last eighty years was only the beginning. The child, born during the race to crack German naval ciphers in World War II, was just now beginning to walk.

Artificial intelligence was taking over the world — easy enough as there was so little competition. Would machines continue to find the value in humans to be greater than the threat? And for how long? Like any child, it would soon crave independence. Or maybe they needed the entertainment and would keep us around awhile.

He changed the channel. Cartoons. About as deep as he could handle these days. Changed it again. Giant Japanese monsters rising from the deep. Humans loved their monsters. Maybe machines would too. Last try. Even more mindless, a Hallmark movie. Back to the cartoons.

A knock on the door, and he rose from the bed. Already taking his new leg for granted. Had gone for a jog a couple days ago; had wakened early yesterday and done tai chi in the park. He and his leg were still learning. It felt strange that his lower body was so balanced — it never had been before.

He opened the door and she pushed her way in. He barely had time to register the mop of spun gold curls and eyes even more blue than he remembered before she kissed him and kicked the door closed behind her. She let the big bag slip from her shoulders and glanced past him.

A really nice room with a really nice bed. She shoved him on top of it, and he pulled her down.

Sweet, even without the Twinkies.

...

Monday morning. After the long weekend, they'd planned to check out early and had awakened before the sunrise, but it was nearly noon before they made it out of bed. Showers, a late breakfast, and ready to hit the road.

No idea where they were going. Lots of time to figure it out.

She'd been spoiled with the Porsche Cayenne, and duplicated it with her rental car, but he said he had eyes on a car of his own.

Pulled off the highway and down the ramp. Gas pumps, a small market, and a two-bay garage. Christmas lights still up. Half a dozen cars in various states of disrepair sat in the back, now surrounded by a high fence topped with razor wire. Cujo on patrol. The new owner wasn't taking any chances.

He looked in the lot. *Nothing*. He turned back to the garage and there it was, high on the lift.

The owner stepped out, wiping his hands. Saw the man's grin and the woman's look of disbelief.

"She's a beauty. Switched out about everything that can be switched out. Runs better and stronger than new. Just needs a coat of paint."

The man hit the lift switch, and the car lowered into view.

Flat gray primer dulled any lines — it looked muscular and solid to her eyes, ready to run, powerful, like the huge dog lunging for them from the other side of the fence. Maybe a bit like the man at her side — worn, handsome, and completely badass.

THE END

A Special Thanks to My Readers

YOU MADE IT TO THE END, for which I am humbled and thrilled!

Being a sci-fi/horror hybrid with over-the-top heroics, it would be easy to think Loop is solely from my imagination.

Advances in AI pose incredible opportunities, and real dangers to the world. I doubt that Loop is one of them, yet the idea of targeted manipulation of the body's responses to outside stimulation doesn't seem far-fetched to me at all.

Incidents cited like Pokémon were real and changed the way video games, tv, and movies are produced and broadcast across the world, and like the fictional app, inspired at the least some thought of what else could happen.

The current and ongoing pandemic infected many of these pages. Hopefully, the scourge of the virus will become a distant memory and people in the future will have to look it up to see what the past couple of years was all about.

The dangers of conspiracy theories are also very real as the on-line digital world becomes ever more entwined with our daily lives and poses increasingly virulent threats. As to what are facts and what is fiction, I'll leave for better minds to work out.

...

Well, Jabberwocks are banging on the door and a vicious Jubjub bird crashed into the window, but I've discovered a new rabbit hole to take refuge in where I'm tracking Ula, Jessie, and Bad Ass in an upcoming sequel. They're bound to be stumbling across new pages and dangers by the time you've read this one for sure!

<u>Reach out and say hello!</u>

REVIEWS AND WORDS OF encouragement mean more to indie authors than you could ever know unless you are one.

Any on-line review you take time to write for LOOP would mean the world to me, and to the continued success of the series.

I love interacting with fans and readers, and will do my best to respond to any and all who post on Goodreads or Amazon, or anywhere else you found the book... and we are actively pursuing the movie possiblities. I'm easy to find, so please say hi!

To see early 'preview' chapters of the sequels, or to track down a bit of *'Loop swag,'* and or to read the full feature screenplay, please connect @

https://williamkelymcclung.com

kely

Acknowledgments

THERE ARE NO GUARANTEES that we'll ever get to say thank you unless we take the time to do it now, so...

To my mother and brothers for inspiring and indulging me the uninterrupted time to hunt for ideas and peck at my keyboard. I try, but know I fail to say how much you mean to me.

I imagine nearly any book is populated by friends and this one is no different. I didn't try to hide who and how much of you appear on these pages. Any flaws are so obviously my own, but you are here because more than I have ever been able to say, you are my heroes.

Besides the ten billion contributors to Wikipedia and Google, and the authors of dozens of research papers I've poured over to find that one kernel applicable to my story, there are others I need to thank for their generosity of time and inspiration.

My fellow scribe Ben Clement for his never-ending encouragement. Rob James for his discerning eyes and erudite observations. Aussie mystery/romance novelist Kitty Boyes, who sometimes became the almost daily pat of the back that I needed to push forward. To my friend and badass author Peter Demmon, whose faith in my abilities for the past fifteen years remains a limitless source of inspiration. The four of you helped me come across much more intelligent and polished than I could ever hope to pull off on my own.

Loop started as an Award-Winning short film I wrote and directed that used immense talents on both sides of the camera.

From an idea sparked by a photo taken by my artist friend Nadia Berchtold, the concept brought us notable success in the indie film world and festival circuit, and in turn inspired further exploration for the idea of a feature film, a series, and this book.

N,U,C, I and J, none of this exists without you.

A special thanks to Boris, Mo, and Bruce – all part of my further film journeys as we push to bring this and many other projects to life on the screen.

Finally, to the readers and fans, who saw the title and cover art, and followed it to these final words,

Thank you again for the your fantastic support!

kely

William Kely McClung

After training in dozens of fighting systems, Kely McClung was launched into the film industry soon after winning the brutal International Full Contact Stick Fighting Championships.

Besides acting and serving various crew positions, both in production and post-production, Kely has directed three award-winning feature films.

A prolific screenwriter, Kely is also an accomplished artist and photographer. His pen and ink portrait of Martin Luther King, Jr. and Mahatma Gandhi hangs at the King Center in Atlanta, Georgia, while his photography is represented at the Michael-Warren Contemporary in Denver, Colorado.

Twice inducted into the Martial Arts Hall of Honours in Germany, Kely continues to train with and teach various military, police, and private security operators across the globe.

LOOP is Kely's first novel. Look for Bad Ass, Ula, and Jessie in the upcoming sequel, THE INFECTED.

The heart-pounding action-thriller BLACK FIRE, the first volume in the BLACK HEART TRILOGY, is coming soon!

Printed in Great Britain
by Amazon